PRAISE FOR

The Paris Wife

"Powerful and devastating . . . McLain pulls off a delicate balancing act, making the macho Hemingway of myth a complex and sympathetic figure."

—*USA Today*

"McLain's vivid account of the couple's love affair and adventures . . . will leave you feeling sad yet dazzled."

—*Parade*

"[A] marvelous . . . tale of love and loss."

—*Marie Claire*

"A gripping love story that tragically seduces us into rooting for the doomed romance."

—*DailyCandy*

"Paula McLain seamlessly blends a romantic novel and a biographical sketch in a way to satisfy the most discriminating reader."

—Fredericksburg *Free Lance-Star*

"*The Paris Wife* is simply a sweet love story with surprising emotional impact."

—*Chicago Sun-Times*

"[A] mesmerizing and helluva-good-time novel."

"Provocative . . . an imaginative homage to Hadley Richardson Hemingway."

—*The Washington Post*

"This is a fascinating, intimate, spellbinding story that is certain to stay with the reader well after the last page has been read. Paula McLain is a master at creating narratives that are so lively, they seem to leap from the printed page."

—*Tucson Citizen*

"*The Paris Wife* is a lyrical novel that is beautifully written on every single page. Stunning!"

—*Historical Novels Review* (Editors' Choice)

"Elegant [and] satisfying."

—*The Washington Times*

"Evocative . . . McLain's novel not only gives Hadley a voice, but one that seems authentic and admirable. . . . To read this novel is to become wholly immersed in Jazz Age Paris."

—*Newsday*

"An insightful, bittersweet novel."

—*The Denver Post*

"McLain's mesmerizing and lyrical work of fiction is filled with life, love, and betrayal."

—*The Wichita Eagle*

"McLain fleshes out [Ernest and Hadley's] poignant story with a poet's gift. . . . [She] manages, as Ayn Rand did in *The Fountainhead*, to write about the creative process genuinely rather than loftily."

—*The Roanoke Times*

"A richly imagined portrait of bohemian 1920s Paris, and of American literature's original bad boy."

—*Town & Country*

"A convincing, heart-beating novel."

—*The Kansas City Star*

"An imaginative, elegantly written look inside the marriage of Ernest Hemingway and Hadley Richardson."

—*Kirkus Reviews* (starred review)

"A compelling, spellbinding portrait of a marriage . . . highly recommended."

—*Library Journal* (starred review)

"Fictionalized though it is, *The Paris Wife* feels like, as Ernest Hemingway himself might say, the real thing."

—*The Dallas Morning News*

ALSO BY PAULA McLAIN

A Ticket to Ride

Like Family: Growing Up in Other People's Houses: A Memoir

THE PARIS WIFE

THE PARIS WIFE

A NOVEL

Paula McLain

BALLANTINE BOOKS TRADE PAPERBACKS

NEW YORK

2012 Ballantine Books Trade Paperback Edition

Copyright © 2011 by Paula McLain
Title-page photo copyright © 2006 Edwin Pijpe
Reading group guide copyright © 2012 by Random House, Inc.

Published in the United States by Ballantine Books, an imprint of The Random House Publishing Group, a division of Random House, Inc., New York.

BALLANTINE and colophon are registered trademarks of Random House, Inc.
RANDOM HOUSE READER'S CIRCLE & Design is a trademark of Random House, Inc.

Originally published in hardcover in the United States by Ballantine Books, an imprint of The Random House Publishing Group, a division of Random House, Inc., in 2011.

Grateful acknowledgment is made to the following for permission to reprint previously published material:

Alfred Publishing Co. Inc.: Excerpt from "Make Believe" by Jack Shilkret and Benny Davis, copyright © 1920 (renewed) WB Music Corp. (ASCAP). All rights reserved. Used by permission of Alfred Publishing Co. Inc.

HarperCollins Publishers: Quote from *Zelda* by Nancy Milford, copyright © 1970 and copyright renewed © 1998 by Nancy Winston Milford. Used by permission of HarperCollins Publishers.

David Higham Associates: Excerpts from *An American and France* by Gertrude Stein and three lines of verse from *Tender Buttons* by Gertrude Stein. Reprinted by permission of David Higham Associates.

Scribner, a division of Simon & Schuster, Inc.: Excerpt from *For Whom the Bell Tolls* by Ernest Hemingway, copyright © 1940 by Ernest Hemingway and copyright renewed © 1968 by Mary Hemingway; two lines from "The Second Coming" from *The Collected Works of W. B. Yeats, Volume 1: The Poems, Revised,* edited by Richard J. Finneran, copyright © 1924 by The Macmillan Company, copyright renewed. All rights reserved. Used by permission of Scribner, a division of Simon & Schuster, Inc.

Library of Congress Cataloging-in-Publication Data
McLain, Paula.
The Paris wife : a novel / Paula McLain.
p. cm.
ISBN 978-0-345-52131-6
eBook ISBN 978-0-345-52132-3
1. Hemingway, Ernest, 1899–1961—Marriage—Fiction. 2. Mowrer, Hadley Hemingway, 1891– —Fiction. 3. Authors' spouses—United States—Fiction. 4. Authors, American—France—Fiction. 5. Expatriate authors—France—Fiction. 6. Paris (France)—Fiction. I. Title.
PS3563.C383495P37 2011
813'.54—dc22
2010037878

Printed in the United States of America

www.randomhousereaderscircle.com

2   4   6   8   9   7   5   3   1

Book design by Caroline Cunningham

It is not what France gave you but what it did not take from you that was important.

—Gertrude Stein

There's no *one* thing that's true. It's all true.

—Ernest Hemingway

PROLOGUE

Though I often looked for one, I finally had to admit that there could be no cure for Paris. Part of it was the war. The world had ended once already and could again at any moment. The war had come and changed us by happening when everyone said it couldn't. No one knew how many had died, but when you heard the numbers—nine million or fourteen million—you thought, *Impossible.* Paris was full of ghosts and the walking wounded. Many came back to Rouen or Oak Park, Illinois, shot through and carrying little pieces of what they'd seen behind their kneecaps, full of an emptiness they could never dislodge. They'd carried bodies on stretchers, stepping over other bodies to do it; they'd been on stretchers themselves, on slow-moving trains full of flies and the floating voice of someone saying he wanted to be remembered to his girl back home.

There was no back home anymore, not in the essential way, and that was part of Paris, too. Why we couldn't stop drinking or talking or kissing the wrong people no matter what it ruined. Some of us had looked into the faces of the dead and tried not to remember anything in particular. Ernest was one of these. He often said he'd died in the war, just for a moment; that his soul had left his body like a silk handkerchief, slipping out and levitating over his chest. It had returned without being called back, and I often wondered if writing for him was a way of knowing his soul was there after all, back in its place. Of saying to himself, if not to anyone else, that he had seen what he'd seen and felt those terrible things and lived anyway. That he had died but wasn't dead anymore.

One of the best things about Paris was coming back after we'd gone away. In 1923 we moved to Toronto for a year to have our son, Bumby, and when we returned, everything was the same but more somehow. It was filthy and gorgeous, full of rats and horse chestnut blossoms and poetry. With the baby our needs seemed to double, but we had less to spend. Pound helped us find an apartment on the second floor of a white stucco building on a tight curving street near the Luxembourg Gardens. The flat had no hot water, no bathtub, no electric lighting—but it wasn't the worst place we'd lived. Not by a long shot. Across the courtyard, a sawmill buzzed steadily from seven in the morning until five at night, and there was always the smell of fresh cut wood, and sawdust filtered in under the windowsills and door frames and got in our clothes and made us cough. Inside, there was the steady report of Ernest's Corona in the small room upstairs. He was working on stories—there were always stories or sketches to write—but also a new novel about the fiesta in Pamplona that he'd started in the summer.

I wasn't reading the pages then, but I trusted his feeling about them and trusted the rhythm of every day. Each morning, he'd wake early and dress and then go upstairs to his room and begin the day's writing. If things weren't hitting for him there, he'd take the notebooks and several well-sharpened pencils and walk to the Closerie des Lilas for a café crème at the marble table he liked best while Bumby and I breakfasted alone, and then dressed for a walk or went out to see friends. In the late afternoon, I'd head home, and if the day had gone well, Ernest would be there at the dining table looking satisfied with some nice cold Sauternes or brandy and seltzer, and ready to talk about anything. Or we would go out together, leaving Bumby with our landlady, Madame Chautard, and find a plate of fat oysters and good talk at the Select or the Dôme or the Deux Magots.

Interesting people were everywhere just then. The cafés of Montparnasse breathed them in and out, French painters and Russian dancers and American writers. On any given night, you could see Picasso walking from Saint-Germain to his apartment in the rue des Grands Augustins, always exactly the same route and always looking quietly at everyone and everything. Nearly anyone might feel like a painter walking the streets of Paris then because the light brought it out in you, and the shadows alongside the buildings, and the bridges which seemed to want to break your heart, and the sculpturally beautiful women in Chanel's black sheath dresses, smoking and throwing back their heads to laugh. We could walk into any café and feel the wonderful chaos of it, ordering Pernod or Rhum St. James until we were beautifully blurred and happy to be there together.

"Listen," Don Stewart said one night when we were all very jolly and drunk as fishes at the Select. "What you and Hem have is perfect. No, no," he was slurring now, and his face contorted with feeling. "It's holy. That's what I meant to say."

"That's swell of you, Don. You're all right, too, you know." I cupped his shoulder lightly, afraid he might cry. He was a humorist, and everyone knew the funny writers were the most serious sort under their skins. He also wasn't married yet, but there were prospects on the horizon, and it was all very important to him to see that marriage could be done gracefully and well.

Not everyone believed in marriage then. To marry was to say you believed in the future and in the past, too—that history and tradition and hope could stay knit together to hold you up. But the war had come and stolen all the fine young men and our faith, too. There was only today to throw yourself into without thinking about tomorrow, let alone forever. To keep you from thinking, there was liquor, an ocean's worth at least, all the usual vices and plenty of rope to hang yourself with. But some of us, a very few in the end, bet on marriage against the odds. And though I didn't feel holy, exactly, I did feel that what we had was rare and true—and that we were safe in the marriage we had built and were building every day.

This isn't a detective story—not hardly. I don't want to say, *Keep watch for the girl who will come along and ruin everything*, but she's coming anyway, set on her course in a gorgeous chipmunk coat and fine shoes, her sleek brown hair bobbed so close to her well-made head she'll seem like a pretty otter in my kitchen. Her easy smile. Her fast smart talk—while in the bedroom, scruffy and unshaven and laid flat out on the bed like a despot king, Ernest will read his book and care nothing for her. Not at first. And the tea will boil in the teapot, and I'll tell a story about a girl she and I both knew a hundred years ago in St. Louis, and we'll feel like quick and natural friends while across the yard, in the sawmill, a dog will start barking and keep barking and he won't stop for anything.

THE PARIS WIFE

ONE

The very first thing he does is fix me with those wonderfully brown eyes and say, "It's possible I'm too drunk to judge, but you might have something there."

It's October 1920 and jazz is everywhere. I don't know any jazz, so I'm playing Rachmaninoff. I can feel a flush beginning in my cheeks from the hard cider my dear pal Kate Smith has stuffed down me so I'll relax. I'm getting there, second by second. It starts in my fingers, warm and loose, and moves along my nerves, rounding through me. I haven't been drunk in over a year—not since my mother fell seriously ill—and I've missed the way it comes with its own perfect glove of fog, settling snugly and beautifully over my brain. I don't want to think and I don't want to feel, either, unless it's as simple as this beautiful boy's knee inches from mine.

The knee is nearly enough on its own, but there's a whole package of a man attached, tall and lean, with a lot of very dark hair and a dimple in his left cheek you could fall into. His friends call him Hemingstein, Oinbones, Bird, Nesto, Wemedge, anything they can dream up on the spot. He calls Kate Stut or Butstein (not very flattering!), and another fellow Little Fever, and yet another Horney or the Great Horned Article. He seems to know everyone, and everyone seems to know the same jokes and stories. They telegraph punch lines back and forth in code, lightning fast and wisecracking. I can't keep up, but I don't mind really. Being near these happy strangers is like a powerful transfusion of good cheer.

When Kate wanders over from the vicinity of the kitchen, he points his perfect chin at me and says, "What should we name our new friend?"

"Hash," Kate says.

"Hashedad's better," he says. "Hasovitch."

"And you're Bird?" I ask.

"Wem," Kate says.

"I'm the fellow who thinks someone should be dancing." He smiles with everything he's got, and in very short order, Kate's brother Kenley has kicked the living room carpet to one side and is manning the Victrola. We throw ourselves into it, dancing our way through a stack of records. He's not a natural, but his arms and legs are free in their joints, and I can tell that he likes being in his body. He's not the least shy about moving in on me either. In no time at all our hands are damp and clenched, our cheeks close enough that I can feel the very real heat of him. And that's when he finally tells me his name is Ernest.

"I'm thinking of giving it away, though. Ernest is so dull, and Hemingway? Who wants a Hemingway?"

Probably every girl between here and Michigan Avenue, I think, looking at my feet to keep from blushing. When I look up again, he has his brown eyes locked on me.

"Well? What do you think? Should I toss it out?"

"Maybe not just yet."

A slow number starts, and without asking, he reaches for my waist and scoops me toward his body, which is even better up close. His chest is solid and so are his arms. I rest my hands on them lightly as he backs me around the room, past Kenley cranking the Victrola with glee, past Kate giving us a long, curious look. I close my eyes and lean into Ernest, smelling bourbon and soap, tobacco and damp cotton—and everything about this moment is so sharp and lovely, I do something completely out of character and just let myself have it.

TWO

There's a song from that time by Nora Bayes called "Make Believe," which might have been the most lilting and persuasive treatise on self-delusion I'd ever heard. Nora Bayes was beautiful, and she sang with a trembling voice that told you she knew things about love. When she advised you to throw off all the old pain and worry and heartache and *smile*—well, you believed she'd done this herself. It wasn't a suggestion but a prescription. The song must have been a favorite of Kenley's, too. He played it three times the night I arrived in Chicago, and each time I felt it speaking directly to me: *Make believe you are glad when you're sorry. Sunshine will follow the rain.*

I'd had my share of rain. My mother's illness and death had weighed on me, but the years before had been heavy, too. I was only twenty-eight, and yet I'd been living like a spinster on the second floor of my older sister Fonnie's house while she and her husband, Roland, and their four dear beasts lived downstairs. I hadn't meant for things to stay this way. I assumed I'd get married or find a career like my school friends. They were harried young mothers now, schoolteachers or secretaries or aspiring ad writers, like Kate. Whatever they were, they were living their lives, out there doing it, making their mistakes. Somehow I'd gotten stuck along the way—long before my mother's illness—and I didn't know how to free myself exactly.

Sometimes, after playing an hour of passable Chopin, I'd collapse onto the sofa or the carpet, feeling whatever energy I'd had while playing leave my body. It was terrible to feel so empty, as if I were nothing.

Why couldn't I be happy? And just what was happiness anyway? Could you fake it, as Nora Bayes insisted? Could you force it like a spring bulb in your kitchen, or rub up against it at a party in Chicago and catch it like a cold?

Ernest Hemingway was still very much a stranger to me, but he seemed to do happiness all the way up and through. There wasn't any fear in him that I could see, just intensity and aliveness. His eyes sparked all over everything, all over me as he leaned back on his heel and spun me toward him. He tucked me fast against his chest, his breath warm on my neck and hair.

"How long have you known Stut?" he asked.

"We went to grade school together in St. Louis, at Mary Institute. What about you?"

"You want my whole educational pedigree? It's not much."

"No," I laughed. "Tell me about Kate."

"That would fill a book, and I'm not sure I'm the fellow to write it." His voice was light, still teasing, but he'd stopped smiling.

"What do you mean?"

"Nothing," he said. "The short and sweet part is our families both have summer cottages up near Petoskey. That's Michigan to a southerner like you."

"Funny that we both grew up with Kate."

"I was ten to her eighteen. Let's just say I was happy to grow up *alongside* her. With a nice view of the scenery."

"You had a crush, in other words."

"No, those are the right words," he said, then looked away.

I'd obviously touched some kind of nerve in him, and I didn't want to do it again. I liked him smiling and laughing and loose. In fact, my response to him was so powerful that I already knew I would do a lot to keep him happy. I changed the subject fast.

"Are you from Chicago?"

"Oak Park. That's right up the street."

"For a southerner like me."

"Precisely."

"Well, you're a bang-up dancer, Oak Park."

"You too, St. Louis."

The song ended and we parted to catch our breath. I moved to one side of Kenley's long living room while Ernest was quickly swallowed up by admirers—women, naturally. They seemed awfully young and sure of themselves with their bobbed hair and brightly rouged cheeks. I was closer to a Victorian holdout than a flapper. My hair was still long, knotted at the nape of my neck, but it was a good rich auburn color, and though my dress wasn't up to the minute, my figure made up for that, I thought. In fact, I'd been feeling very good about the way I looked the whole time Ernest and I were dancing—he was so appreciative with those eyes!—but now that he was surrounded by vivacious women, my confidence was waning.

"You seemed awfully friendly with Nesto," Kate said, appearing at my elbow.

"Maybe. Can I have the rest of that?" I pointed to her drink.

"It's rather volcanic." She grimaced and passed it over.

"What is it?" I put my face to the rim of the glass, which was close enough. It smelled like rancid gasoline.

"Something homemade. Little Fever handed it to me in the kitchen. I'm not sure he didn't cook it up in his shoe."

Over against a long row of windows, Ernest began parading back and forth in a dark blue military cape someone had dug up. When he turned, the cape lifted and flared dramatically.

"That's quite a costume," I said.

"He's a war hero, didn't he tell you?"

I shook my head.

"I'm sure he'll get to it eventually." Her face didn't give anything away, but her voice had an edge.

"He told me he used to pine for you."

"Really?" There was the tone again. "He's clearly over it now."

I didn't know what had come between these two old friends, but whatever it was, it was obviously complicated and well under wraps. I let it drop.

"I like to think I'm the kind of girl who'll drink anything," I said, "but maybe not from a shoe."

"Right. Let's hunt something up." She smiled and flashed her green eyes at me, and became my Kate again, not grim at all, and off we went to get very drunk and very merry.

I found myself watching for Ernest the rest of the night, waiting for him to appear and stir things up, but he didn't. He must have slipped away at some point. One by one nearly everyone did, so that by 3:00 a.m. the party had been reduced to dregs, with Little Fever as the tragic centerpiece. He was passed out on the davenport with long dark wool socks stretched over his face and his hat perched on his crossed feet.

"To bed, to bed," Kate said with a yawn.

"Is that Shakespeare?"

"I don't know. Is it?" She hiccuped, and then laughed. "I'm off to my own little hovel now. Will you be all right here?"

"Of course. Kenley's made up a lovely room for me." I walked her to the door, and as she sidled into her coat, we made a date for lunch the next day.

"You'll have to tell me all about things at home. We haven't had a moment to talk about your mother. It must have been awful for you, poor creatch."

"Talking about it will only make me sad again," I said. "But this is perfect. Thanks for begging me to come."

"I worried you wouldn't."

"Me too. Fonnie said it was too soon."

"Yes, well, she would say that. Your sister can be smart about some things, Hash, but about you, nearly never."

I gave her a grateful smile and said good night. Kenley's apartment was warrenlike and full of boarders, but he'd given me a large and very clean room, with a four-poster bed and a bureau. I changed into my nightdress then took down my hair and brushed it, sorting through the highlights of the evening. No matter how much fun I'd had with Kate or how good it was to see her after all these years, I had to admit that number one on my list of memorable events was dancing with Ernest Hemingway. I could still feel his brown eyes and his electric, electrifying energy—but what had his attentions meant? Was he babysitting me, as Kate's old friend? Was he still gone on Kate? Was she in love with him? Would I even see him again?

My mind was suddenly such a hive of unanswerable questions that I had to smile at myself. Wasn't this exactly what I had wanted coming to Chicago, something new to think about? I turned to face the mirror over the bureau. Hadley Richardson was still there, with her auburn waves and thin lips and pale round eyes—but there was something new, too, a glimmer of potential. It was just possible the sun was on its way. In the meantime, I would hum Nora Bayes and do my damnedest to make believe.

THREE

The next morning, I walked into the kitchen to find Ernest leaning lazily against the refrigerator, reading the morning newspaper and devouring half a loaf of bread.

"Did you sleep here?" I asked, unable to mask my surprise at seeing him.

"I'm boarding here. Just for a while, until things take off for me."

"What do you mean to do?"

"Make literary history, I guess."

"Gee," I said, impressed all over again by his confidence and conviction. You couldn't fake that. "What are you working on now?"

He pulled a face. "Now I'm writing trash copy for Firestone tires, but I mean to write important stories or a novel. Maybe a book of poetry."

That threw me. "I thought poets were quiet and shrinking and afraid of sunlight," I said, sitting down.

"Not this one." He came over to join me at the table, turning his chair around to straddle it. "Who's your favorite writer?"

"Henry James, I suppose. I seem to read him over and over."

"Well, aren't you sweetly square?"

"Am I? Who's your favorite writer?"

"Ernest Hemingway." He grinned. "Anyway, there're lots of famous writers in Chicago. Kenley knows Sherwood Anderson. Heard of him?"

"Sure. He wrote *Winesburg, Ohio*."

"That's the one."

"Well, with your nerve, you can probably do anything at all."

He looked at me seriously, as if he were trying to gauge whether I was teasing or placating him. I wasn't. "How do you take your coffee, Hasovitch?" he finally said.

"Hot," I said, and he grinned a grin that began in his eyes and went everywhere at once. It was devastating.

When Kate arrived for our lunch date, Ernest and I were still in the kitchen talking away. I hadn't yet changed out of my dressing gown, and there she was sharp and fresh in a red wool hat and coat.

"I'm sorry," I said, "I won't be a minute."

"Take your time, you deserve a little indolence," she said, but seemed impatient with me just the same.

I went off to dress, and when I came back, Kate was alone in the room.

"Where did Nesto run off to?"

"I haven't the faintest," Kate said. And then, because she clearly read disappointment in my face, "Should I have invited him along?"

"Don't be silly. This is our day."

In the end, we had a lovely afternoon. Out of all the girls in my class at Mary Institute, Kate was the boldest and most fearless, able to talk to anyone and make fun out of nothing at all. She was still that way and I felt bolder, too, walking along Michigan Avenue with her, and years younger. We had lunch at a restaurant across from the marble vastness of the Art Institute, where two regal lions presided over traffic and an ever-shifting sea of dark coats and hats. It was a chilly day, and after lunch, we huddled arm in arm along State Street, tucking into every interesting shop we came to. She tried to urge me to open up about things at home, but I didn't want to lose my good mood. Instead, I got Kate talking about her summer up in Michigan, the fishing and swimming parties and general rambunctiousness. All of her stories seemed to involve rowboats and ukuleles, full moons and campfires and grog. I was desperately jealous.

"Why do you get all the young men?"

"They're not mine, I'm just borrowing them." She smiled. "It's having brothers, I guess. And anyway, sometimes it's a nuisance. I spent half the summer trying to encourage this one and discourage that one and all the signals got mixed and in the end no one even kissed anyone else. So there, see? Nothing to be envious of."

"Is Carl Edgar still proposing to you regularly?"

"Ugh, I'm afraid so. Poor old Odgar. Sometimes I wonder what would happen if I actually said yes—as an experiment."

"He'd fall over."

"Or run away in terror, maybe. Some men seem to only want the girls beating a path in the other direction."

"What about Ernest?"

"What about him?" Her eyes snapped to attention.

"Does he like his women on the run?"

"I wouldn't know."

"How young is he, anyway? Twenty-five?"

She smirked. "Twenty-one. A boy-o. I know you're more sensible than that."

"What do you mean?"

"I thought I saw some interest." She gazed at me with intensity.

"I'm just bored," I said. But I'd always been a terrible liar.

"How about a new hat instead?" she said, and pointed to something towering and feathery I couldn't see myself standing beneath in a million years.

By the time we made it back to the apartment late that afternoon, the place was chock-full again. Kenley and his brother Bill, the youngest of the Smith clan, were trying to get together a card game. A fellow named Brummy was playing a ragtime tune on the piano while Ernest and another cohort, Don Wright, circled each other on the carpet in a spontaneous boxing match. They were stripped to the waist, bobbing and weaving with their fists up, while a group stood around egging them on. Everyone was laughing, and it looked like great fun until Ernest lit out with a right hook. Don managed to dodge most of it, and the match went on good-naturedly, but I'd seen the killer look on Ernest's face when he threw the punch and knew it was all very serious to him. He wanted to win.

Kate seemed unfazed by the boxing and everything else going on in the apartment. Apparently the place was always this crazy in the evenings, a good-time Grand Central. Prohibition had been under way for the better part of a year, and that "noble experiment" had spurred the popping up, nearly overnight, of speakeasies in cities everywhere. There were supposed to be thousands of these in Chicago alone, but who needed a speakeasy when Kenley, like many resourceful young men, had stockpiled enough hooch to pickle a herd of elephants? That night, there was plenty of open wine in the kitchen, so Kate and I had some of that, and then some more. As dusk fell, purpling and softening the room, I found myself on the davenport squeezed in between Ernest and Horney while they talked over me in Pig Latin. I couldn't stop collapsing into fits of giggles—and when was the last time I giggled anyway? It was surprisingly, intoxicatingly easy now.

When Horney got up to join Kate on the improvised dance floor, Ernest turned to me and said, "I've been thinking all day about how to ask you something."

"Really?" I didn't know if I was more surprised or flattered.

He nodded. "Would you want to read something of mine? It's not a story yet, more like a sketch." He tucked his chin nervously and I almost laughed with relief. Ernest Hemingway was nervous and I wasn't, suddenly. Not in the least.

"Sure," I said. "But I'm no literary critic. I'm not sure I can help you."

"It's all right. I'd just like to get your take on it."

"Okay, then. Yes," I said.

"I'll be right back," he said, and bolted halfway across the carpet before turning around. "Don't go away, all right?"

"Where would I go?"

"You'd be surprised," he said, mysteriously, and then ran off to fetch the pages.

Essentially, the story wasn't a story, he was right. It was a darkly funny sketch called "Wolves and Donuts" set in an Italian restaurant on Wabash Avenue. But even though the piece was unfinished, the voice was acid sharp and hilarious. We went into the kitchen for better light and a little quiet, and as I read, Ernest paced the room, his arms swinging and pawing the air as he waited for me to answer the question he couldn't bring himself to ask: *Is it good?*

When I'd turned the last page, he sat in the chair opposite me with an expectant look.

"You're very talented," I said, meeting his eyes. "I've probably spent too much time on Henry James. Your stuff isn't that."

"No."

"I'm not sure I get it completely, but I can tell you're a writer. Whatever that thing is, you have it."

"God that's good to hear. Sometimes I think all I really need is one person telling me that I'm not knocking my fool head against the bricks. That I have a shot at it."

"You do. Even I can see that."

He looked at me intently, boring a small hole with those eyes. "I like you, you know. You're a good clear sort."

"I like you, too," I said back, and it struck me how comfortable I felt with him, as if we were old friends or had already done this many times over, him handing me pages with his heart on his sleeve—he couldn't pretend this work didn't mean everything to him—me reading his words, quietly amazed by what he could do.

"Will you let me take you to dinner?" he said.

"Now?"

"What's stopping us?"

Kate, I thought. *Kate and Kenley and the whole drunken throng in the living room.*

"No one will even notice we're gone," he said, reading my hesitation.

"All right," I said, but slunk off like a thief to get my coat anyway. I wanted to go with him. I was dying to go, but he was wrong about no one noticing. As we ducked out the door together, I felt Kate's green eyes flashing hotly over my back and heard her silent shout, *Hadley, be sensible!*

I was tired of being sensible. I didn't turn around.

It was a sheer pleasure to walk the chilly Chicago streets with Ernest at my side, talking and talking, his cheeks flushed, his eyes beaming. We went to a Greek restaurant on Jefferson Street where we had roasted lamb and a cucumber salad with lemon and olives.

"I suppose it's embarrassing, but I've never had olives before," I said when the waiter arrived with our order.

"That should be illegal. Here, open."

He put the olive on my tongue, and as I closed my mouth around it, oily and warm with salt, I found myself flushing from the deliciousness but also the intimacy, his fork in my mouth. It was the most sensual thing that had happened to me in ages.

"Well?" he prodded.

"I love it," I said. "Though it's a little dangerous, isn't it?"

He smiled and looked at me appreciatively. "A little, yes." And then he ate a dozen himself, one after the other.

After dinner we walked under the elevated train and headed toward the Municipal Pier. The whole time he talked fast about his plans, all the things he wanted for himself, the poems, stories, and sketches he was burning to write. I'd never met anyone so vibrant or alive. He moved like light. He never *stopped* moving—or thinking, or dreaming apparently.

When we reached the pier, we walked along it all the way out to the end of the streetcar line.

"Did you know they had barracks and Red Cross units out here during the war? I worked for the Red Cross over in Italy, as an ambulance driver."

"The war seems very far away now, doesn't it?"

"Sometimes." A line of worry or doubt appeared on his forehead. "What were you doing in those days?"

"Hiding out, mostly. I sorted books in the basement of the public library. I'm told they eventually went to soldiers overseas."

"That's funny. I hand-delivered those books. Chocolate bars, too. Letters, cigarettes, candy. We had a canteen set up, but sometimes I went out to the line at night, on a bicycle. Can you picture it?"

"I can. It's a wobbly red bicycle, right?"

"The boy was wobbly too after he got blown all to hell."

I stopped walking. "Oh, Ernest, I'm sorry. I didn't know."

"Don't worry. I was a hero for a day or two." He leaned against the railing and looked out at the lake, gray on gray, with just a ghost of white. "You know what I think about now?"

I shook my head.

"Silkworms. I spent a night in San Pedro Norello, a village on the front. Horney was there—that's where I met him—and our cots were set up on the floor of this building, right? It was a silkworm factory. They were up over our heads, in the eaves, chewing away in racks full of mulberry leaves. That's the only thing you could hear. No shell fire, no nothing. It was terrible."

"I've never thought of silkworms that way. Maybe I've never thought of silkworms at all, but I can hear them now, the way you did."

"Sometimes when I can't sleep, I think I hear them chewing. I have to get up and turn the lights on and look up at the ceiling."

"Are they ever there?" I smiled, trying to lighten the mood.

"Not yet."

We headed away from the brightly lit shops and turned toward home—and I was struck by how rare it was to hear a near stranger share something so essential about himself. He told it beautifully, too, with real feeling. I think I was a little dumbstruck. Just who was this Ernest Hemingway?

Suddenly he stopped walking and faced me on the sidewalk. "Listen, Hash. You're not going to run off on me are you?"

"I'm not much of an athlete," I said.

"I like your spine. Did I tell you that?"

"You did."

"I like it more than that, then," he said. Then he gave me a winning smile and started to walk again, tucking my gloved hand under his arm.

The next morning Kate came into my room without knocking. I wasn't even dressed yet.

"I waited past midnight. Where were you?"

"I'm sorry. Ernest invited me to dinner. I wasn't sure how I could say no."

"*No* is the easiest word there is. *Children* learn to talk by saying no."

I pulled my robe more tightly around my waist and sat down on the bed. "All right. I didn't want to say no. It was just dinner, Kate. There's no harm done."

"Of course," she said, obviously still flustered. "I just feel protective of you and don't want to see you get tangled up in something awful."

"Why awful? He doesn't seem like a bad fellow."

"He's not bad, exactly." I could see she was trying to choose her words carefully. "He's just young. He likes women—*all* women, apparently. And I see you throwing yourself at him, blindly trusting him, and it worries me."

"I'm not throwing myself at anyone," I said, suddenly angry. "I had dinner with the man. Honestly, Kate."

"You're right, you're right," she said. "I'm getting carried away." She sat down beside me on the bed and reached for my hand. "Forget I said anything, okay? You're a levelheaded girl. You'll know what to do."

"*Nothing* happened."

"I know. I'm terrible." She rubbed my hand with hers and I let her, but my head was fairly spinning.

"This is all too much to think about before breakfast," I said.

"You poor thing." She stood, smoothing her skirt, and then she smoothed her expression, too, while I watched, righting and simplifying everything. It was a good trick. I wished I could do it.

The rest of that morning passed in a daze as I brooded over Kate's words and her concern for me. Was Ernest really someone to watch out for? He seemed so sincere and forthcoming. He'd confessed to writing poetry, for goodness' sake, and those stories about being wounded at the front—and the silkworms! Was this all part of some elaborate ploy to take advantage of me? If so, then Kate was right, I was falling for it, heaving myself at him like a dumb country mouse—likely one of dozens. I could barely stand to think about it.

"Maybe we should hightail it out of here before anyone stirs," Kate said when we'd finished our coffee. "I don't have to be at work at all today. What shall we do? The sky's the limit."

"You decide," I said. "I don't much care." And I didn't.

Another kind of girl might have suspected Kate of jealousy, but I was very simple and trusting, then. More than this, I was inexperienced. At twenty-eight I'd had a handful of beaux, but had only been in love once, and that had been awful enough to make me doubt men and myself for a good long while.

His name was Harrison Williams and he was my piano teacher when I was twenty and just returned home to St. Louis after a single year at Bryn Mawr. Although he was only a few months older than I was, he seemed much older and more sophisticated to me. I found it both appealing and intimidating that he'd studied overseas with famous composers and knew loads about European art and culture. I could listen to him talk about anything, and I suppose that's how it started, with admiration and envy. Then I found myself watching his hands and his eyes and his mouth. He wasn't an obvious Casanova, but he was handsome in his way, tall and slender, with dark thinning hair. Most appealing of all was his impression of me as exceptional. He thought I could make it as a concert pianist and I thought so, too, at least for the hours I sat at his piano bench working through finger-cramping études.

I worried a lot about my hair and dress those afternoons at Harrison's. As he paced and corrected and occasionally praised me, I did my best to decode him. Did the tapping of his fingertip on his temple mean he had or hadn't noticed my new stockings?

"You have a lovely alignment at the bench," he said to me one afternoon, and that's about all it took to send me spiraling into a fantasy of my alignment in white lace, his alignment in morning tails and gorgeous white gloves. I played terribly that day, distracted by my own swooning.

I loved him for a full year and then, in one night, all my wishing came apart. We were both at a neighbor's evening party, where I forced myself to tip back two glasses of too-sweet wine so I could be braver near him. The day before we'd gone for a walk together in the woods just outside of town. It was fall, crisp and windless, with the clouds overhead looking like perfect cutouts of themselves. He lit my cigarette. I stamped at some yellow leaves with the toe of my lace-up shoes, and then, in the middle of a very nice silence, he said, "You're such a dear person, Hadley. One of the best I've known, really."

It was hardly a declaration of love, but I told myself he did care for me and believed it—long enough for the gulping of the wine in any case. I waited for the room to tip just that much off its center, then walked up to Harrison, picking each foot up and putting it back down again, getting closer. I was wearing my black lace. It was my hands-down favorite dress because it never failed to make me feel a bit like Carmen. And maybe it was the dress as much as the wine that lifted my hand toward Harrison's coat sleeve. I'd never touched him before, so it was probably clean surprise that stopped him still. We stood there, locked and lovely as statues in a garden—and for several dozen heart-beats I was his wife. I had already borne his children and secured his loyalty and was well beyond the thorny rim of my own mind, that place where hope got itself snagged and swallowed over and over. I could have this. It was already mine.

"Hadley," he said quietly.

I looked up. Harrison's eyes were the pale blue of drowned stars, and they were saying no—simply and quietly. Just *no*.

What did I say? Maybe nothing. I don't remember. The music lurched, candlelight blurred, my hand dropped to the lace of my skirt. A minute before it had been a gypsy's dress, now it was funereal.

"I have a terrible headache," I said to my mother, trying to explain why I needed to go home that instant.

"Of course you do," she said, and her expression softened. "Let's get our girl to bed."

Once home, I let her lead me up the stairs and help me into my muslin nightgown. She tucked me into layers of quilting and put a cool hand on my forehead, smoothing my hair. "Get some rest now."

"Yes," I said, because I couldn't begin to explain that I'd *been* resting for twenty-one years, but that tonight I'd tried for something else.

That was my one brush with love. Was it love? It felt awful enough. I spent another two years crawling around in the skin of it, smoking too much and growing too thin and having stray thoughts of jumping from my balcony like a tortured heroine in a Russian novel. After a time, though more slowly than I wanted, I came to see that Harrison wasn't my failed prince and I wasn't his victim. He hadn't led me on at all; I'd led *myself* on. The thought of love could still make me queasy and pale, though, more than half a decade later. I was still gullible, clearly, and needed someone's guidance—Kate's, for instance.

We tramped all over Chicago that day looking first for world-class corned beef and then for new gloves. I let Kate chatter away and distract me and felt grateful that she had warned me about Ernest. Even if his intentions were entirely above suspicion, I was far too susceptible just then. I'd come to Chicago wanting escape and I'd gotten it, but too much dreaming was dangerous. I wasn't happy at home, but drowning myself in fanciful notions about Ernest Hemingway wasn't going to solve anything for me. My life was my life; I would have to stare it down, somehow, and make it work for me.

I spent another full week in Chicago and every day of that time brought some new excitement. We went to a football game, saw a matinee showing of *Madama Butterfly,* roamed the city by day and by night. Whenever I saw Ernest, which was often, I strove to keep my head clear and just enjoy his company without conjuring up any drama in one direction or another. I might have been a little more reserved with him than I'd been before, but he didn't say anything and didn't force any intimacy until my last evening in town.

It was freezing that night—too cold to be out, really—but a group of us grabbed armfuls of wool blankets, poured rum into flasks, and then piled into Kenley's Ford and headed out to Lake Michigan. The dunes were steep and pale in moonlight, and we invented a game around them, climbing to the top of one—drunkenly, of course—and then rolling down like logs. Kate went first because she loved to be the first at anything, and then Kenley went, singing his way down. When my turn came, I crawled up the dune as sand shifted under my feet and hands. At the top, I looked around and everything was bright frosted stars and distances.

"C'mon, then, coward!" Ernest yelled up at me.

I closed my eyes and let myself fall, barreling down over the hard bumps. I'd had so much to drink I couldn't feel a thing—nothing but a thrilling sense of wildness and freedom. It was a kind of euphoria, really, and fear was a key part of it. For the first time since I was a girl, I felt the heady rush of being afraid and liked the sensation. At the bottom, I'd barely come to a stop when Ernest whirled me up out of the dark and kissed me hard. I felt his tongue for a hot instant against my lips.

"Oh," was all I could say. I couldn't think about whether anyone had seen us. I couldn't think at all. His face was inches from mine, more charged and convincing and altogether awake than anything I'd ever seen.

"Oh," I said again, and he let me go.

The next day I packed my bags for my return trip to St. Louis feeling a bit lost. I'd been so swept away by living for two weeks, I couldn't really imagine going back home. I didn't want to.

Kate was working that day and we'd already said our good-byes. Kenley had to be at work as well, but had been kind enough to offer to drive me to the station on his lunch break and save me the cab fare. After everything was stowed and ready, I put on my coat and hat and went to wait for him in the living room. But when a body appeared in the hall to fetch me, it was Ernest's.

"Kenley couldn't get away after all?" I asked.

"No. I wanted to do it."

I nodded dumbly and collected my things.

It wasn't much of a distance to Union Station and we passed it mostly in silence. He wore wool trousers and a gray wool jacket, with a dark cap pulled down nearly to his eyebrows. His cheeks were pink with cold and he looked very beautiful. *Beautiful* was exactly the right word for him, too. His looks weren't feminine but they were perfect and un-marred and sort of heroic, as if he'd stepped out of a Greek poem about love and battle.

"You can let me out here," I said as we neared the station.

"Would it kill you to give a guy a break?" he said, finding a place to park.

"No. Probably not."

A few minutes later, we stood together on the platform. I clutched my ticket and my pocketbook. He held my suitcase, shifting it from hand to gloved hand—but as soon as my train appeared, its silver-brown body trailing smoke and soot, he set it down at his feet. Suddenly he was holding me tight against his chest.

My heart beat fast. I wondered if he could feel it. "I don't think I've ever met anyone like you," I said.

He didn't say anything at all, just kissed me, and through that kiss I could feel all of him radiating warmth and life. There was so much I didn't know about Ernest and even more I wouldn't let myself ask or even imagine, but I found myself surrendering anyway, second by second. We were surrounded by people on the platform, but also entirely alone. And when I finally boarded my train a few minutes later, my legs were shaking.

I found a seat and looked out my window into the crowd, scanning the dark suits and hats and coats. And then there he was, pushing closer to the train, smiling at me like a maniac and waving. I waved back, and then he held up one hand like a sheet of notebook paper, and the other like a pencil, pantomiming.

I'll write to you, he mouthed. Or maybe it was *I'll write* you.

I closed my eyes against hot, sudden tears, and then leaned into the plush seat as my train carried me home.

FOUR

*I*n 1904, the year I turned thirteen, St. Louis was host to the Louisiana Purchase Exposition, better known as the World's Fair. The fair grounds covered twelve hundred acres in and around Forest Park and Washington University, with seventy-five miles of paths and roads connecting the buildings and barns and theaters. Many of these structures were plaster of Paris over wooden framing, built to last only a few months, but they looked like opulent neoclassical palaces. Our crown jewel, the Palace of Fine Arts, boasted a sculpture garden fashioned after the Roman Baths of Caracalla. There were lagoons you could paddle along, enormous man-made waterfalls and sunken gardens, exotic animal zoos and human zoos with pygmies and primitives, bearded girls and pinheaded boys. All along the Pike, hundreds of amusements and games and food stalls enthralled the passersby. I had my very first ice-cream cone there and couldn't stop marveling at how the sugary cylinder wasn't cold in my hand. The strawberry ice cream inside it seemed different, too. Better. It might have been the best thing I'd ever tasted.

Fonnie was with me on the Pike that day, but she didn't want ice cream. She didn't want cotton candy or puffed wheat or iced tea or any of the other novel offerings either, she wanted to go home where our mother was preparing to host her weekly suffragette meeting.

I'd never understood why Fonnie was drawn to Mother's group. The women always seemed so unhappy to me. To hear them talk, you would think that marriage was the most terrible thing that could happen to a woman. My mother was always the loudest and most emphatic one in the room, nodding sharply while Fonnie passed plates of teacakes and watercress sandwiches, trying very hard to please everyone.

"Another half hour," I said, trying to bargain with Fonnie. "Don't you want to see the Palace of Electricity?"

"Stay if you like. I'm surprised you can enjoy yourself." And then she flounced imperiously off into the crowd.

I *was* enjoying myself or had been until she reminded me I was supposed to be sad. It was probably very selfish of me to want to stay and smell the salt on the popcorn, and hear the braying from the barns. But it was April and the cherry trees around the lagoons were flowering. I could close my eyes and hear fountains. I could open them and imagine I was in Rome or Versailles. Fonnie grew smaller in the crowd, her dark skirt blotted by riotous color. I wanted to let her go without caring what she thought of me or said to our mother, but I couldn't. I took a last dejected look at my ice-cream cone and then dropped it into a trash barrel as I trotted off after my sister toward home, where the curtains were drawn and the lights were banked, and had been for some time. We were in mourning. My father had been dead two months.

Ours was the quintessentially good family, with Pilgrim lineage on both sides and lots of Victorian manners keeping everything safe and reliable. My father's father founded the St. Louis Public Library and the Richardson Drug Company, which became the largest pharmaceutical house west of the Mississippi. My mother's father was a teacher who started the Hillsboro Academy in Illinois and later a private high school in St. Louis called the City University. Fonnie and I went to the best schools wearing navy-blue skirts with knife-sharp pleats. We sat for private lessons at one of our two Steinway grand pianos, and spent summers in Ipswich, Massachusetts, at our beach cottage. And everything was very good and fine until it wasn't.

My father, James Richardson, was an executive at the family drug company. He'd go off in the mornings in his bowler hat and black string tie smelling of shaving cream and coffee and, just underneath, a ghost of whiskey. He kept a flask in his dressing gown. We all knew another lay tucked in his desk drawer in the study, which he locked with a tiny silver key. Still another waited behind stacked jars of stewed fruit in the pantry, where our cook, Martha, pretended not to see it. He tried not to be home very often, and when he was, he was quiet and distracted. But he was kind, too. My mother, Florence, was his perfect opposite—all sharp creases and pins, full of advice and judgments. It's possible my father was too soft and too cowardly around her, inclined to back away into his study or out the door rather than face up to her about anything, but I didn't fault him for this.

My mother always preferred Fonnie, who was twenty-two months older than me. We had an older brother, Jamie, who was off to college before I started kindergarten, and there was Dorothea, eleven years older but very dear to me just the same, who married young and lived nearby with her husband, Dudley. Because of the closeness in our ages, Fonnie was my primary companion as a girl, but we couldn't have been more different. She was obedient and bendable and good in a way my mother could easily understand and praise. I was impulsive and talkative and curious about everything—far too curious for my mother's taste. I loved to sit at the end of our driveway, my elbows on my knees, and watch the streetcar trundle along the center of the boulevard, wondering about the men and women inside, where they were headed, what they were thinking, and if they noticed me, there, noticing them. My mother would call me back to the house and send me up to the nursery, but I'd simply stare out the window, dreaming and musing.

"What could you possibly be fit for?" she often said. "You can't keep your head out of the clouds."

It was a legitimate enough question, I suppose. She worried about me because she didn't understand me in the least. And then something terrible happened. When I was six years old, I managed to dream myself right out the window.

It was a spring day, and I was home sick from school. When I grew bored with the nursery, which generally happened quickly, I began to watch Mike, our handyman, pushing a wheelbarrow across our yard. I was crazy about Mike and found him infinitely more interesting than

anyone in my family. His fingernails were square and nicked. He whis-
tled and carried a bright blue handkerchief in his pocket.

"What're you up to, Mike?" I said, shouting out the nursery window,
craning over the sill to better see him.

He looked up just as I lost my balance and fell crashing to the paving
stones below.

For months I lay flat in bed while the doctors wondered if I would walk
again. I recovered slowly, and as I did, my mother had a baby carriage
specially adapted for me. She liked to push me around the neighborhood, stopping at each of our neighbors' houses so they could exclaim
about the wonder of my survival.

"Poor Hadley," my mother said. "Poor hen." She said it over and
over, until her words became stitched onto my brain, replacing any
other description of me, as well as every other possible outcome.

It didn't matter that I healed completely, learning to walk without a
limp. My constitution was a great worry in the house and stayed that
way. Even the slightest sniffle, it was thought, would damage me further. I didn't learn to swim, didn't run and play in the park as my friends
did. I read books instead, tucked into the window seat in the parlor, surrounded by swirls of stained glass and claret-colored drapes. And after
a time, I stopped struggling even internally against the prescribed quietness. Books could be an incredible adventure. I stayed under my blanket and barely moved, and no one would have guessed how my mind
raced and my heart soared with stories. I could fall into any world and
go without notice, while my mother barked orders at the servants or entertained her disagreeable friends in the front room.

When my father was alive, I often watched him come home while
the women were still gathered. Hearing them he'd freeze and then re-
trace his steps, slinking back out the door. *Where did he go?* I wondered.
How far did he have to walk and how much whiskey did it take to quiet
my mother's voice in his head? Did he remember the way he used to
love his bicycle? I did. There was a time when he would happily ride
anywhere in St. Louis, choosing it over any other mode of transporta-
tion, probably because of the freedom it offered. Once he hitched a cart

to the back and took Fonnie and me along the paths in Forest Park, singing "Waltzing Matilda." He had the most beautiful baritone, and as threads of song floated back to us in the cart that day, his happiness seemed so real and so strange to me, I was afraid to move in case I might startle it away.

It was a cold morning in February when a single shot rang through the house. My mother heard it first and knew instantly what had happened. She hadn't let herself think the word *suicide*, that would be too terrible and too common, but she'd been half expecting it just the same. Downstairs, behind the locked doors of his study, she found my father lying on the carpet in a pool of blood, his skull shattered.

For weeks after, the noise of my father's death rang through the house. We learned he'd lost tens of thousands of dollars in the stock market, that he'd borrowed more and lost that too. We already knew he drank but not that he did little else in his last weeks, plagued by throbbing headaches that made sleep impossible.

After he was gone, my mother stayed in her room, crying and confused and staring at the drawn curtains while the servants took over. I'd never seen this kind of chaos in my house and didn't know what to do with it but play Chopin's nocturnes and cry for my father, wishing I had known him better.

The door to my father's study stayed closed for a time, but not locked. The carpets had been cleaned but not replaced, the revolver had been emptied and polished and placed back in his desk—and these details were so terrible I couldn't help but be magnetized by them. Again and again, I imagined the last moments of his life. How alone he must have felt. How deadened and how hopeless, or else he couldn't have done it, lifting the muzzle and tripping the trigger.

My mood grew so low that my family began to worry I might hurt myself. Everyone knew that children of suicides stood a greater risk of taking that route. Was I like him? I didn't know, but I had inherited his migraine headaches. Each one resembled a dreadful visitation, pressure and nausea and a dull but constant thrumming from the base of my skull while I lay absolutely still in my airless room. If I stayed there long enough, my mother would come in and pat my hand and tuck the covers around my feet, saying, "You're a good girl, Hadley."

I couldn't help but notice my mother responded to me more warmly when I was ill, so it's no surprise that I often was or thought I was. I missed so much school as a junior and senior that I was forced to stay another year as all my girlfriends went away to college without me. It was like watching a train leave the station for some far-off and exciting place, with no ticket myself and no means to purchase one. When letters began to arrive from Barnard and Smith and Mount Holyoke, I suddenly felt sick with jealousy of my friends' excitement and promise.

"I want to apply to Bryn Mawr," I told my mother. Her sister Mary lived in Philadelphia, and I thought having a relative nearby would put my mother at ease.

"Oh, Hadley. Why do you insist on overreaching yourself? Be realistic."

Fonnie came into the room and sat near Mother. "What about your headaches?" she said.

"I'll be perfectly fine."

Fonnie's brow furrowed skeptically.

"Mary can care for me if something happens. You know how competent she is." I put particular stress on the word *competent* because my mother loved and was often persuaded by it. For the moment, however, she only sighed and said she would give it serious thought, which meant that she would take the matter up with our neighbor Mrs. Curran and the Ouija board.

Mother had long been interested in matters of the occult. There were séances in our house occasionally, but many more of them down the street at Mrs. Curran's. According to my mother, she was a savant of the supernatural and had a very familiar and persuasive way with the board. I wasn't invited to attend the session, but when Mother returned home from Mrs. Curran's she reported that I could go to Bryn Mawr after all, and that everything would be well.

Later I had to wonder about Mrs. Curran's prophecy because it seemed blatantly false to me. I did go away, in 1911, but the whole venture was doomed before it even began. The summer before I left for Bryn

Mawr, my older sister Dorothea was badly burned in a fire. Though she was well out of the house during the years I was growing up, Dorothea had always been the kindest and most supportive member of my family, and I felt she understood me in a way no one else did or wanted to. When things at home grew too stifling and restrained, I'd walk to her house and watch her two young boys wrestling around her, feeling calmed and restored.

Dorothea was very pregnant that summer. She was home alone with the boys a great deal, and one afternoon the three were out on the front porch when Dorothea saw that a fire had started in a pile of rubber tires in the empty lot next door. The boys were curious about it, but Dorothea was afraid it might spread to her own yard. She ran over and tried to stamp out the flames with her feet, but her long summer kimono quickly caught fire. Her stockings did, too, badly burning her all the way to the waist before she fell to the ground and rolled, snuffing out the flames.

When her husband, Dudley, called us with the news, we were at our vacation cottage on Ipswich Bay. We were all worried sick about Dorothea, but Dudley reassured us she was in the hospital getting the best of care. She had no fever, and the doctors believed she would re-cover fully. The next day, she delivered a stillborn baby girl. Dorothea and Dudley were both devastated, but the doctors were still saying she'd live. They kept saying that until she died, eight days after the fire. Mother got on a train for the funeral, but the rest of us stayed in Ips-wich, heartbroken and numb.

I remember feeling that I might not survive Dorothea's loss, and maybe that I didn't want to. Mother came back from St. Louis, bring-ing Dudley and the boys with her. They stepped off the train looking wretched, and what comfort could I offer? *They have no mother,* I found myself thinking over and over.

One afternoon shortly after the funeral there was a terrible storm in Ipswich Bay, and I talked one of the boys from a neighboring cottage into taking me out in it, in a rowboat. Waves slashed at the bow and came stinging over the sides and into our faces. I couldn't even swim, but he didn't turn back, even when the lighthouse captain signaled us to come in. The clouds were low and terrible and the air was drenched and salty. I felt as I if was drowning the whole time, over and over again. And even when we made it back to shore that day, the feeling that I was still out in the bay, sinking deeper and deeper, stayed with me through the rest of that summer and long afterward.

In September I boarded the train and went off to Bryn Mawr as planned, but my classmates seemed to be running on a different frequency. The girls in my dorm spent their afternoons in the salon drinking tea and frothy hot chocolate, talking about dance mixers and potential conquests. I felt well removed. As a girl I knew I was pretty, with bright red hair, nice eyes, and fair skin—but now I couldn't seem to care whether boys noticed me or not. I stopped taking an interest in my clothes and my coursework, too. I began to fail exams, which was difficult and surprising to me, since, aside from my appalling pile of absences, I'd been a good student all of my life. Now I found I couldn't summon any focus or attention or even interest.

The next fall, I let Fonnie and my mother persuade me to stay home. I can't say it was any better for me there than at school. There was nowhere to go in the house to escape my dark thoughts. I couldn't sleep, and when I could, I had terrible, obsessive dreams about Dorothea and my father, replaying the last awful moments of their lives. I'd wake to a panicked feeling and the promise of more joyless days and nights. And if I said that I remained in this kind of coma for eight more years, then you'd understand how ready I was to live just as my mother began to die.

My mother was sick with Bright's disease for years, but things got quickly worse in the summer of 1920. Throughout the hottest weeks of July and August, I hardly ever left the upstairs apartment, and when I did leave, she worried endlessly.

"Elizabeth? Is that you?" she called out weakly as soon as she heard me on the stairs. I wasn't sure why she was using my given name after all these years, but much about her baffled me just then. She didn't resemble the steel-spined and difficult woman who had always been able to dissolve me with a single word. She was frail and anxious, calling out again as I hurried up the stairs: "*Elizabeth?*"

"I'm here, Mother." I came into the main room where she rested on the worn pink velvet settee. I put down my shopping bags and un-pinned my hat. "Are you too warm? Can I open a window?"

"Is it warm?" Her hands kneaded the afghan in her lap. "I'm chilled to the bone."

I pulled a chair over to the settee and took up her hands, rubbing them to bring blood to the surface, but wherever I touched, the impres-sions of my fingertips became set, as if her skin had become bread dough. I let her go and she started to whimper.

"What can I do?"

"Bring your sister. I need Fonnie with me now."

I nodded and stood to leave, but her eyes opened wider. "Don't go, please don't leave me." So I sat again, and this is how it went, all that long night. She took a little broth and slept lightly for a few hours. Then, near midnight, she became suddenly calm.

"I worry greatly for you, Elizabeth," she said. "What will become of you when I'm gone?"

"I'm a grown woman, Mother. I'll be fine. I promise."

"No." She shook her head. "Years ago Mrs. Curran and I spoke to Dorothea about you." Her breath was labored, and I didn't want to see her struggle this way.

"Shh. It doesn't matter."

"It does. We asked her about you several times and she rebuffed us. She had nothing to say."

I'd always been skeptical of the occult—the board, the hushed, candlelit séances and automatic writing sessions with red scarves on the lamps—but now I felt a rush of cold through me. Was it possible that Mother *had* been in touch with Dorothea? And if so, why had my sis-ter, dead for nine years, turned her back on me? Did she know some-thing hard and sad about my fate? The idea terrified me and yet there was no way to be certain. I couldn't ask my mother to elaborate on the session; she was exhausted and more anxious than ever. I also wasn't entirely sure I wanted to know. What if the future was worse than the present? What if it didn't exist at all?

All that August night I stayed in the straight-backed chair next to the settee. I swabbed Mother's forehead and neck with a damp cloth and looked out at the warm summer night, the dark sky and darker trees, everything as remote as exhibits in a museum. And I knew that I too could die in this room. This was one way my life's wheel could turn.

Hours later, near dawn, my mother died without a sigh or rattle or ragged breath. How very different from the way my father had gone— the crack of his revolver shaking the doors in their jambs—but no less final. While everyone else was downstairs sleeping, I looked at the face I'd hated sometimes and felt sorry for at other times. Her hands were curled to each side of her thin body, and I traced one with my fingertips, feeling a terrible and complex love for her. Then I went downstairs to wake Fonnie and Roland and call the doctor. I made breakfast and had a bath, and then sat with Fonnie in the parlor to see about the funeral arrangements. Mother's body was still upstairs waiting for the coroner, and I could feel her there, still pressing on me. She'd always seemed to take pleasure in the quietness of my life, as if I'd become what she thought I would, which was not much of anything at all. This tugging was very old and powerful, and I knew I could easily give in to it, in to nothingness. Or I could push with everything I had the other way.

FIVE

*E*verything all right, miss?" the cabdriver asked.

"It will have to be," I said, and opened the door.

I was back in St. Louis after a long day on the train, a day that had been stretched further by the feeling that I'd failed at something in Chicago. Now here I was again, back at Fonnie and Roland's house on Cates Avenue. It was all I could do to pay the man and get out of the car.

Outside, the air was crisp and chill. The driver walked behind me, delivering my bags to the porch; our footfalls rang hollowly on the flagstones. Inside, I dropped my luggage at the bottom of the steps and went up to my apartment, which had a cold, unlived-in feel. Though it was late and I was exhausted, I lit the lamps and built a fire to warm myself. I sat on the pink settee and wrapped my own arms around my shoulders and wondered if some part of my mother was still there in the room, swaddled in an afghan, maybe, and looking at me pitifully: *Poor Hadley. Poor hen.*

The next morning I slept later than usual, and when I came downstairs, Fonnie was waiting for me in the dining room. "Well? I want to hear everything. What did you do? What kind of people did you meet?"

I told her all about the parties and games and the interesting people who moved through Kenley's apartment in swells—but I didn't tell her about Ernest. What was there to tell? I wasn't sure where we stood at all, even as friends.

As Fonnie and I talked, Roland came into the room, fastening his cuffs, moving in a cloud of soap and piney hair tonic. He sat down and Fonnie eased her chair ever so subtly away from his so that she didn't have to see him eat. That's how they were at this point. Their marriage was a disaster and always had been and it made me feel badly for them both.

"Well," Roland said. "Was Chi-Town everything you imagined?"

I nodded, spreading marmalade on toast.

"And did you conquer dozens of new beaux?"

Fonnie made an almost inaudible huffing noise, but said nothing.

"I wouldn't say dozens," I said.

"You must have made at least one conquest. This letter just arrived for you." He pulled a crumpled-looking artifact from his suit pocket. "Special delivery," he said. "It must be serious." He smiled and handed over the letter.

"What's that?" Fonnie said.

"Special delivery," I repeated in a kind of trance. Ernest's name was on the envelope, scrawled but clear enough. He must have mailed it just after he put me on the train, paying the extra ten cents to make sure it arrived first thing. *I'll write to you. I'll write* you. I fingered the envelope, half afraid to open it.

"What's your fellow's name?" Roland asked.

"I wouldn't call him my fellow, but his name is Ernest Hemingway."

"Hemingway?" Fonnie said. "What kind of name is that?"

"I have no idea," I said, and carried the letter out of the room to open it. It was as clutched and creased as if it had spent days in his pocket—and I already loved that, no matter what the letter held. I found a quiet corner in the sitting room near my piano and discovered that inside the pages were rumpled, too, and scratched at with dark ink. *Dear Hasovitch*—it began—*You on the train and me here and everything emptier now you're gone. Tell me are you real?*

I put the letter down because I almost couldn't bear the feeling that he'd crawled into my head. *Are you real?* I wondered exactly the same about him—and had more right, too, I thought, particularly after Kate's warning. I was as solid as the ground he walked on, too solid probably. But what about him? His attentions to me had never faltered during my visit, but that didn't mean he was reliable, only that for the time being he thought I was worth pursuing. The truth was I didn't know what to think about him, and so I kept reading, devouring the rest of his letter very quickly, all he had to say about what he was doing and wanted to do, his work, his thoughts. He said there might be a job for him at a monthly magazine called the *Co-operative Commonwealth* if he'd give in to doing the whole thing himself—as writer, reporter, editor, the whole ball of wax. *Not crazy about the terms but will probably take it,* he wrote. Though there was a good deal of unquiet chatter in my mind about him, I couldn't help liking his voice and vibrancy and how his words on paper sounded like the Ernest who invented reasons to pop into my room in Chicago. His letter was doing that now, bringing Ernest into the sitting room that had been dark and airless a moment before.

"Well?" Fonnie said, coming into the room with a swish of her somber wool skirt. "What does he have to say?"

"Nothing out of the ordinary," I said, but of course that wasn't true. Everything about Ernest Hemingway was out of the ordinary.

"Well, it's nice to have new friends, anyway. I'm happy you've found a pleasant distraction." She sat and took up her lacework.

"Are you?"

"Of course. I want you to be happy."

That was probably true, but only if *happy* meant I was locked upstairs for the rest of my life, the lonely maiden aunt.

"Thank you, Fonnie," I said, and then excused myself to my room, where I started in on my answer. I didn't want to be too enthusiastic. I didn't want to make my reply mean more than it did—but I found that I liked writing to him. I made my reply last all day, putting things down as they happened, wanting to be sure he could picture me moving from room to room, practicing the piano, sitting down to a perfect cup of ginger tea with my friend Elsa Blackman, watching our gardener prune the rosebushes and swaddle them in burlap for winter. *I miss the lake tonight,* I wrote. *Lots of other things too. Do you want to meet me in the kitchen for a smoke?*

My mother had kept a snapshot of me in a bathing suit, splashing knee-deep in the Meramec River with Elsa, both of us happy and washed over with sunshine. This version of Hadley hardly ever made an appearance these days, it was true, but I thought Ernest would like her open face and anything-goes smile. I tucked the photo into an envelope with my letter, and then, before I could have second thoughts about anything, walked down the street to the letter box at the corner. It was dark out, and as I walked, I looked into houses as if they were glowing bowls. Everything glowed faintly—and for a moment I could imagine light speeding over all the knobby cornfields and sleeping barns between St. Louis and Chicago. When I arrived at the box, I gripped my letter, kissed it on impulse, and then pushed it into the slot and let it go.

SIX

I have so many schemes about writing—so much I want to see and feel and do. Say, do you remember playing the piano with your hair glinting full on and how you got up and came over to me on the davenport and said, "Do you gather me, Begonia?"

Do you gather me, Hash?

Will you come up here already and give me some of that dead-sure stuff that's you?

His letters came crushed and strangled, full of deliciousness, sometimes two and three a day. I tried to be more reserved at first, vowing to write only once a week, but that fell apart immediately. Before long I found myself in a real bind. The letters were flying back and forth, but what did they mean? Kate's voice often filled my head—*He likes women, all women, apparently*—and I debated over whether or not I should tell her about our quickly progressing friendship. I couldn't imagine her not feeling hurt and angry; I was blatantly, willfully disregarding her advice after all. But if I confessed everything, she might give me *more* advice, and then I'd have to listen and perhaps act on it.

I was torn between wanting to know if I could trust Ernest and wishing I could stay blind enough to keep things exactly as they were. His words already meant so much—too much. Each of his letters was a perfect tonic and writing him, too, was a tonic, and before long I learned I could hear the mail boy on his bicycle from several blocks away even if he didn't ring his bell. I told myself that Kate didn't know *everything* about Ernest. Who knew everything about anyone? There were qualities coming through in his letters—tenderness, for instance, and palpable warmth—that she might never have seen in all those summers in Michigan. It was possible. It had to be, because the happiness that grew out of Ernest's interest in me was seeping over into the rest of my life. I was suddenly busier and more content at home than I'd ever been. Two friends, Bertha Doan and Ruth Bradfield, had moved into the upstairs apartment with me as boarders, and for the first time in almost a decade, I wasn't lonely in my own house. I also had young men interested in me, and even if they weren't anything extraordinary, they were a nice diversion. I let them take me dancing or to the theater and even let a few of them kiss me good night. Not one of them had Ernest's great big square head or padding feet and hands; not one asked his wonderful questions or made me want to say, *Do you gather me, Begonia?*

I kept up with it, though, going out with nearly anyone who asked because Ernest, dear soul that he was, was theoretical—a lovely hypothesis—and hundreds of miles away. In St. Louis, where I was fated to live my actual life, there was Dick Pierce, the brother of a good friend. I liked his company and knew that if I encouraged him at all, he'd fall in love with me and perhaps even propose, but I felt little or nothing for him. There was also Pere Rowland, a pleasantly rumpled boy who knew a lot about books and music, but romantic dates didn't appeal to me as much as when a group of us would jam into someone's car and go to a movie in town or the dance hall where everyone was happy and free. Afterward, Ruth and Bertha and I would sit up in our nightgowns with tea and talk through the events of the night.

I had just turned twenty-nine, but in a way I felt younger and more carefree than I did my first year at Bryn Mawr, when I couldn't enjoy the smallest happiness or intimacy. It was as if I was experiencing a long-delayed coming out, and I was grateful for every minute of it.

And then there were the letters from Chicago arriving every day, always beautifully crumpled and full of busy news. Ernest told me all about his articles for the *Commonwealth*, his ideas for sketches and novels. But more and more he was also sharing stories about his growing up about the long summers up in Michigan when his father, Ed, who was a practicing obstetrician and natural outdoorsman, had taught him how to build a fire and cook in the open, how to use an ax, land and dress a fish, hunt squirrel and partridge and pheasant.

Whenever I think of my father, he wrote, *he's in the woods flushing jack-snipe or walking through short dead grass or shocks of corn, or splitting wood with frost in his beard.* I read these sentences with tears in my eyes because I had so few warm memories of my own father. When I did think about him, the first image that came to me was his revolver, and then the noise it made ringing through the house. Remembering his death and the way I used to painfully fixate on it disturbed me so much I had to walk twice around the block in a stinging wind before I was calm enough to return to Ernest's letter.

But if I was jealous of his relationship with his father, his mother was troubling in other ways. Nearly every time he mentioned her in a letter, she was *that bitch.* He described her as utterly dominant in the household, quick to criticize and full of unbendable ideas about how life should proceed, down to every detail. Before he could read, she'd taught Ernest to memorize Latin and German phrases and lines of "essential" poetry. Although he tried to respect her creative spirit—she sang opera and painted a little and wrote poetry—Ernest ultimately believed she was a selfish mother and wife, intent on her own needs at the risk of destroying everyone around her, particularly her husband. She forced Dr. Hemingway into giving in to every one of her demands, and seeing this made Ernest despise her.

Though Ernest's passionate rejection of his mother gave me chills, I couldn't help but recognize it. Learning just how alike our parents' relationships were was eerie, and yet what struck me hardest was how even though I'd often detested my mother's indomitable will and even blamed her for my father's suicide, I'd never expressed this hatred to a soul. It had seethed and roiled inside me. On the occasions it forced its way to the surface, I took up my feather pillow and screamed my feelings into it, choking them off at the root. Ernest spat out his rage freely. Whose response was the most terrifying?

Ultimately, I felt a growing respect for the way he could express even the worst bits of himself and was drawn in by his confidences. I looked forward to Ernest's letters as I did little else. But his candor, I soon learned, applied to everything equally. In early December, not long after my birthday, he wrote that he'd been attracted the night before by a girl in a flashing green dress at a party. It made me sick to read this. I had no flashing green dress, and even if I did, he wouldn't see it. He was hundreds of miles away, absorbed by the details of his days and nights there. We were friends and confidants, yes—but he didn't owe me anything, had made me not a single promise, not even a false one. He could follow that green dress like a siren into the lake if he wanted. I had no hold on him.

No one seemed to have any hold on anyone, in fact. That was a sign of the times. We were all on the verge now, bursting with youth and promise and little trills of jazz. The year before, Olive Thomas had starred in *The Flapper*, and the word suddenly meant jazz and moved like it, too. Girls everywhere stepped out of their corsets and shortened their dresses and darkened their lips and eyes. We said "cat's pajamas" and "I'll say" and "that's so jake." Youth, in 1921, was everything, but that was just the thing that could worry me sick. I was twenty-nine, feeling almost obsolete, but Ernest was twenty-one and white hot with life. What was I thinking?

"Maybe I'm not up to this game," I told my roommate Ruth after I'd gotten Ernest's siren letter. Bertha was out, and Ruth and I were making dinner together, moving easily around each other in the small kitchen, snapping beans and boiling water for spaghetti, as if we were two maiden aunts who'd done this for decades.

"I'm not sure any of us are," Ruth said, measuring salt and tossing some over her shoulder for luck. She had wonderfully strong hands, and I found myself watching them and wishing I could be more like her. She turned to face me and gave me a wry smile. "But what else is there? If we give up now, we're done for."

"I might just crawl under my bed and not come out until I'm old and doddering and can't remember feeling anything for anyone at all."

She nodded. "You want to, but you won't."

"I won't." I moved around the small table, setting the plates and second-best silver, smoothing our two napkins. "I'll try very hard not to."

stones under our feet. He wanted everything there was to have, and more than that.

I slept and read at our hotel the next afternoon while Ernest arranged for an interview with Mussolini. He'd recently been elected to the Italian Chamber of Deputies, and this fascinated Ernest. The man seemed to be a mass of contradictions. He was strongly nationalistic, and wanted to bring Italy back to its former glory by reaching into its Roman past. He seemed genuinely invested in the plight of the working class and of women, all of which he'd laid out in *The Manifesto of the Fascist Struggle*. And yet he also managed to endear himself to the aristocracy and the bourgeoisie, guaranteeing their continued existence. He seemed to want to be all things to all people, traditional and revolutionary, loved by the military, the business class, and the liberals. The National Fascist Party was gathering steam so quickly it all seemed terribly inevitable.

"Are you nervous?" I asked as he was organizing his notebooks and preparing to leave.

"Of what? He's just a big bully, isn't he?"

"I don't know. Some say he's a monster."

"Maybe, but monsters don't always look that way. They have clean fingernails and use a knife and fork and speak the King's English."

I buttoned his coat and brushed the fabric over his shoulders with my hands.

"You're fussing, wife. Take a nap, and don't worry."

He was gone for two hours, and when he came back to the hotel to type up his notes, he seemed all too pleased to tell me he'd been right. "The man's up to here with bluff," he said, gesturing to his neck, "and nothing on top."

"Was he wearing his black shirt?" I asked, very much relieved.

"He was, they all were." He sat down at the desk and put fresh paper in his Corona. "He's bigger than you'd guess, too, with a wide brown face and very pretty hands. A woman's hands, really."

"I wouldn't write that if I were you."

He laughed and began to type rapid fire in his usual way, his fingers stabbing quickly with very little breaking or breathing. "I'll tell you what else," he said without looking up, "there was a beautiful wolfhound pup with him in the room."

"So the fascist monster is a dog lover."

"Maybe he planned to eat it later," he said, grinning.

"You're terrible."

"Yes," he said, his index fingers poised for another violent attack on his machine. "That was a fine dog."

The next day we boarded a bus to Schio, where Ernest wanted to show me the mill and the wisteria and every part of the town that had managed to stay so fine in his memory, no matter what else had happened around it. But on the way, the sky dimmed and grew gray. It began to rain and didn't stop. When we finally arrived at the town, Ernest seemed surprised. "It's so much smaller," he said.

"Maybe it's shrunk in the rain," I said, trying to lighten the mood, but quickly realizing that it wasn't going to be possible. For the whole visit, Ernest wrestled with memory. Everything had changed and grown dingy in the four years since he'd last been here. The wool factory—closed down during the war—spewed black muck into the swimming hole where Ernest and Chink had bathed on so many hot afternoons. We walked up and down the winding streets in the rain, but everything looked dull and lonely, the shopwindows full of cheap dishes and tablecloths and postcards. The taverns were empty. We went into a wine shop where a girl sat carding wool.

"I can barely recognize the town," Ernest said to her in English. "So much is new."

She nodded and continued with her work, drawing the paddles back and forth, the white fibers becoming long and smooth.

"Do you think she understands you?" I said to Ernest quietly.

"She understands me."

"My husband was here during the war," I said.

"The war is over," she answered without looking up.

Deflated, we gave up on sightseeing and went to check in at the Two

Spades, but it had changed, too. The bed creaked, the linens were worn and sad looking, and the lightbulbs were filmed over with dust.

In the middle of a tasteless dinner, Ernest said, "Maybe none of it happened."

"Of course it did," I said. "I wish Chink were here. He'd find a way to cheer us up."

"No. He wouldn't be able to take it either."

We slept badly that night, and when morning came the rain went on and on. Ernest was still determined to show me Fossalta, where he'd been wounded, and so we found a driver who would take us as far as Verona and then boarded a train to Mestre, where we had to find another car and driver. On and on, all day, and for the whole of the trip, Ernest studied maps and tried to match up what he saw in the countryside to what he remembered seeing years before. But nothing was the same. Fossalta, when we finally arrived, was worse than Schio because there wasn't a single sign of ravage. The trenches and dugouts had vanished. The bombed houses and buildings had been changed out for new. When Ernest found the slope where he'd been wounded, it was green and unscarred and completely lovely. Nothing felt honest. Thousands of men had died here just a few years earlier, Ernest himself had bled here, shot full of shrapnel, and yet everything was clean and shiny, as if the land itself had forgotten everything.

Before we left, Ernest combed the hedgerows, and finally came away with a single rusted shell fragment, not much larger than a button.

"Chasing your past is a lousy, rotten game, isn't it?" He looked at me. "Why did I come?"

"You know why," I said.

He turned the fragment over in his hand a few times and I guessed he was thinking about our talk with Chink, and how the war in his head couldn't be counted on any longer. Memory couldn't be counted on. Time was unreliable and everything dissolved and died—even or especially when it *looked* like life. Like spring. All around us, the grass grew. Birds made a living racket in the trees. The sun beat down with promise. From that moment forward, Ernest would always hate the spring.

SIXTEEN

*W*e didn't return to Paris until late in June, and before long the Bastille Day celebrations had begun, and there was dancing and singing in the street at all hours. It was hot and noisy, and we shouldn't even have tried to sleep. I could see Ernest's restless outline in the dark, one arm over his eyes.

"It will be our anniversary soon," I said.

"Should we go away?"

"Where would we go?"

"To Germany, or maybe to Spain."

"We wouldn't have to," I said. "We could stay home and get very drunk and make love."

"We could do that now." He laughed.

"We could," I said.

The clarinetist outside our window played a series of low notes, waiting for accompaniment, then fell silent again. Ernest turned on his side and reached to stroke my bare shoulder. His touch gave me a delicious run of chills, and then he pulled me toward him and rolled me over onto my stomach without saying anything, covering my body with his. He was heavy and warm, and I could feel his lips and forehead against my neck.

"Don't move," he said.

"I'm hardly breathing."

"Good."

"I like it slow this way."

"Yes." His arms were bent to each side of me so he wouldn't crush me completely, but I wanted to be crushed a little.

Afterward, as we lay in the dark, the same laughter rose from the street, and the music was louder, if anything, and more chaotic. Ernest grew very quiet again, and I wondered if he was thinking about Schio and all that wouldn't be found there, and of the sadness he'd carried home with him.

"Should I get up and shut the window?"

"It's too hot, and it won't help anyway. Just go to sleep."

"Something's on your mind. Do you want to tell me?"

"Talking won't do a lick of good either."

I could hear that he'd fallen into a very low place, but I believed, naïvely, that I could help if I could get him to talk about it. I continued to gently press and finally he said, "If you really want to know, it's making love. There's something about it that makes me feel emptied out afterward, and lonely too."

"How awful," I said, feeling the sting of his words. We'd just been so very much with each other, or at least I'd felt that way.

"I'm sorry. It's nothing you've done."

"The hell it's not. Let's not ever do it again. We won't have to. I won't care."

"We do, though. You see that. I know you do."

"No."

He pulled me closer then. "Please don't worry, just tell me you love me."

"I love you," I said, and kissed his hands and eyelids and tried to forget what he'd said. But I couldn't. I couldn't forget anything he'd ever said to me. That's how it was.

"Go to sleep now."

"All right," I said.

He rose and dressed. It must have been three o'clock in the morning, or maybe four.

"You're not going to work now?"

"Maybe not," he said. "But I'm going to try."

I heard him leave, his steps on the stairs, all the way down, and then fell asleep for a few hours. When I woke up he was still away working, and it was already hot and close in the apartment. I kicked the bedsheet away and put my robe on and went into the kitchen to make the coffee. Musicians from the night before were still in the street and it made me feel tired just to hear them. I didn't know how they managed to keep playing. Did they sleep standing up in doorways? Did they sleep at all?

After breakfast, I washed and dressed and sat at the piano for a few hours, but it wasn't satisfying work. The day was too hot and I was too distracted by the night before. I lay down again, and then heard Marie Cocotte in the kitchen, clearing dishes. We'd gotten her name from the concierge in our building, and now she came in every morning as our *femme de ménage*, taking care of all the washing and cooking for two francs an hour. Marie was childless and nearing middle age, petite and sturdy, with quick and competent hands. She'd earned her nickname, *cocotte*, which was French slang for "wench," from a dish she made often and beautifully for us, *poulet en cocotte*. Several days a week, she returned in the late afternoon to prepare our dinner, and because she made everything so well, I'd asked her to teach me French cooking. But now that it was high summer, I didn't want to be in the kitchen at all and was happy to eat fruit or nothing until Ernest was finished with his work. Then we'd go to a café for an aperitif when it was dark and much cooler and felt right again to eat and be hungry.

"Good morning, madame," Marie Cocotte said, coming into the bedroom where the curtains were still open from the night before. We'd never closed them.

"Will the music ever stop?" I asked in my still-graceless French, pointing to the window.

"Not today," she said, laughing.

"I think Bastille Day will last forever," I said, and she laughed again.

"That is how we like it," she said.

The summer stretched on this way, becoming several summers in a row, with time not moving at all. The days grew harder to fill. I felt my headaches coming back, and though I knew I shouldn't resent Ernest's working or try to keep him from it, I was always happiest when he woke up and said he wasn't going to try to write at all that day, and that we should go to the boxing matches instead, or drive out to the country to see the bicycle races.

One afternoon Gertrude and Alice invited us to lunch at their country house in Meaux. We went out all together, in Gertrude's Model T, and had a picnic feast with two kinds of eggs and potatoes and roast chicken. We drank several bottles of chilled wine and then three-star Hennessy, and everything was beautiful—the valleys and bridges, the charming house and its flowering trees. After lunch, we lay in the grass and talked and felt free.

Ernest had taken to showing Gertrude all of his work, and reading hers as well. Though he'd felt put off by the difficulty of her writing at the beginning of their friendship, he'd grown to appreciate the strangeness of it and was becoming more and more interested in what she was doing. She even began to influence his style, particularly the habit she had of naming and repeating concrete objects, places, and people, not trying to find variation, but reveling in how any word took on a striking power when you used it again and again. In some of the new Nick Adams passages, I saw how he was doing this, too, with the simplest language and things—*lake, trout, log, boat*—and how it gave the work a very distilled and almost mythic feel.

Ernest's connection to Gertrude was obviously very important to them both, and I loved that we were all becoming good, easy friends with one another, though there was still a persistent pairing off when we met. Ernest and Gertrude were the artists, and when they talked, their heads close together, they seemed almost like siblings. Alice and I were the wives, even without the four walls of the salon to define us, and she seemed content with this. Was I? Ernest utterly supported my playing and often referred to the piano as my "work," as if I were an artist, too. I loved to play and felt it was very much a part of my life, but I wasn't at all convinced I was special, as Ernest was. He lived inside the creative sphere and I lived outside, and I didn't know if anything would ever change that. Alice seemed to feel easier in her role as an artist's wife, throwing herself wholly behind Gertrude's ambition, but maybe she'd just been doing it longer and could hide her jealousy better.

I gazed into my glass of brandy—at the kaleidoscope it made on the pale blanket, which was some kind of Irish wool. We were here together now, I told myself. Everything was lovely and fine. I should just know it and hold on to it and be happy. I would. I would try.

The next day we woke late and I still felt the Hennessy. Ernest must have been feeling it, too, because we weren't even out of bed yet before he said, "The work won't be any good at all today. I shouldn't bother."

"You could go and try anyway, just for a few hours," I said, feeling a small sting because I didn't mean it.

"No," he said. "It won't come to anything. I already know."

We rose and had our breakfast, and then decided we would go out to Auteuil, to the horse races. It would be cooler out of the city. Marie Cocotte would pack a basket with sandwiches and wine, and then we'd get the racing forms and read them on the train. As soon as it was settled, I felt the pressure in my head leave, whooshing out quickly like a ghost being exorcised from a house. I felt guilty for how happy it made me not to share him—guilty and happy, all at the same time.

Ernest and I both loved Auteuil. We always went over the racing form together and then visited the paddocks to see the animals. I loved the deep smell of the horses and the track itself and the noises of the happy crowd taking its luck as it came. Ernest was fascinated by everything—the beautiful rippling of horse flesh, the stumpy-looking jockeys in their silks, the trainers standing at the rails and seeming to know something mysterious, the slang of the boys in the stable, and the smell of horse piss. We never had a lot to spend at the races, but we always had something, and it felt good to be out together in the sun. Ernest would spread his coat in the grass and we'd lunch there, and then I'd nap or just watch the clouds and wait for the next race. When we won, we had champagne, and sometimes when we lost, too, because we were happy to be there and be together, and what was money to us anyway? We never had enough to make a difference if we lost it.

That day, the favorite was a shiny dark beauty, a good jumper with a quick way. He had tight sharp lines on the jump, making you think you'd barely seen it at all. We didn't bet on the favorite, but on another, lighter horse called Chèvre d'Or that was running a hundred and twenty to one. Sometimes we picked the horses together, after walking the paddock or standing at the rails and seeing how the horses moved and waiting for a feeling. Sometimes Ernest found someone he knew who'd give him a name or two, good odds. That day I followed my own hunches and found the horse myself. I could be lucky for us that way. It had happened before, and that day I felt sure it would happen again. Chèvre d'Or wasn't quick and dark but moved like brandy in a glass. I watched his smooth legs and told Ernest he was the one.

"Let's really bet on him," I said. "Do we have enough?"

"Maybe we do," he said.

"Let's spend it anyway, even if we don't."

He laughed and went off to place the bet, still smiling at me. He loved it when I was bold.

"Are you still stuck on this horse?" he asked when he came back.

"I am."

"Good. He's got six months of living expenses on him."

"You don't mean it."

"I do," he said, and we crowded up to the rail with the rest, both of us tingling with risk.

My horse took the lead from the start. By the second hurdle, nothing could touch him. He was four lengths ahead by the fourth hurdle, a brandy-colored blur.

"He's doing it," I said, feeling flushed. My stomach was taut and knotted.

"He's doing it all right," Ernest said, watching the other horses break. But it was too late for any of them because Chèvre d'Or was too fast and too far ahead—too good as he was, ten lengths ahead, then more. The favorite gained and took the others, his jockey's whip slicing, but my horse was in his own race.

He was twenty lengths ahead and twenty paces from the finish when it happened. As beautiful as the rest had been, that's how ugly it was when he fell at the last jump. If he was brandy before, now he was a busted wheelbarrow. He was sticks and string, a child's toy breaking with a crack. It was so terrible, I couldn't watch. I buried my face in

Ernest's shoulder and didn't see the end of the race, the horses parting around the fallen animal, the favorite taking everything he hadn't earned.

I cried half the way home on the train, through the gloomy neighborhoods with the clotheslines and the garbage and the children dressed in rags, trying to forget the day and what we'd seen.

SEVENTEEN

When our anniversary came, we decided to spend it with Chink. First we traveled to Frankfurt, then took a boat down the Rhine to meet him in Cologne. The weather was still very warm then, and the days were lovely and long, and we were all very happy to be together. He was good for us, and we were good for him, and Cologne was beautiful.

One afternoon I was lying back on the grass watching Ernest and Chink fish. Ernest reached into the duffel bag on the bank next to him and pulled out a bottle of cold white wine that he uncorked with his teeth. In his other hand he held the rod, its line well out, the water moving around it in gentle eddies. There was a nice breeze, and yellow pollen blew by in small clouds and sifted down on us from the trees.

"You boys look like something out of a painting," I said, squinting up at them.

"We have an admirer," Ernest said to Chink.

I got up out of the grass and walked over to Ernest and watched him closely for several minutes. "Show me how it's done," I said.

"Tired of admiring already?"

"No." I smiled. "But I'd like to give it a try."

"All right, then." He stood behind me on the soft, grassy bank and showed me how to point the rod. I swung my arm back and forward again in a smooth arc, just as he said, and managed to release the reel perfectly. It sailed out into the current like a dream.

"That felt good," I said.

"That's how you know you've done it right," Chink said.

"What now?"

"Now you wait," Ernest said, and walked over to the rod case. Before he'd even reached it I felt a small tug at the line, then another stronger tug. On instinct, I pulled up and the hook struck. I could feel the fish working against it.

"Hey," Chink said, watching. "She's a ringer."

Ernest rushed back and helped me land the trout, and then the fish was on the grass, pale brown and spotted.

"I feel a little sorry for him," I said.

"You can throw him back if you'd like," Chink said.

"Like hell she will," Ernest said, laughing.

"No, I want to eat him. I want to know if it tastes different when you catch it yourself."

"Good girl," Ernest said. "It does, you know."

"I thought so."

"This one's got the killer instinct," Chink said, and we all laughed.

"You might as well know it all," Ernest said later when I had landed three trout, one after the other. He showed me how to clean and gut the fish and rinse the body well in the stream for cooking.

"I'm not disgusted," I said as we worked.

"I know it. I can tell."

We roasted my three over the fire on sticks, as well as the other half dozen Chink and Ernest had caught between them.

"I like mine best," I said, licking salt off my fingertips.

"I like yours best, too," Ernest said, and opened another bottle of wine as the sky softened and evening came on.

In Cologne itself, the mood was more troubled. At the British Occupation Garrison, where Chink had recently been stationed, an angry mob had vandalized a statue of Wilhelm II on horseback, wrenching down the huge iron sword and shattering off the spurs. Other rioters had murdered a German policeman, chasing him into the river and then severing his fingers when he tried to hold on to a bridge to save himself. From a distance, the city looked like something out of a fairy tale, with red-roofed houses, colorful villagers, and a stunning cathedral that ri-valed Notre-Dame, but like the rest of Allied-occupied Germany, it was in a state of supreme unrest.

A few days later, on September 14, we were in a café catching up on our newspapers when we learned that the Turkish port city of Smyrna was burning. The Greco-Turkish war had been raging for three years, since the repartitioning of the Ottoman Empire that came out of the war, but the conflict had finally broken with this fire. No one knew who was responsible. The Greeks blamed the Turks and vice versa, and the only clear thing was the tragic results. The harbor had been set alight with petroleum, as had many of the Greek and Armenian quarters in the town. People were driven out of their houses and into the streets. Scores drowned in the harbor, and others were slaughtered where they stood. Refugees were fleeing into the hills. We felt very chastened where we sat in the café, having our fine lunch, for not having been more aware of the conflict.

"I imagine I'll be there soon enough," Chink said. His expression was stern.

"Maybe I will, too," Ernest said, and I felt a cold rush go through me.

"You don't really think so," I said.

"I don't know. It's possible."

"I've always wanted to see Istanbul," Chink said.

"*Constantinople*'s a better word, though," Ernest said. "Or *Byzantium*."

"Right," Chink said. "Well, either way, it's in the crapper now, isn't it?"

Back in Paris, we hadn't even unpacked before a telegram came for Ernest from the *Star*. John Bone was sending him to Turkey to report on the conflict, just as he'd suspected. He would leave in three days' time. He'd just read the news, the torn envelope still in his hands, when I felt myself come crashing down.

"What is it?" Ernest said, watching my face fall. "I won't be long. It will be like Genoa, the same as that. And then I'll be home and we'll be together again."

But I had never told him about how low I'd been when he was away in Genoa, how every day without him had been a struggle against my-self.

"I don't want you to go," I said.

"What?"

"Tell them you can't, that I'm ill."

"You're not making any sense."

"But I am, don't you see? I'm telling the truth for once."

"No, you're being childish. This is a tantrum, and I want you to stop it now."

That's when I began to cry, which was worst of all; he hated tears.

"Please stop," he said. "We've just had a wonderful time in Cologne, haven't we? Why can't we just be happy?"

"That's all I want," I said, but the tears still came. I opened my suit-case, then closed it again and went into the kitchen to boil water for tea. I thought maybe he'd gone into the bedroom, but he was there, just be-hind me, pacing.

"It's too far away," I finally said.

"That's the point, isn't it? You don't want a war breathing down your neck."

"Can't we just pretend the telegram never came?"

"No, we can't." His face grew suddenly hard then, because I was ask-ing him to choose me over his work. "To hell with the tea," he said, but I kept at it, measuring leaves for the pot and pouring water through the porcelain sieve. He strode back and forth behind me in the tiny kitchen, waiting for me to apologize. When I didn't and didn't even turn around, he finally stormed out of the apartment.

I knew he'd gone to a café. I could have found him easily and it might have been fine, then, if I had. We could have had a brandy and water and agreed to put it behind us. Or asked the waiter to bring the absinthe and let it erase everything beautifully. But I stayed where I was and drank the damn tea, though I didn't even want it.

By the time Ernest came home, I was drunk and pretending to sleep. I'd abandoned the tea and taken up a bottle of whiskey instead. I'd eaten nothing, and just drank the whiskey, several glasses, warm without water. When I was drunk enough to do it, I took up the lovely china teapot which had come so far with us and let it drop to the floor with a crash. I meant to leave the pieces there for him to see, but once I'd done it, it was too small and childish—the act of a tantrum, like he'd said. I hated feeling so desperate and out of control, but couldn't seem to rein it in either. I picked up the mess, one wet ruined shard at a time, and put it in a small paper sack. Then I went to bed. My head swam viciously on the pillow, but I closed my eyes and tried to slow my breathing. Much later, I heard him on the stairs, then in the room.

"Hadley," he said, sitting next to me on the bed. He touched my face and neck lightly, but I didn't move. "Let's don't do this, Feather Cat."

I pinched my eyes tight to keep the tears from coming, and tried to appear as if I were sleeping. But he knew I wasn't.

"Damn you," he said, when I wouldn't open my eyes or answer him. He gave my shoulder a rough shove. "It's the job. You know I have to go."

"You don't have to. You want to go."

"To hell with you anyway," he said, and left to sleep elsewhere.

Maybe he went back to his room on the rue Descartes that night or slept on the long bench downstairs in the dance hall. I don't know. He stayed out until after noon the next day, and then came in to pack and make arrangements. He moved around the apartment, throwing things into a bag, getting his notebooks together.

"Is this how it's going to be then?"

I stared out the window at nothing.

"You said you'd never do this, you know."

He was right. Over and over I'd sworn I'd never stand in the way of his work, particularly when we were just beginning, when I saw his career as my own and believed it was my role or even my fate to help him carve a way. But more and more I understood that I didn't know what those promises really meant. Part of me wanted him to be as unhappy as I was. Maybe then he'd give in and stay.

But he didn't. We didn't speak or touch for three days, and when he left, on September 25, he was so hurt and angry I could barely stand to look at him. I stood at the door and watched him struggle with his bags on the stairs. Toward the bottom, he dropped the valise holding his Corona. It fell hard, bounced with a sickening clatter, and then fell again. He kicked it angrily before he picked it up. When he got to the door at the bottom of the stairs, he kicked that, too, and then I heard nothing.

EIGHTEEN

It might be malaria breaking through the quinine, but everything is strangely yellow. The long road is a tamped and stark ocher color and the mountains in the distance are darker. There's a river, the Maritza, and it's running high and fast because it's been raining for five days and the rain, too, is yellow.

He hasn't slept well since he left Paris, and this makes the rain harder to walk through. There isn't an end to any of it, the rain or the walking. Columns of refugees surge and spill onto the Karagatch Road. They've loaded their carts with everything they can't bear to leave behind, the ones who have carts, and the rest are strapped to bundles and carry other bundles or carry children. The children carry what they can and cry when they get too tired or scared. Everyone's scared and wet and the rain keeps coming.

He is here to bear witness, he understands that, and so makes himself see everything and not look away from any of it, though much he sees gives him a sick feeling in his stomach. It's his first taste of war since he was inside the war, and that alone started a terrible shaking in him the first two days. The shaking is gone now. He's forced it back and now can do what he came to do.

Along the Karagatch Road, he talks with many who've come from Smyrna and seen the fires there and worse. A man with a bright red face watched his sister run down to the quay screaming and alight to the tips of her hair. Another man is bandaged from his hand to his shoulder, the cloth filthy and sodden, and even in the rain you can smell the gangrene, a sweet smell like roasting almonds. The man speaks through an interpreter and says he hid under the pier at Smyrna for most of a day and a night, the water up to his chest sometimes. It was the mussels on the footings of the pier that cut his hand and arm when the tide came in and pushed him against the hard shells.

"There were searchlights in the harbor," the man says. "And you didn't want to see the things floating there, all around you."

In the end he came out of the water and found his family and took to the road, like so many others. He was cut deep in several places but he wasn't bleeding. He had thought the salt would cure his wounds and that he'd be fine without a surgeon.

"You can see I'm not fine," the man says through the interpreter, and keeps walking.

"Yes, anyone can see that," Ernest says.

They walk next to a cart pulled by a single great ox streaming with rain, and in the cart the man's wife is in labor. The bedding in the cart is wet through, and there's another blanket, tented and dripping, that two of her children hold over her as she bears down. An old woman crouches between her knees while the children try to look away, and it makes Ernest sick to see this and to hear her screaming, which won't be helped until the child is born, and maybe not even then.

The man is still walking and looking ahead through the rain and says, "My wife knows I'm a coward. I hid under the pier. I meant to leave them all."

Ernest nods and looks up to see they're coming to a bridge over the river, a wooden structure that looks slick but sound for all the weight on it, carts and oxen and camels, the bodies packed in and no one moving forward or back.

In the distance, over the heads of the living, he sees the fine white spires of a mosque, minarets rising out of the yellow muck, detached from the very real things happening on the road, the mud and the screaming and the cowardice and the rain. In the pocket of his jacket there's a blue notebook folded in half and two pencils. The paper's drenched through, he knows it without having to check, but he couldn't write any of this anyway. He'll send a dispatch from the hotel tonight, if it hasn't floated off in the rain. For now, all he can do is make himself see everything and not shake and not look away.

A week passes but it feels as if he's never been anywhere else. It's one of the things war does to you. Everything you see works to replace moments and *people from your life before, until you can't remember why any of it mattered. It doesn't help if you're not a soldier. The effect is the same.*

He sleeps on a cot in a hotel in Adrianople wrapped in a dirty blanket and covered with sores from the lice. He spends his days talking to refugees and writing and sending dispatches to the Star and to the INS under the name John Hadley. Sometimes he's too tired and sends the same story twice. He could give a damn; let them fire him. They'll have to find him first and he's nowhere.

When night falls, he goes to a bar where a very dark Armenian girl with deep shadows under her eyes wears a colored dress that ties at the waist. He can see the shape of her breasts under the cloth and wants to touch her, and it all becomes very simple. Another man comes along, a British soldier, and puts his hands on the girl's waist and she smiles. That's when Ernest flares forward and punches the soldier. He hasn't meant to do it exactly. He just knows he needs to move if he wants the girl. They never come to you, and why would you want them to? He feels his fist connect with the soldier's jaw and the jaw springing loose. He doesn't feel anything yet himself. The soldier drops to one knee, and then comes up again fast, his eyes bright and very wide. He lunges, but isn't quick or low enough. Ernest hits him in the gut this time, and feels the man's breath collapsing around his hand.

The girl says something he doesn't understand, but it sounds like "Enough." He takes her hand and they leave. There's a taxi outside and they go to her room without saying anything. Behind the door, she unties the dress, and then reaches for his belt. He pushes her hands away. He'll do it all himself, though his right hand is bleeding. He sits on a small wooden chair and pulls her down on top of him and feels how rough and silky she is straddling him. He is the one moving her, as if she's a doll, and he knows it has to be this way because it makes him feel that he won't die, at least for tonight. He groans when it's over, and it's over quickly the first time. He stays with her in her filthy bed, and in the morning, he leaves the address of his hotel on a sheet of notebook paper and also two American dollars. He thinks he probably won't see her again, but that it would be all right if he did. He has more money to spend, and maybe if he saw her again, he wouldn't feel so sick, like he does now, and maybe it will be better and maybe it will fix something.

He goes into the street, where it's still very early and cool and hasn't yet started to rain again. He walks back to his hotel thinking, You've done it now, haven't you? It's too late to take anything back and you wouldn't anyway. You need to remember that later, when you see your wife and want to die for hurting her. Remember no one made you do anything. It's never anyone but you who does anything, and for that reason alone you shouldn't be sorry.

Now it is raining again, a very fine drizzle that seeps into the fabric of his shirt and trousers. He feels the small buildings push toward him along the muddy road, and there is the very real thought, again, that there isn't any other world. What does it matter if you know your being with another will kill your wife, if you have no wife? You don't have Paris, either, or anything else. You might as well see the dark girl again. You might as well bring yourself down and make yourself stinking sick with all you do because this is the only world there is.

NINETEEN

When he was gone, I felt sad and guilty, hating myself instantly. I looked at the whiskey bottle on the shelf and even held it for a moment before putting it back. Not before lunch. I would never make it through that way. So I made some coffee instead and peeled an orange and tried not to think about him on the train. He would be two days traveling, at least, and then he'd be in another world, and a dangerous one. All I could do was hope that he'd be safe, and that the thread that bound us was strong enough to weather the damage done.

Except for two scribbled postcards sent before he was over the border into Turkey, I didn't hear from Ernest when he was gone and I blamed the cable service for it because I didn't want to think what else his silence might mean. I read his first story in the *Star* when it arrived two weeks later, but thinking too specifically about what was happening there—not just violence but disease, too, apparently, cholera and malaria in epidemic proportions—only made things worse, so I burned the paper and went for a walk.

Marie Cocotte came every afternoon. "You need to get out of your bed," she said, and brought me an apron to tie around my robe. Together we made *boeuf bourguignon* and *blanquette de veau* and cassoulet, and it was all lovely, though I couldn't make myself eat it.

Lewis Galantière came by and sat at the terrible dining table and tried to drag me out to Michaud's.

"James Joyce has apparently fathered six more children just this week. They're all there, eating an enormous mutton and spouting milk out their nostrils. Tell me you don't need to see it for yourself."

I made myself smile and then dressed, putting on my coat and my least unfashionable shoes. "Let's go around the corner, though," I said. "Not Michaud's tonight, all right?"

"I'm your humble servant, madame."

I didn't tell Lewis or anyone else how bad things had gotten between us. I was too embarrassed. In the mornings I wrote letters and lied, telling Grace and Dr. Hemingway that all was fine and well. I explained how smoothly Ernest's work had been going for the *Star*, how promising his career looked. I didn't say he'd recently decided to break his exclusive contract with them and file stories under a pseudonym for the International News Service. All of this had been negotiated in secret and meant lying and stickiness when something for INS hit the wire before his "exclusives" for the *Star* did, but he'd claimed it was worth it for the money. He'd work it out with his own conscience. I had a harder time with this dishonesty, because it seemed to speak of something larger. The way he was always out for himself, whatever the cost.

But thinking this way got me nowhere. Nowhere but back to the whiskey, that is, so I put my thinking down with the stack of letters and walked to the Musée du Luxembourg instead, to visit the Monets. I stood and looked into the brightest patches of his lilies and the lovely purpling in the water and tried not to see anything else at all.

At the end of October, in the very early morning, Ernest stepped off his train at the Gare de Lyon looking as if he'd been in a terrible battle and lost. He was weak and exhausted and feverish with malaria. He'd shed twenty pounds or more, and I hardly recognized him. He moved into my arms and collapsed there, and then we went home where he leaned over the basin and let me shampoo his head, which was crawling with lice.

"I'm so sorry for everything, Tatie," I said when his eyes were closed.

"Let's not say anything about it. It doesn't matter now."

I took up the scissors and cut his hair very close to his head and picked the rest of the lice out one by one, bringing the lamp over so I

could see everything. Then I rubbed his body all over with cream and
helped him into fresh clean sheets where he slept for twenty-four hours.
When he woke up, I brought him eggs and toast and ham and mustard,
and he ate this all gratefully, and then he slept again.

He didn't leave the bed for a week, and sometimes I just watched
him sleep and knew by the look of him that he'd suffered in ways he
wouldn't be able to talk about, not for a long time. The breach between
us had been terrible and the silence, too, but his time in Turkey had
come to outshadow all of that. And maybe he was right that it didn't
matter. He was home now, and we were together again, and maybe it
would all be all right as long as we didn't think about it or give it any
room or air.

After a week, he could get out of bed and bathe and dress and was
almost ready to see friends. He went to his duffel bag and moved the
notebooks aside to bring out presents rolled in newspaper and layers of
cloth. He'd brought me a bottle of attar of roses and also a heavy amber
necklace with big, rough beads that were threaded with black coral and
silver.

"It's as beautiful as anything ever," I said, holding up the necklace.

"It belonged to an extremely important Russian diplomat who's now
a waiter."

"I hope you paid him well for it."

"I did, and got him drunk to boot," Ernest said, nearly himself now.

I waited for him to say more about it all, but he just sat at the table
and drank his coffee and asked after the newspapers.

I knew he loved me again; I could see that. No matter what each of
us had felt or thought about the other in our weeks apart, that time was
over now. I opened the bottle of attar of roses, which was a deep yellow
and smelled like pure rose, the absolute thing. Somehow, without finding or fixing any words to it, the next part of our story had begun.

TWENTY

Careful now," Ernest said. "You know you're inviting the devil in."

"Am I?"

"You know you are."

"He can come then, as long as he comes this way, all in green vapor."

We were at the Select with Pound and Dorothy, whom we'd taken to calling Shakespear. Pound had just taken on the editorship of a new literary press called Three Mountains and was keen to publish something of Ernest's. We were all in high spirits that night, and I'd only meant to have the one glass of absinthe, to celebrate.

"You must go more slowly," Pound said.

"Must I?" I said, but he wasn't talking to me at all, but to the waiter pouring water over a sugar cube into the drink, which was going from a wickedly clear yellow-green to a cloudy white as the water dripped in. Absinthe was illegal in France and had been for years. So was opium, but you could find both everywhere in Paris if you knew where to look. I loved the delicate licorice taste and the way the ritual of the cube and specially perforated spoon made raindrops, sugar drops. Our waiter was doing it beautifully, I thought, but Pound grabbed the pitcher with force, taking over.

"You're drunk, darling," Shakespear said to him in her civilized whisper.

"I'm trying to picture you drunk," Ernest said to her. "I'm betting you never spill a drop."

She laughed. "If I don't, it's because I won't touch absinthe."

"It's licorice candy and smoke," I said.

"You'll wish it were only that tomorrow," Ernest said.

"Maybe, but it makes everything easier now, doesn't it?"

"Yes, it does," Ernest said, touching my glass with his. "So have it and to hell with tomorrow."

"Hear, hear," said Pound leaning forward in his rumpled tweed jacket and putting his elbows on the table. I was growing to like him more all the time—but I was generally liking everyone. I thought I might be in love with our waiter. He had the prettiest mustache, unwaxed and pure and fresh as flowers. I wanted to touch it or eat it.

"You should grow your mustache like that," I said to Ernest, pointing not at all subtly.

"I am, dear. It's just the same."

I looked at him square. "So it is," I said. "Where have you been?" And we all laughed.

Later, when we'd moved on to the Dôme, Pound started talking about the States.

"I'd never return to the Middle West," he was saying, "I renounce it, in fact. Indiana's full of prigs and idiots."

"Oh, that old story," Shakespear said in her low perfect whisper.

I looked into the long smoky mirror and touched my face, then the glass. "I can't feel anything," I said to Ernest. "Isn't it wonderful?"

"Have another, Tatie," Ernest said. "You're very beautiful."

Shakespear smiled at us with her curved mouth and her eyes smiled, too. "Look at our pretty lovers," she said to Pound.

"Indiana's always been an intellectual wasteland, mind you," he said, and then blew a smoke ring that circled before being swallowed by the rest of it, the blue halo that was everywhere, blending and blurring. All of us breathing it in and out.

"All they have is the moral high ground," he went on. "There's nothing else within reach. I was useless teaching at Wabash. What did those young people with cornhusks between their ears want to hear me rant on about? Not Yeats, that's for certain. Not poetry."

"The actress was a small bit of poetry," Shakespear said.

"The most scrumptious knees I've ever seen on a woman," Pound said.

"Do go on," Ernest said. "I'm getting hungry."

"There was rain that night—it's always raining in Indiana, intellectually speaking, you understand—and the actress . . . what was her name?"

"Bertha," Shakespear said.

"Not Camille?" Ernest said.

"No, no. She wasn't consumptive. Just didn't want to get her hair damp. She had lovely hair. I'd suggested we go out to dinner, but then there was the matter of dampness."

"One of my favorite problems," Ernest said.

Everyone laughed and then Pound said, "When word got out I'd entertained her in my room, you'd think I'd murdered the girl instead of roasted a chicken."

"Poor Ezra," Shakespear said. "They fired him next day."

"Poor Ezra nothing. I'd be in Indiana still, teaching poetry to stalks of corn."

"And roasting the occasional chicken," I said.

"Even chicken won't save you from Indiana," Ezra said.

Late that evening, after we'd abandoned the Dôme for the Ritz, Ernest and Pound began heatedly discussing the merits of Tristan Tzara. Pound thought the Surrealists might be onto something, possibly, if they could stay asleep long enough. Ernest thought they were idiots and they might just as well wake up so we could all move on to something else.

"I'm dropping off just listening to you all," Shakespear said, and the two of us moved to the other side of the room and sat at a small table.

"You and Hem really are beautiful together," she said.

"Are we?" I'd been drinking only warm water for an hour, and could finally feel my tongue.

"I wonder how that happens. Love, I mean." She touched the sweep of her hair, still smooth and perfect.

"Don't you and Pound have it?"

"Oh, no." She laughed with a small puff of air. "We have what we have, though."

"I'm not sure I understand you."

"I'm not sure I do either." She laughed a dark laugh and then became quiet, stirring her drink.

The weather turned wonderful that fall, and although we knew the cold, damp season would be coming soon enough, we were living deep into what we had and feeling happy and strong. Ernest was working well on his Nick Adams novel and new stories and saw so clearly the books they could be, it was almost as if they already fully existed. In our circle, everyone believed things would hit for him, and that it was only a matter of time.

"You're making something new," Pound told him one day in his studio. "Don't forget that when it starts to hurt."

"It only hurts to wait."

"The waiting helps you boil it down. That's essential, and the hurting helps everything along in its way."

Ernest put this wisdom in his pocket the way he did everything Pound said.

Soon enough, the light began to change in the streets in the late afternoon, thinning and waning, and we started to wonder if we had it in us to face the long winter.

"I've been thinking about writing to Agnes," Ernest said to me one evening. "It's been on my mind since Milan. Do you mind?"

"I don't know. What do you want out of it?"

"Nothing. Just for her to know I'm happy and thinking of her."

"And that your career is going just as you said it would."

He smiled. "That's the cherry on top, is all."

"Send your letter."

"Yes," he said. "I already have."

I felt a flare of jealousy. "You were so sure I wouldn't mind?"

"Maybe. But if you did, I knew I could make you see it was all right. It's just a letter, in any case, and we have each other."

"That's what Shakespear said the other night."

"Shakespear? What does she know about love?"

"Maybe more than we do, because she doesn't have it. She's not in the thick of it."

"That's why I can't write about Paris now, because it's everywhere."

"So you write about Michigan."

"It feels so close. As if I could never lose it." He'd been reading over the day's work from a notebook on the table in front of him. He rested his hand on the pages, his fingertips brushing over the boldly slanted sentences. "But it's not just the real place. I'm inventing it, too, and that's the best part."

Over his writing desk he'd pinned a pale blue map of northern Michigan, and all the essential places were there—Horton Bay, Petoskey, Walloon Lake, Charlevoix—the precise locations where important things had happened to him, Ernest, but also to Nick Adams. Ernest and Nick weren't the same guy, but they knew a lot of the same things, like where and when to look for bait hoppers heavy with dew, and how the water moved and what it told you about where the trout were. They knew about mortar shelling in the middle of a still night, and what it felt like to see a place you'd loved burned down and hollowed out and changed. Nick's mind wasn't altogether right and you could sense the pressure coming up inside him, in a story like "Big Two-Hearted River," though Ernest never had him look at it directly or name it.

"I love your Michigan stories," I said.

He squinted at me through the lantern light, across the table. "Is that true?"

"Yes, of course."

"Sometimes I wonder if you want me writing at all. I think it makes you feel lonely."

"It's not the writing that makes me lonely, it's your being gone. It's been so long since you've even tried to write here at home. Maybe it would work now and I could see you. I wouldn't have to talk or disturb you."

"You know I need to go away to make anything happen." He closed the notebook and put his pencil on top, rolling it back and forth with his fingertips. "I have to be alone to get it started, but if I really was alone, that wouldn't work either. I need to leave that place and come back here and talk to you. That makes it real and makes it stick. Do you get what I'm saying?"

"I think so." I walked behind him and put my head on his shoulder, rubbing my face into his neck. But the truth was I didn't, not really. And he knew.

"Maybe no one can know how it is for anyone else."

I straightened and walked over to the window where the rain came down in streams and pooled on the sill. "I'm trying."

"Me too," he said.

I sighed. "I think it's going to rain all day."

"Don't kid yourself. It's going to rain for a month."

"Maybe it won't after all."

He smiled at me. "All right, Tiny. Maybe it won't."

TWENTY-ONE

*N*ear Thanksgiving 1922, the *Star* sent Ernest to cover a peace conference in Lausanne that would decide the territorial dispute between Greece and Turkey, the thing that had started the terrible business at Smyrna and had generally kept them killing each other for the better part of three years. When the cable came, I saw Ernest's nervousness. He almost couldn't open it and I knew why. We couldn't take another fight like the last. We might not survive it.

"Lausanne," he said finally. "We have the money. You'll come, too."

"I needn't," I said. "I can be good."

"No," he said. "I want you there."

I was relieved he'd insisted and agreed to go—but by the time the trip was launched, I was sick in bed, my head stuffed and aching. I couldn't eat anything without retching. We decided he would go alone, and that I would join him when I could travel. My old friend Leticia Parker from St. Louis happened to be coming through Paris just then, and she said she wanted to visit every day and take care of me when Ernest was gone. It wouldn't be like his time in Turkey at all, or even like Genoa.

By the time I felt well enough to join him, it was early December. I packed happily, knowing that when the conference was over and the reporting done, we'd have a long skiing holiday at Chamby and have Christmas there with Chink and then go on to Italy and Spain. All in all, we wouldn't be back in Paris for four months, and I was ready for a nice long break from the cold and dampness. I hadn't been out of bed for a week and wasn't sure I'd have the energy for skiing, but I was damned well going to try.

Along with the travel plans passing back and forth between us, Ernest had also cabled to say that Lincoln Steffens, one of the journalists he'd met in Genoa, was in Lausanne and highly impressed with his dispatches. He wanted to see everything Ernest had written so far, but he only had one thing with him, "My Old Man," a story about a boy and his ruined jockey father. Steffens thought the story was wonderful and compared it to Sherwood Anderson. Ernest didn't like being compared to anyone, and it seemed worse, somehow, that it was Anderson, a friend and champion, but it helped that Steffens had offered to send the story on to an editor friend at *Cosmopolitan*. Ernest had one published piece at that point, in a small art magazine out of New Orleans called the *Double Dealer*. There was only that, and the promise from Pound about printing something for Three Mountains. This was much more promising, thrilling even.

As I packed my big suitcase, I thought about how long we'd be gone, and how anxious Ernest would be to return to his stories and the novel. It went without saying that he'd like to show more of his work to Steffens, so I headed for the dining room, to the cupboard where Ernest kept all his manuscripts. I gathered everything together and packed it in a small valise. This was my surprise for him, and I felt buoyed by it as I left the apartment for the Gare de Lyon.

The station was busy, but I had never seen it any other way. Porters scrambled by in their red jackets—past the waxed wooden benches and the ornamental palms and the well-dressed travelers headed home or away with anticipation. By morning, I would be with Ernest again and all would be well, and this was my only thought as I moved through the station and handed my bags to a porter. He helped me onto the train, put the big suitcase with my clothes on the rack up high, and placed the small valise under my seat, where I could reach it. The train was nearly empty. We had half an hour before departure, so I went to stretch my legs and get a newspaper. I threaded through the station, past the vendors with their apples and cheese and Evian water, the rented blankets and pillows and warm wrapped sandwiches and little flasks of brandy.

When the conductor called for boarding I hurried onto the train with
the stream of passengers and found my compartment just as it was before. Except for the small valise.

It wasn't under my seat. I didn't see it anywhere.

In a panic, I called for the conductor.

"Is there something I can do?" my seatmate said while I waited for
him to appear. She was a middle-aged American who seemed to be
traveling alone. "I can lend you something of mine to wear."

"It isn't clothing!" I shrieked, and the poor woman turned away, un-
derstandably horrified. When the conductor finally arrived, he didn't
seem to understand, either. I couldn't stop crying long enough to find
the right words in my terrible French. Finally he called over two French
policemen, who led me outside the train and interrogated me while
everyone stared. They asked for my identification cards, which one
officer examined while the other asked me to describe the bag and my
actions in detail.

"It was yours, this valise?"

"My husband's."

"Is he on board?"

"No, he's in Switzerland. I was bringing it to him. It's his work.
Three *years'* worth of work," and here I lost any remaining composure.
I felt sick with rising dread. "Why are you standing here questioning
me?" My voice pitched shrilly. "He's getting away! He's probably long
gone by now!"

"Your husband, madame?"

"The thief, you idiot!"

"We cannot help you if you're going to be hysterical, madame."

"Please." I felt as if I might lose my mind. "Please just search the
train. Search the station."

"Can you estimate the value of the case and its contents?"

"I don't know," I said in a fog. "It's his *work.*"

"Yes, so you said. We'll do what we can." And the two men walked
off officiously.

The conductor agreed to hold the train for another ten minutes
while the police performed their search. They walked from one end of

the train to the other asking the passengers if they'd seen the bag. I didn't for a moment believe that whoever had stolen it was still on the train. It had obviously been a common pickpocket who'd seen an opportunity and taken it, hoping for valuables. Instead, it contained every thought and sentence Ernest had sweated over since we came to Paris and well before, the Chicago stories and sketches, every poem and fragment. He never threw anything away, and it was all there.

The two officers came off the train empty-handed. "Nothing yet, madame," one of them said. "We'll continue to look, but if you still intend on traveling to Switzerland, I suggest you take your seat."

I gave them our address and the phone number for the dance hall, since there wasn't a phone in our apartment, but I didn't hold out much hope they'd succeed in their efforts. Paris was vast and too much time had passed. I imagined the thief hurrying to an empty alleyway, opening the case and then shutting it immediately. He'd have dropped it where he stood or pitched it into a rubbish pile. It could be in any alleyway or gutter or burning trash barrel in Paris. It could be listing, at that moment, toward the bottom of the Seine.

"I'm very sorry for your trouble," my seatmate said when I'd finally made my way back to the compartment.

"No, I'm sorry," I said, beginning to weep again. "I'm not usually this discomposed."

"Is it very dear, what you've lost?"

The train grumbled beneath us, then lurched away from the platform with finality. There was no stopping or changing anything now. No avoiding the truth of what had happened. I felt dread settle in to fill me completely and a new hard-won certainty. There was only one answer to her question. "Priceless," I said, and turned away.

TWENTY-TWO

*W*hat followed was the longest night of my life. The mountains closed in as we headed into Switzerland, and blackness fell. I thought about how I would tell Ernest the work was gone, but I couldn't imagine it. There were no words.

When we finally pulled into Lausanne the next morning, and I saw Ernest on the platform with Steffens right beside him, it was all I could do to stand and walk toward them. I was crying. Ernest looked at Steffens and shrugged as if to say, *Who can understand a woman,* but then I couldn't stop and Ernest knew something was very wrong.

Still, it was ages before I could say the words. Steffens excused himself, telling Ernest he'd phone to arrange a meeting. When he was gone, Ernest made me sit down at a café table near the entrance of the station. All around us couples and families kissed good-bye or bade each other farewell, and they seemed so painfully untroubled to me. A fresh wave of tears came.

"What is it?" Ernest asked again and again, first worried and tender, then angry, then worried again. "Whatever it is, we'll get through it. Nothing can be that bad."

But it was. It was exactly that bad. I shook my head and cried harder, and it went on this way until finally I was able to tell him about packing the case and stowing it for the journey.

I didn't need to say more. His face grew pale and very serious. "You lost it on the train."

"It was stolen out from under me."

He nodded, taking it all in, and I watched his eyes carefully, how they changed and steadied, changed and steadied. He was trying to be brave for me, I knew. Because he wasn't sure what I'd do.

"You couldn't have packed everything. Why would I need it all?"

"If you were going to be making changes in the originals, I thought you'd want the copies, too, so that everything would be right."

"You must have left something," he said.

I shook my head and waited. Would he snap from the strain and fly into a rage? I'd certainly earned that. I'd taken what was his—what was most his in the world—without his asking me to, as if I had that right. And now it was gone.

"I have to go back. I need to know it for myself."

"I'm so sorry, Tatie." I shook with remorse and heartsickness.

"It's going to be all right. I made it. I can make it all again."

I knew he was bluffing if not outright lying, but I held him tight and let him hold me, and we said all the words people say to each other when they know the worst has come.

Late that night, he boarded a train back to Paris while I waited in Lausanne in a wet knot. Steffens took me to dinner and tried to calm my nerves, but even with several whiskeys in me, I jangled.

He was gone for two days and sent no cable. But just as I could see myself reaching into the cupboard over and over, packing everything away in the valise, I could see him coming into the quiet apartment and discovering for himself that it was all really gone.

Turning on all the lights, he first looks at everything in plain sight, the table and the bed, the kitchen. He looks at the floor and walks between the two rooms slowly, saving the cupboard until he's seen everything else, because that's the last place, and there won't be anywhere to look after and no hope left at all. He has a drink first, then another, but finally he has to see it. He puts his hand on the knob and pulls the door open and then he knows everything. There isn't a page left in the cupboard. Not a note or a scrap. He looks and looks, standing there, wrenched out and hollow. As desolate as the cupboard is, that's how he is too because the pages belong to him and are him. It's like someone has taken a broom to his insides and swept them out until everything's clean and bright and hard and empty.

TWENTY-THREE

When Ernest came back from Paris, he was tender with me and kept saying over and over that all was forgiven, but his eyes were bruised looking and changed. There was still work to do at the conference, and he did it as he always did, throwing himself into the day and coming home tired and glad for a drink. I passed my time walking through the town looking for gifts to send home for Christmas. Even more than our first year in France, I was desperate to see something that captured the holiday as I remembered it from childhood. I wandered for hours, peering in shopwindows, but search as I might, nothing in Lausanne looked like Christmas to me.

At the end of the week, we readied our things for the trip to Chamby. "It doesn't seem right to simply follow our plans through after all that's happened," I said to Ernest as we packed.

"Maybe," he said. His voice sounded tired. "But what should we do instead?"

"Go back to Paris?"

"That would be worse, wouldn't it?"

"I don't think I can bear Christmas Day feeling like this. Everything's such a bust. Maybe it's time we think about going home."

"Stateside? And admit failure? Are you trying to kill me?"

"I'm sorry. It's just hard to know how to go on."

"Yes," he said. He picked up his Corona and carefully nestled it in its black case before snapping the case closed. "It certainly is."

When we arrived at Chamby, the town was the same. Our chalet was perfect and exactly as before, as were the snow-covered mountains and our proprietors, the Gangwisches, who greeted us as if we were long-lost family members. It was all so welcome after our heavyhearted time in Lausanne that we surrendered completely. Before we'd even un-packed, we put on our skiing togs and caught the last train up the mountain to Les Avants. The sun was fading as we tied on our skis and flew down the powder-laced slope toward the village. With the wind roaring in our ears and stinging our cheeks, we raced along, Ernest just ahead of me, his bad knee bandaged with strong black cloth. He favored it a little, but looked lighter in his body than I'd seen in some time. I was grateful and relieved and sent a small prayer of thanks out to the snowy firs and the creamy sky turning every shade of pink, and Lake Geneva in the distance, flat and polished as glass.

The next day we slept late in our big soft four-poster bed and didn't even wake when the maid tiptoed in to start the fire. We roused our-selves later, when the room was warm and the porcelain stove purred with the blaze.

"We were right to come, Tatie," I said and nestled behind Ernest, kissing his neck and the buttons of his spine.

"Yes," he said. "Let's enjoy every minute and not think about any-thing else."

"There isn't anything else," I said. I rolled to cover him, straddling his flat, strong belly. I pushed my nightgown over my hips and then reached to draw him inside of me.

He groaned and closed his eyes, giving himself over completely.

Chink arrived on Christmas Day, and in the end, our holiday wasn't sad at all. We'd hung stockings for each other and for Chink, and we opened those, and then had a dinner fit for kings. It was only when we sat by the fire late that night, warm brandy in our bellies and more in our glasses, that Ernest brought up the terrible business of his lost manuscripts.

"Oh, kid," Chink said when Ernest reached the end of the story. "Can you really start over with nothing?"

"I don't know. I wrote the damned stuff once, didn't I?" Ernest said. "I have to, in any case."

Chink nodded seriously.

"I've been working like a dog for the *Star*," Ernest went on, "and now we have enough to live on for eight months. Eight months, and I'm going to give all of them to fiction. Only that."

"That's my Tatie," I said. Chink raised his glass, and we all toasted Christmas and each other.

But as the days passed, Ernest's notebooks and pencils stayed packed away. His Corona never left its black case. He said nothing about this and I didn't either; I knew better. Meanwhile, we skied all day and sometimes well into the evening, when the sun bled through the cloud line and seemed to be showing us something no one had seen before. We enjoyed every moment of Chink's good company and each other's, too. We made love every day, sometimes twice a day—that is, until I told Ernest I'd left our usual precautions back in Paris.

We had always tracked my monthly cycles carefully. Ernest did this himself, the way he kept accounts of everything in our marriage. There was a notebook for recording expenses and incoming monies, another for correspondence, another for noting story ideas and how many words he'd written each day. And there was a notebook marked *Hadley*, devoted to the rising and falling of my fertility each month so we could have unprotected intercourse as often as possible. In the beginning, in the unsafe times, we used the withdrawal method the way most couples did. "Not so very different from Russian roulette," Ernest used to joke, and it wasn't. You could get condoms at the chemist's or the barbershop, but these were thick and coarse, made of rubber cement—uncomfortable at best and sometimes riddled with holes.

When we first arrived in Paris, Gertrude, who could be wonderfully frank this way, asked if we knew about the diaphragm. Without too much trouble, we found a doctor and got me fitted for one, and this is what we'd used ever since. Ernest knew better than I did which were safe and which weren't. About a week into our time in Chamby, he reminded me we'd come to the end of our window.

"Could you make the necessary arrangements?" he said when we were in bed one night. This was his usual code. My role was to say, "Yes sir," as if I were his secretary, and he'd just asked me to make a lunch reservation or send a telegram. But this particular night, I didn't laugh and didn't get up to search my stocking drawer for the case. Instead, I said, "Oh dear."

"Don't tell me you've left it in Paris."

I could only nod.

"Your timing stinks." His face was red. I could tell he was very angry.

"I meant to tell you in Lausanne, as soon as I realized, but that was hardly the time either."

"What else are you keeping from me?"

"Nothing. I'm sorry. I should have told you."

"I'll say." He threw back the bedclothes, then got up and began to pace the room in his underwear, fuming. "Sometimes I wonder who I married exactly."

"Please be fair, Tatie. It's not as if I meant to forget it."

"No?"

"Of course not." I crossed the room and stood near enough to see his face in the dim. "I didn't. And yet I'd also be lying if I said I don't think a baby would be a wonderful idea."

"Now it comes out. I knew it. We've always said I'd get a really good start on things before we'd even talk about a baby. We agreed."

"I know we did," I said.

"I'm just finally getting going. Do you really want to ruin it for me?"

"Of course not," I said. "But I have worries, too. I'm thirty-one."

"Just. And you've never been crazy about children. You don't care at all for other people's."

"It's different to want one of your own. I don't have all the time in the world."

"I don't either. Life doesn't often give you more than one shot. I want to take mine now." His eyes were clear and challenging, the way they always were when he was asking for loyalty. "Are you for me?"

"Of course I am." I put my arms around his neck and kissed him, but his lips didn't soften under mine. His eyes, just a few inches from mine, were open and questioning.

"I suppose you think I'm going to lie down with you now."

"Ernest! I'm not trying to trap you!"

He said nothing.

"Tatie?"

"I need a drink." He headed for the door, grabbing his robe as he went.

"Please stay so we can talk about this."

"Go to sleep," he said, and left the room.

I couldn't sleep, though, for all my fretting. He didn't come to bed at all, and in the morning, I dressed and went down to look for him. He was in the dining room having his morning coffee, already wearing his skiing togs.

"Can we please make up, Tatie?" I said, going to him. "I'm just sick about everything."

"I know you are," he said, and sighed. "Listen. We have to be together on this. If we're not, then nothing's any good. You see that, don't you?"

I nodded and leaned into his shoulder.

"If you really want a baby, the time will be right someday."

"But not now."

"No, little cat. Not now."

Chink came into the room, saying good morning. Then he stopped, eyeing us carefully for a moment. "Is everything all right then?"

"Hadley's under the weather."

"Poor Mrs. Popplethwaite," Chink said tenderly. "You should be in bed."

"Yes. Go and try to get some rest," Ernest agreed. "We'll be up to check on you at lunch."

They went off to ski alone while I did my best to find some peace. I put on some nice thick socks and my Alpine slippers and then curled up in a chair by the fire to read *The Beautiful and Damned.* "Fitzgerald's a poet," Shakespear had said when she recommended it, just before she and Pound left for several months in Italy. The writing was exquisite, I had to admit, but it was making me sad to read about Gloria and Anthony. They talked prettily and had nice things, but their lives were hollow. I didn't have the stomach for such a dire picture of marriage, not just now.

I'd put the novel down and climbed into bed to try for a nap when Ernest came in. His hair was damp and crushed from his wool hat, and his face was pink from the cold. He sat on the bed near me and I saw that his eyes had softened considerably. Time away with Chink had done him some good.

"You look very warm," he said. "Do you mind if I share your cocoon?"

"Of course. If you think that's a good idea."

"I stopped at the chemist's in the village," he said, and took the little tin of condoms out of his trouser pocket.

"I'm surprised. You always say you hate them."

"Not as much as being away from you."

I looked at his trim belly and flanks as he undressed. "You're very beautiful," I said.

"So are you, Tatie."

As he climbed into bed, his skin chilly against mine, it began to snow outside. We pressed ourselves together in a crush on the feather-bed, his hands wonderfully rough, his hip bones sharp against my thighs. Later I would see plum-colored bruises there, and the skin on my face and breasts would be chapped and pink from where he hadn't shaved, but for now there was only wordless desire and a feeling of return. He'd left me for a time. He'd doubted me, but now he was mine again and I wanted to keep him here in a tangle of limbs and bedsheets until I'd quieted every last voice and we were only right again.

After three weeks at Chamby, when we were well fed and sun chapped and had parted ways with Chink, we headed off to Rapallo, on the Italian Riviera, where the Pounds had a rented villa.

"Ezra thinks he's discovered the place," Ernest said on the train. "Though Wordsworth and Keats had a go at it before him."

"Ezra thinks he's discovered trees and the sky."

"You have to admire the guy anyway, though, don't you?"

"I don't have to, but I will, I guess. For you."

After traveling south for a full day and more, we were finally near Genoa, where the countryside grew ever more springlike and lovely.

"This is heaven," I said. "I had no idea it would be so beautiful." Through our window I caught glimpses of the sea, quick bursts of frothed blue, then dark rock again, then the sea. "Aren't we lucky to be so happy, Tiny?" I said, just as we entered a mountain tunnel.

"Sure we are," he said and kissed me. The sound of the train bounced against black rock, roaring in our ears.

When we arrived at Rapallo, I thought the town was charming, with its pale pink and yellow hotels on the shoreline, its quiet empty harbor. Ernest disliked it on sight.

"There's no one here," he said when we got to our hotel.

"Who should be?"

"I don't know. It just doesn't seem to have any life, this place." He stood at the window in our room that faced the shore. "Doesn't the sea seem a bit spineless to you?"

"It looks like the sea," I said, and came up behind him and put my arms around him tightly. I knew it wasn't the place that was troubling him. During our last week at Chamby, I had woken several mornings to find him at the small desk in our room, the sharpened pencil lifeless next to his hand, his blue *cahier* open but empty. He still wasn't working, and the longer that went on, the harder it would be to start again. He was utterly determined to do it. He *would* do it. But how?

We played tennis every day in Rapallo and had long lunches with the Pounds in their terraced garden. Another couple arrived to join us on holiday, Mike Strater, a painter friend of Pound's, and his wife, Maggie. They had a delicious-looking baby girl, with wisps of yellow hair and gray eyes. I liked to watch her exploring the world just beyond her blanket, plucking fistfuls of grass and staring at her hand intently, as if it held the secret to something. Meanwhile, Ernest and Mike ducked and lunged in a boxing match on the nearby flagstones. Aside from being a very good painter, Mike was athletic and game for a good deal, and I could tell Ernest liked him immediately. Mike was a much better physical match for Ernest than Pound, who tried very hard in his blustery way but had a poet's delicate hands.

February was a changeable time in Italy. Some days were hung with mist, blotting out the hills behind the town until we felt very remote. The palm trees dripped and the swallows hid away somewhere. Sometimes the air was humid and drenched with sun. We could walk in the piazza or along the promenade to see fishermen on the concrete pier, dangling their poles out into the tide. The village was famous for its lace, and I liked to scan the shopwindows looking for the best pieces to send home as gifts while Ernest took long walks into the rocky hillside with Ezra, talking about Italian troubadours and the questionable virtues of automatic writing. Ernest liked to say he didn't want his mind shut off when he was working because it was the only thing he had going for him. True enough, but when he was through for the day, he couldn't turn his thoughts off without a glass of whiskey, and occasionally not even then. When he wasn't writing at all, like now, it was often more than he could take. This was hard to watch and I worried about him.

A week into our stay in Rapallo, I had something new to unsettle me, however. I woke feeling dizzy, with a strange roaring in my head. I tried to eat breakfast but couldn't stomach it, and returned to bed.

"It must have been the mussels we had last night," I said to Ernest, and stayed in our room until midday, when the feeling passed.

The next morning, when the same symptoms hit at precisely the same time, I forgave the mussels and began instead to count the days forward and back. We'd arrived in Chamby just before Christmas and a few days after my monthly bleeding. It was now February 10, and I hadn't had another period. When Ernest left the room to meet Ezra, I found his cache of notebooks and studied the one in particular that could illuminate my situation. Sure enough, for the last year I'd never been late by more than a day or two. This was a week at least, maybe ten days. I felt a small thrill of excitement, but didn't say anything to Ernest. It wasn't a certainty yet, and I was too afraid of what he would say.

I couldn't keep my secret forever, though. I could hardly stand the sight of food and even the smell of whiskey or a cigarette turned me green. Ernest was thankfully content to blame the exotic food, but Shakespear was growing suspicious. One afternoon as we sat at a table in the garden watching Ernest and Mike practicing tennis serves at one another, she looked at me with her head cocked and said, "There's something different about you these days, isn't there?"

"It's my newly revealed cheekbones," I said. "I've lost five pounds."

"Maybe," she said thoughtfully, but there was a strange clarity in her look that made me think she'd guessed the truth.

I tried to ignore it and said, "You seem to be reducing, too, my dear. You're fading away."

"I know. It's this business with Olga Rudge," she said with a sigh.

She'd long since told me about Olga, a concert violinist who'd been Pound's mistress for more than a year. "What's happened?" I asked. "Has something changed?"

"Not really. I expect him to be in love with half a dozen women, that's simply who he is, but this one seems different. The affair's not waning for one thing. And she's appearing in the *Cantos,* well disguised in myth, of course. But I can see her." She shook her pretty head as if to clear the image. "She's dug in. I wonder if we'll ever be free of her now."

"I'm so sorry," I said. "But it seems to me you're awfully tolerant of him. I don't understand marriage this way at all. I suppose I'm a Puritan."

She shrugged gracefully. "Mike Strater's in the middle of something now, too. An actress, I hear."

"Oh, God. Does Maggie know?"

"Everyone knows. He's gone off his head."

"He doesn't look it."

"No," Shakespear said, "but they never do. Men are stoics when it comes to matters of the heart."

"You seem very stoic to me, too."

"Yes," she said. "But I work impossibly hard at it, darling."

Ezra was famous for his roving affections; I expected nothing less from him. But the news about Mike Strater had thrown me, because he and Maggie looked so solid. I'd been watching and admiring them and their daughter, and stitching a fantasy about how our child—mine and Ernest's could squeeze in naturally at ringside and change very little about our lives or Ernest's work. Now that dream was punctured. This baby was almost certainly coming, but into what?

Marriage could be such deadly terrain. In Paris, you couldn't really turn around without seeing the result of lovers' bad decisions. An artist given to sexual excess was almost a cliché, but no one seemed to mind. As long as you were making something good or interesting or sensational, you could have as many lovers as you wanted and ruin them all. What was really unacceptable were bourgeois values, wanting something small and staid and predictable, like one true love, or a child.

Later that afternoon, when we went back to our room at the Hotel Splendide, it began to rain hard and looked as if it wouldn't ever stop. I stood at the window and watched it, feeling a growing worry.

"Mike Strater's in love with some actress in Paris," I said to Ernest from the window. "Did you guess?"

He sat on top of the bedclothes reading W. H. Hudson's *Green Mansions* for the hundredth time. He barely looked up. "I don't think it means anything. Ezra says he's quite the philanderer."

"When *does* it mean something? When everyone finally gets smashed to bits?"

"Is this what's gotten into you today? It doesn't concern us in the least."

"Doesn't it?"

"Of course not. You don't catch infidelity like the measles."

"You like him, though."

"I do. He's a good painter. He wants to come by here tomorrow and do my portrait. Yours, too, maybe, so you'd better find a less troubled face by then." He smiled lightly and went back to his book.

Outside the rain picked up and the wind canted it sideways, so that the boats in the harbor tipped dangerously.

"I'm hungry," I said.

"Then eat something." He didn't look up.

"If it would stop raining, we could eat in the garden on the flagstones."

"It's going to rain all day. Just eat something already or be quiet."

I walked over to the mirror and studied myself impatiently.

"I want to grow my hair out again. I'm tired of looking like a boy."

"You don't," he said to the book. "You're perfect."

"A perfect boy. I'm sick of it."

"You're just hungry. Have a pear."

I watched him with his head bent over into his book. He'd been letting his hair grow, and now it was nearly the same length as mine. We had begun to look a bit alike, in fact, just as Ernest said he wished we might, long ago on a star-hung rooftop in Chicago. But we wouldn't look this way for long. In a few months I would feel and see the roundness at my waist. It was unavoidable.

"If I had long lovely hair, I'd tie it up at my neck and it would be silky and perfect and I wouldn't care about anything else."

"Hmmm?" he said. "So do it."

"I will. I'm going to."

There was a pair of tiny nail scissors on the bureau under the mirror. On impulse, I took them up and trimmed a little hair under one ear, and then the other.

He watched me and laughed curiously. "You've lost your mind, you know."

"Maybe. Now you." I went over and straddled his waist, then snipped away at the hair under his ears until it matched mine. Tucking the hair into my shirt pocket, I said, "Now we're just the same."

"You're a strange one today."

"You're not in love with any actress in Paris, are you?"

"God, no." He laughed.

"Violinist?"

"No one."

"And you'll stay with me always?"

"What is it, Kitty? Tell me."

I met his eyes then. "I'm going to have a baby."

"Now?" The alarm registered immediately.

"In the fall."

"Please tell me it's not true."

"But it is. Be happy, Tiny. I want this."

He sighed. "How long have you known?"

"Not long. A week, maybe."

"I'm not ready for this, not nearly."

"You might be by then. You might even be glad for it."

"It's been a hell of a few months."

"You'll work again. I know it's coming."

"Something's coming," he said darkly.

The next few days were tense and difficult for us. Some part of me had hoped that Ernest's arguments against a baby only went so deep, and that as soon as he knew one was really coming, he'd be happy, or at least happy for *me*. But he didn't seem to be budging an inch in my direction. Our days looked very much the same as before, but I felt the distance between us and wondered how we'd bridge it to find each other again.

Then, in the midst of my brooding, a new guest arrived at the Pounds' villa. His name was Edward O'Brien, and he was a writer and editor staying in the hills above the town, near the Albergo Montallegro monastery. Ezra had heard he was there and invited him down for lunch.

"O'Brien edits a collection of the year's best stories," Pound said, making the introductions out on the terrace near the tennis courts. "He's been doing it since the war." Turning to Ernest, he said, "Hemingway here writes a damned good story. He's really very good."

"I'm gathering material for the 1923 edition now," O'Brien said to Ernest. "Do you have anything on hand?"

It was only luck that he did. Out of his satchel, he pulled a ragged copy of the jockey story, "My Old Man," which Lincoln Steffens had since sent back. He handed it over to O'Brien, and then told an abbreviated story of how his work had been lost. "So this piece," he said dramatically, "is all I have left. Just this last thing, like a small piece of the prow of a ship that's rotting at the bottom of the sea."

"Well, that's very poetic," O'Brien said, and he took the story up the hill to consider it.

When he'd left, I said to Ernest, as quietly as I could, "I wish you hadn't talked that way to O'Brien. It makes me sick to my stomach."

"Maybe that's the baby, then."

"Are you angry with me?"

"Why would I be?"

"You don't think I've done this on purpose?"

"What, lost the manuscripts?"

I felt as if he'd slapped me. "No. Fallen pregnant."

"It's the same in the end, isn't it?"

By that point, our whispering had gotten fierce, and it was clear to the other two couples that we were in the middle of a serious argument. They began to drift discreetly toward the house.

"I can't believe you really mean that," I said, my eyes hot with tears.

"I'll tell you what Strater says. He says no other writer or even painter—no one who makes something with all their soul—could ever have left that valise on the train. Because they'd have known what it meant."

"That's cruel. I suffered for those pieces too."

He sighed loudly and shut his eyes. When he opened them again he said, "I'm sorry. I've promised myself not to talk about it. It won't do any good anyway."

I stormed off in one direction and he went in another, and though by the time dinner was served everyone in our party seemed intent on pretending they'd overheard nothing, I knew perfectly well they had and thought it best to just come clean.

"We wanted you very fine people to be the first to know we're having a baby," I said, reaching for Ernest's hand. He didn't pull away.

"Well done," Shakespear said, rising to embrace me warmly. "I thought you seemed more substantial," she whispered into my ear.

"Damned good show," Mike said.

"Yes, yes," Pound said. "It's the happy fate of the monkey."

"Ezra!" Shakespear said sharply.

"Do I lie?"

"Congratulations," Maggie Strater said and hugged me. "We monkeys have to stick together."

The next afternoon, we watched the three men play tennis. Ernest was a terrible player, but this didn't stop him from doing it with force. He swung his racket wide and hard around, like a golfer. Mike hit a lovely shot that skimmed the net and fell nearly at Ernest's feet. He missed it anyway, and then cursed loudly and foully and threw his racket to the ground.

Maggie cringed. "He'll get used to the idea of the baby eventually," she said. "Mike did."

"Of course he will," Shakespear agreed. "His pride will take over at some point, and then he'll believe it was all his idea."

"I'm not so sure," I said.

I actually had a terrible feeling about the way Ernest was tangling up the lost manuscripts with the coming baby in his mind. If he felt—even in his darkest, most remote recesses—that I was capable of trying to sabotage his work and his ambition, how would we ever recover? Broken trust could rarely be repaired, I knew, particularly for Ernest. Once you were tarnished for him, he could never see you any other way.

I felt very low indeed until Edward O'Brien drove down the hill full of extravagant praise for Ernest's story. It was splendid and he wanted to publish it, even though it would break with the series' tradition of selecting from pieces that had already been published in magazines. Not only that, he wanted to lead the edition with the story and include it in his introduction; he felt that strongly about it.

O'Brien's timing couldn't have been more perfect; he answered my prayers and Ernest's too. His confidence, which had been sorely lacking, had a new boost and there was something solid to aim for and look forward to. Everyone who mattered would read his story when the collection was published. His name would mean something. He hadn't, in fact, been toiling for nothing.

The next morning when I woke, Ernest was at the desk by the window and he was writing.

We had two more weeks in Rapallo and they passed fruitfully for both of us. Ernest seemed to be less threatened by the baby, probably because the words had come back, and he felt the pulse of them. I wasn't as anxious about the future because Ernest was himself again, buoyed up by all he wanted to accomplish. I could finally be happy about the baby. The only thing that marred the experience at all was Ezra's taking me to one side as we were leaving. "You know I've never been keen on children. That's another matter. But in this case, with Hem, I think it would be a terrible mistake if you tried to utterly domesticate him."

"I like him the way he is. Surely you believe me."

"Of course. That's how you feel now. But mark my words, this baby will change everything. They always do. Just bear that in mind and be very careful."

"All right, Ezra, I promise," I said, and moved away toward Ernest and our train. Pound was Pound and given to speech-making, and I didn't take him seriously that day. I was far too optimistic about everything to heed any warnings, but years later his parting remarks would come back to me sharply. Pound was Pound, but about this one thing he had been dead right.

TWENTY-FOUR

*W*hen we returned to Paris in early April, I was very ready to be home. The trees were newly flowering, the streets were washed clean and hung with fresh laundry; children ran along the gravel paths in the Luxembourg Gardens. Ernest was working with intensity, and though I missed him when he was away, I was happier to be on my own than before.

It sounds funny to say it, but for the first time I had my own project. I took long walks every day for my health and tried to eat well and get plenty of rest. I bought yards and yards of soft white cotton and spent hours sitting in the sun and hand-stitching baby clothes. In the evenings I read the letters of Abélard and Héloïse, a love story that suited me far more than Fitzgerald's disintegrating Jazz Age couple. I felt hopeful about absolutely everything as spring passed into early summer. My middle thickened and my breasts grew fuller. I was tan and strong and content—more *substantial,* as Shakespear had said—and began to believe that I'd finally discovered my purpose.

When he wasn't toiling away in his room on the rue Descartes, Ernest spent a lot of time with Gertrude. She had commiserated when he told her about the lost manuscripts, of course, but was less sympathetic about his concerns over the coming baby.

"You'll do it anyway. You'll push through."

"I'm not near ready," he said.

Gertrude had narrowed her eyes at him and said, "I've never known a man who was. You'll do just fine."

"What were you hoping she'd say?" I asked when he relayed the story to me.

"I don't know. I thought she might have some advice."

"And did she?"

"No, actually. Nothing beyond 'Do it anyway.'"

"That's perfect advice for you. You *will* do it anyway."

"Easy for you to say. All you have to do is cut and sew baby clothes."

"That and *make* the baby, thank you very much. It's not coming out of the sky."

"Right," he said distractedly, and went back to work.

Not long after we returned to Paris, Jane Heap, the editor of the *Little Review*, wrote asking Ernest to contribute something to the next issue. Among the lost sketches in the valise was a series of vignettes he was collectively calling *Paris, 1922*. They all began with the phrase "I have seen" and painted memorable and often violent moments he'd witnessed or read about in the past year. One depicted Chèvre d'Or's ruinous collapse at Auteuil. Another described how Peggy Joyce's Chilean lover had shot himself in the head because she wouldn't marry him. Everyone had followed the actress's desperate story in the headlines, but Ernest's take on it was more vivid and alive than anything you could find in a newspaper. Whether he'd gotten the knowledge secondhand or not, each piece was graphic and brutal and completely convincing. Ernest believed he'd never done anything sharper or stronger, and Gertrude agreed. He was writing knockout punches.

"You might not want to hear it," Gertrude said, "but I think your losing everything has been a blessing. You needed to be free. To start with nothing and make something truly new."

Ernest nodded solemnly, but I knew he was tremendously relieved. So was I.

"I want to take another shot at the Paris vignettes for Jane Heap. But I don't want to simply revive their corpses. New is new. I'm thinking of pushing them out into paragraphs, so they really begin to move." He was watching her face carefully as he spoke, feeding off her encouragement. "Each would be less a sketch than a miniature wound up and let go."

"By all means," she said, and in a very short time, he was ready to show her a draft that captured the goring of a matador with ferocious intensity. He was particularly anxious to get her take on it because the scene was based on a story she herself had told him about the bullfights in Pamplona. You wouldn't have known, reading the passage, that he'd never been.

"This is exceptional," Gertrude said. "You've reproduced it exactly."

"That was the point," he said, clearly pleased to hear it. "But I want to know how bullfighting works firsthand. If I went myself, I could gather material for more sketches. Mike Strater's keen to go and so is Bob McAlmon. Bob's got plenty of money. He could front the whole trip."

"Go," Gertrude said.

"You should," I agreed. "Everything's pointing that way."

When we got home that night, I asked Ernest if I could read all of the miniatures he'd done so far and was stopped cold by one about his time in Turkey. It was set on the Karagatch Road and described, among other things, a woman giving birth like an animal in the rain.

I handed the pieces back, praising them to high heaven, as they deserved, but also couldn't help saying, "You don't have to hide how scared you are about this baby coming. Not from me."

"Sure I'm scared. How will I work? What will happen to our good time?"

"Not just that. I know you're worried about me."

"A little."

"Please don't. Nothing bad will happen."

"How could you possibly know that? Something could always go wrong. I've seen it myself."

"It's going to be fine. I can feel it."

"Just the same, I've been wondering if we shouldn't have the baby in Toronto. I could get full-time work at the *Star*. The hospitals are supposed to be very fine there, and I would have a steady job. We'll need the money for sure."

"Aren't you a good papa already," I said, and kissed him softly on the mouth.

"I'm trying to want this. To ward off all the troubling thoughts, too."

"And stuff in as much living as you can before the baby comes?"

"That too, yes."

The coming weeks brought a flurry of plans about Spain. He met often with Strater and Bob McAlmon in cafés, planning the itinerary, but for whatever reason Ernest always came back from these meetings peevish and irritated with the other men. McAlmon was a poet and friend of both Ezra and Sylvia. He was married to the British writer Annie Ellerman, who wrote under the pseudonym Bryher. It was very widely known that Annie was a lesbian and that Bob was keener on men than women. The marriage was one of convenience. On and off, Annie had been very involved with the poet H.D., another of Pound's "pupils," and although none of this seemed to trouble Bob in the least, it got under Ernest's skin. I wasn't exactly sure why. We were surrounded by every combination of sexual pairing and triangulation, so I didn't think it was the homosexuality that got to Ernest per se. It was more likely the dis-tribution of power. Annie was an heiress. Her father was a shipping magnate who happened to be the wealthiest man in England. Although Bob had money of his own, it wasn't anywhere near what Annie had, and there was the impression that she kept him on a leash and that he needed her if he was going to go on running his brand-new press, Con-tact Editions. Bob was dependent on Annie, and Ernest might someday be dependent on Bob, if he wanted to be published. Contact Editions was new but earmarked for greatness and actively looking for the sharpest, freshest writing possible.

Knowing that he *should* impress Bob meant that Ernest was in-eluctably drawn to offend him. By the time Bob, Ernest, and Mike Strater had left for Spain, Ernest and Bob were barely even speaking. The trip became an awkward one in many ways. Bob (with help from Annie) was footing all the bills, and this brought out the very worst in Ernest. He was always critical of the rich and hated to feel obligated. I learned later from Mike that Ernest had also immediately taken over as the "expert" on the trip, lecturing the other men incessantly. He loved bullfighting from the very first moment. In his letters to me, he talked only of the courage of the toreros and the bulls, too. The whole thing was a great and moving tragedy that you could see and feel, close enough to raise the hair on your neck.

When he came back a week later, he was brimming with enthusiasm. He practiced the dramatically flared passes he'd learned in Ronda and Madrid with a tablecloth in our apartment.

He turned parallel to our table, the only bull available for the moment. "There's an incredible calm as the matador watches the animal come, only thinking of what he has to do to bring him in correctly and not about the danger. That's where the grace is. And the difficulty, of course."

"I'd love to see it," I said.

"You might find it hard to watch," he said.

"Maybe, but it sounds like something I wouldn't want to miss. The fights might even be a good influence on the baby," I said.

"Yes, he'll be a real man before he's even born."

"What makes you so sure it's a boy?"

"What else would it be?"

We made plans to go back together in July, to the Fiesta de San Fermin in Pamplona, where Gertrude and Alice had gone the summer before. It was supposed to be the very best arena for bullfighting, drawing the most murderous bulls and highest-skilled toreros. Although I'd expressed only excitement at the prospect, Ernest was determined to prepare me for the violence.

"Not everyone can stomach it," he said. "McAlmon drank brandy all through his first bullfight. Every time the bull rushed the horses, it made him go green. He said he couldn't imagine anyone ever finding anything to love about it, and if they did, they were deranged."

"I don't think the two of you are meant to be friends."

"Maybe not, but it's looking like he and Annie want to do a book of stories for me. Or maybe stories and poems."

"Really? If you hate him so much, why would you want him to do the book?"

"Someone's got to. Now I only have to write the damned thing."

. . .

All of Pamplona was awake when our bus lumbered into the walled city in the middle of the night. The streets were so crowded with bodies that I wondered how the bus could budge at all, but the dancers moved in a ripple away from the rumbling engine and then filled in again once we'd passed. We continued to climb the narrow streets toward the public square, and when we reached it there was such a blur of noise and motion—dancers whirling, musicians drumming and blasting reed pipes, fireworks exploding in loud bursts of white smoke—we nearly lost our luggage. Once we had it securely in hand and found our hotel, our reservations, which Ernest had made weeks before, had been given away.

Back on the street again, Ernest told me to stay and wait for him while he looked for lodging. I watched him borne away by the crowd without feeling much hope that he'd find a room, much less make his way back to me. The streets themselves seemed to be shifting. I backed against a thick stone wall and tried to stand my ground as dancers spun by in blue and white. The women wore flaring full skirts. They circled each other, snapping their fingers and stamping their black-heeled shoes on the cobblestones. Their hair was loose and beautiful. Some carried tambourines or bells, and though the music sounded chaotic to me, with shrill fifing and drumming that shook the bones of my knees, the women seemed to hear a clear rhythm and move to it perfectly, their legs lifting in time, their arms arcing out from their sides. The men wore blue shirts and trousers, with red kerchiefs at their necks, and danced together in large groups. They called out to one another with happy yelps that were instantly absorbed. It was all like nothing I'd ever seen.

Somehow Ernest navigated the madness. He returned to collect me, and though all the hotels were booked and had been for weeks, he'd managed to secure us a room in a private house nearby, six nights for twice what we paid in rent each month in Paris.

"So much?" I said, feeling a bit ill at the amount. "How can we possibly afford it?"

"Chin up, Tiny. We'll be paid back in sketches. I need to be here. I feel that so powerfully."

I couldn't argue with his instinct and was dead on my feet besides. We took the room and were grateful for it, but in the end we might as well have stayed on the streets all night like everyone else. The whole city had been waiting all year for this week, this joyful night. They could dance forever, it seemed, and it struck me as funny that we'd been keen to come here to escape the chaos of Bastille Day in Paris, when this was as frenetic if not worse.

I finally got out of bed near 6:00 a.m., knowing there would be no rest for me, and walked out onto the balcony. On the street beneath me, there were as many people about as the night before, but they seemed more focused and directed. It was nearly time for the running of the bulls, but I didn't know that. I only knew something was happening. I went inside and dressed quietly, but Ernest woke anyway from his very light sleep, and by the time we were back at the balcony together, a cannon had sounded with a crack. We saw its white smoke scatter above the public square, and then the crowd gathered there began to sing. Our room was perfectly situated. We could see and hear everything from where we stood at the railing. A group of men and boys sang a passionate song in Spanish. I understood nothing, but didn't really need to.

"I think it's about danger," I said to Ernest over the din.

"Happy danger," he said. "They're excited to test themselves. To see if they can outrun their fear."

He knew the bulls would be released soon. Gertrude and Alice had relayed in great detail all they'd seen at the fiesta the year before, and so had Mike Strater. But Ernest wasn't content to hear what it was like; he wanted to know it firsthand. And if I hadn't been there with him, I knew he wouldn't be standing on the balcony at all. He really wanted to be down in the square, preparing himself to run.

"*Viva San Fermin,*" the crowd shouted. "*Gora San Fermin!*"

The cannon sounded again as the bulls were set loose, and we saw the runners coming very fast along the cobbled streets below. Everyone wore white shirts and pants with bright red scarves around their waists and necks. Some carried newspapers to wave the bulls away and all wore an expression that seemed ecstatic. After the runners, six bulls thundered past with such power the house shook under our feet. Their hooves rang on the cobblestones and their thick dark heads ducked low, looking murderous. Some of the men were overcome and had to scramble up the side of the barricades lining the street. Onlookers reached to help them escape, but there was also a palpable anticipation as the crowd waited to see if some unlucky one wouldn't be fast or limber enough.

There was no goring that day, at least not that we saw, and I was very relieved when the bulls were safely in the arena. The entire ritual took only a few minutes, but I realized I'd been holding my breath.

We breakfasted on wonderfully sweet café con leche and dense rolls, and then I tried to nap in our room while Ernest walked the streets of Pamplona taking notes on everything he saw. It was all poetry to him, the heavily lined faces of the old Basque men, each one with the same blue cap. The young men wore wide-brimmed straw hats instead and carried hand-sewn wine skins over their shoulders, their arms and backs well muscled from hard labor. Ernest came back to the room excited by it all, and talking about the lunch he'd just eaten, perfectly crisped river trout stuffed with fried ham and onions.

"The best fish I've ever eaten. Get dressed. You have to try it."

"You really want to go back to the same café and watch me eat?"

"Watch nothing. I'm going to have it again."

Later that afternoon when the first fight began, we sat in good *barrera* seats right up next to the action. Ernest had paid a premium to make sure we had an excellent view of the action, but he was also protective of me.

"Look away now," he said when the first horseman set the long, barbed *banderilla* into the withers of the bull, and the blood ran freely. He said it again when the first horse was gored badly, and again when the fine young torero, Nicanor Villalta, killed his bull with deft precision. But I didn't look away.

We sat in the *barrera* seats all that afternoon and saw six bulls die, and the whole while I watched and listened and felt swept up by it all. Between fights, I cross-stitched a white cotton blanket for the baby.

"You've surprised me," Ernest said, near the end of the day.

"Have I?"

"You weren't brought up to know how to watch something like this. I guessed you'd go weak. I'm sorry, but I did."

"I wasn't sure how I'd feel, but I can tell you now. Safe and strong." I'd come to the end of a row of stitches and tied a neat, flat knot, the way my mother had taught me to do when I was a girl. As I smoothed the floss with my fingertips, satisfied with my work, I couldn't help but think how shocked she would be to see me in this passionate, violent place and not cringing the least, but weathering it like a natural.

"When I was very young, I used to be fearless. I've told you."

He nodded.

"When I lost it, I think my family was happy."

"I don't know that you ever really lost it. I see it in you now."

"I'm stronger because of the baby. I can feel him moving when the pipes sound and the crowd roars. He seems to like it."

Ernest smiled with obvious pride, and then said, "Families can be vicious, but ours won't be."

"Our baby will know everything we know. We'll be very honest and not hold anything back."

"And we won't underestimate him."

"Or make him feel terrified of life."

"This is getting to be a very tall order, isn't it?" Ernest said, and we laughed happily, buoyed by our wishing.

Late that same night, when again we weren't sleeping for the fireworks and the drumming and the *riau-riau* dancing, Ernest said, "What about Nicanor as a name for the baby?"

"He'll be a fine torero with that name. He can't help it."

"We've had some fun, haven't we?" He squeezed me tightly in his arms.

"It's not all over."

"No, but I figure I have to be steady when the baby comes. I'll earn the bread and be the papa and there won't be time to think about what I want."

"For the first year, maybe, but not forever."

"A year of sacrifice, then. And then he'll have to take his chances with the rest of us."

"Nicanor," I repeated. "It rings, doesn't it?"

"It does, but that doesn't mean the little bugger gets more than a year."

TWENTY-FIVE

I wanted muskmelons and a really nice piece of cheese, coffee and good jam and waffles. I was so hungry thinking about this I couldn't sleep.

"Waffles," I said to Ernest's curled back near dawn. "Wouldn't that be lovely?"

When he didn't rouse, I said it again, louder, and put my hand on his back, giving him a friendly little shove.

"Oh, for crying out loud," he said, rolling out of bed. "It's gone now."

"What's gone?"

He sat on the edge of the thick mattress, scratching one knee. "The right words for the sketch."

"Oh, sorry then," I said.

I watched him dress and move toward the kitchen. Within minutes I could hear the coffee boiling and smell it and it made me hungrier. I heard him get his coffee and then heard the chair squeak back as he sat at the table. Silence.

"Tiny?" I said, still in bed. "What do you think about the waffles?"

He groaned and pushed his chair back. "There it all goes again."

The months were closing in on us. Our baby was due at the end of October and we were set to sail for Canada in late August. That would give us six or seven weeks to find an apartment and prepare. As the time grew closer, Ernest worked hard and worried harder. He was panicked he'd never have time to set down the rest of the miniatures for Jane Heap and the *Little Review*. He was working on five new ones simultaneously, each describing some aspect of bullfighting. When he came home from his studio, he often needed several drinks back to back before he could tell me about his work, which was going well, but seemed to be taking everything he had.

"I'm trying to keep it alive," he said. "To stay with the action, and not try to put in what I'm feeling about it. Not think about myself at all, but what really happened. That's where the real emotion is."

This was one of his newest ideas about writing, and because the miniatures would test it, he was killing himself to get them right. I had no doubt they would hit and be perfect, but in the meantime, it was hard to see him so overworked.

He was also slaving over proofs for Bob McAlmon. Even after their prickly time in Spain, Bob had made good on his offer to do a book for Ernest through Contact Editions. The volume would be titled *Three Stories and Ten Poems,* and although Ernest was crowing with excitement at the prospect, he was worried he'd never get the proofs corrected on time. He worked by candle late into the night; when he'd finally finished his notes and mailed everything back to McAlmon, it was time for good-byes.

In a series of sad dinners, we saw the Straters, the Pounds, Sylvia, Gertrude and Alice—each time saying we'd be back in a year, when the baby was ready to travel.

"Mind it's not longer," Pound said ominously. "Exile weighs on the mind."

"It's not quite exile, is it?" Ernest said.

"Limbo then," Pound said, retreating slightly.

"A softer word only if you don't bring in the Old Testament," Ernest said with a grumble.

Ten days later, we sailed.

It was early September when we arrived in Quebec, and by the time we got to Toronto, there was an enthusiastic note waiting from John Bone and another from Greg Clark, a reporter friend from Ernest's past, welcoming us warmly to town. All seemed to be boding well, but when

Ernest reported for work on September 10, he learned that Bone wouldn't be his immediate supervisor, as he expected, but Harry Hindmarsh, who was the *Star*'s assistant managing editor. After one meeting, Ernest knew the relationship would be a troubled one. Hindmarsh was heavy physically and also in word and deed; he liked to throw his weight around.

"Right off, he sized me up," Ernest said when he returned to our room at the Hotel Selby. "I hadn't said three words before he decided I was too big for my britches." He paced the room, scowling. "What about *him*? If he weren't married to the publisher's daughter, he'd be sweeping sidewalks."

"I'm sorry, Tiny. I'm sure he'll come around to your wonderfulness," I said.

"Fat chance. He seems bent on treating me like some cub reporter. I won't be getting a byline, and he's sending me out of town."

"When?"

"Tonight. To Kingston to cover some escaped convict. It's only five or six hours on the train, but I don't know how long the story will keep me there."

"Does Hindmarsh know this baby could turn up anytime?"

"I don't think he cares."

I sent Ernest off with a kiss and repeated assurance that all would be well. He made me swear to find reinforcements, and I did. Greg Clark had a lovely wife, Helen, who warmly agreed when I asked her for help in finding an apartment. Money was as much of a concern for us as it had always been, even more so because we were putting away every possible dime for the baby. We couldn't afford some of the nicer neighborhoods she recommended, but we did find something that would do on Bathurst Street. It was a railroad flat on the fourth floor, with a clawfoot tub and a pull-down Murphy bed in the bedroom, which was oddly squeezed between the kitchen and living room. Although the apartment itself lacked warmth and charm, it looked down on one corner of a ravine on the Connables' estate.

Ernest had known Ralph and Harriet Connable since just after the

war, when he'd come to Toronto to try and find newspaper work. Ralph
owned the Canadian chain of Woolworth five-and-dime stores and was
as wealthy as a god as far as we were concerned. He and his wife were
both very kind to me as soon as they learned we were neighbors, and
I was happy to have someone, anyone, close by as I neared my due date.

Ernest came home from Kingston looking tired and irritable, and
then left again, just days later, to do a mining story in Sudbury Basin,
easily twice as far from Toronto as Kingston. He barely had time to visit
and approve of the apartment.

"Oh, Cat. I feel terrible I won't be here to help you get settled."

"There's not much to do. I'll hire someone to do the lifting."

"I can't help but think we were foolish to come here. You're alone all
the time. I'm working like a slave for what? Spotty bits of news in
nowhere locations? What a bust."

"I know you're overworked, Tiny. But everything will make sense
once the baby comes."

"I hope to Christ you're right."

"I am. You'll see," I said. And kissed him good-bye.

I was doing far too much of that for my comfort, it was true, but
I did believe coming to very cold and lonely Toronto would be worth it
once our baby was born healthy and well. In the meantime, I tried to
make the new space as homey as I could. We'd brought crates from
Paris with our clothes and dishes and pictures packed inside. I hired a
cleaning woman and an ancient-looking janitor to cart our things up
the four flights. We didn't have much in the way of furniture, and for
the first weeks, as Ernest crisscrossed Ontario like some kind of traveling salesman, I camped out on the Murphy bed, wrapped in blankets
against the dropping temperatures and finishing the letters of Abélard
and Héloïse.

I was keen for any distraction, and it was easy to lose myself in their
words and their story. Some days I only got up to make tea or stuff blankets under the doors and windowsills where the chill crept in. I also
wrote letters to Paris, to the friends we were missing there, and home to
the States. Fonnie had been trying to muster happiness for me about

the coming baby, but she was close to the breaking point on many fronts. Roland had recently suffered a nervous breakdown and was recuperating in a mental hospital in Massachusetts. *It's a highly regarded facility,* Fonnie said in a letter, *as those places go. But the children are confused and ask if he'll ever come home again. I don't know what to tell them.* I felt very sorry for them all, but not surprised that such a thing could happen. There had always been too much unrest between them, as with my own parents. And when tensions are that high for so long, something *has* to snap. How can it not?

I also wrote to Ernest's parents. He was too busy to answer his own letters, but his stinginess with his parents was more complicated than that. He'd never wanted them overly involved in his life, particularly Grace. When he left for Paris, I think he felt he had freedom for the first time to completely reinvent himself. His parents reminded him of his beginnings, which he would rather have thrown off altogether. I understood his need for independence, but here we were a few weeks away from the baby's arrival, and Ernest hadn't said a thing to them. I felt they had a right to know, and I continued to tell him so when he came home ever so briefly between assignments.

"I'll do it if you insist," he finally agreed. "But it's a mistake. They'll just come sniffing around the way wolves always do."

"You don't really mean that."

"The hell I don't. Can you imagine my mother *not* forcing her way into everything with this baby, pummeling us with her opinions and advice? We don't need her. We don't need anyone."

"She and Ed would love any small opportunity to help."

"So let them, but I'm not asking for a hot dime."

"Fair enough," I said, but was grateful when they responded to Ernest's cable quickly and extravagantly, sending trunks full of wedding gifts we'd been storing with them and furniture, too, from our long-ago apartment on Dearborn Street. None of it was especially nice, but having our own things around us made our lot on Bathurst Street seem less provisional. And it all arrived just in time.

·   ·   ·

Hindmarsh sent Ernest off again, the first week in October, this time to cover the arrival of British prime minister David Lloyd George in New York City.

"It's like a personal vendetta," I said as I watched him pack for his trip.

"I can take it, I guess," Ernest said. "But what about you?"

"The doctor said we have until the end of the month, maybe until the first of November. You'll be here."

"This is the last trip," he said, snapping shut the new valise. "I'm going to ask John Bone to talk some sense into Hindmarsh."

"If it comes directly from Bone, he'll have to lay off, won't he?"

"That's the idea. Take good care of the baby cat."

"I promise."

"And the mama cat, too."

"Yes, Tiny, but you'd better hurry. They won't hold your train."

Several days later, on October 9, Harriet Connable called on me with a dinner invitation.

"I'd love to," I said. "But I'm so very large now nothing fits me. I'll have to wear table linens."

"I'm sure you'll carry them off beautifully, dear," she said with a gracious laugh. "We'll send a car around for you at eight."

In the end I was very glad she insisted. All afternoon I'd been feeling something I was calling indigestion. Of course it was more than that. My body was readying itself, but I tried to ignore it. I thought if I just stayed calm and didn't overexert myself, the baby would hold off until Ernest returned home. I spooned up my delicious soup as quietly as a mouse and then sat on the Connables' rich velvet sofa listening to Harriet play a lively rendition of "I'll Take You Home Again, Kathleen" without so much as tapping my foot. But of course the baby was coming whether I was prepared or not, and this became more and more obvious as the evening passed.

"Hadley, dear, I don't think you're feeling well," Ralph Connable said when he could no longer politely disregard the strained and serious expression on my face.

"I'm perfectly all right," I said, stubborn to the last, but then I began to cry as soon as I'd said it, my emotions bursting right through my carefully made dam. The pain was too much now. I bent over with it and began to shake.

"Oh, you poor girl," Harriet said. "Don't worry about anything. We'll make sure you're very well cared for."

They drove me to the hospital, Harriet patting my hand and making soothing noises while Ralph sped along with determination. The streets glowed faintly under gaslight.

"Can you try and reach someone at the *Star*? There must be a way to let Ernest know."

"We'll move mountains if we have to," Harriet assured me. "There's still a little time, I think."

But there wasn't. Half an hour later, I was gowned and draped on the surgical table, coached by the doctor and several nurses to begin pushing. This was why we'd come to Toronto—to have these very capable and trained professionals oversee everything. In Paris I would have had a midwife who boiled water on my own cooktop to sterilize her instruments. Even in the States, doctors were just beginning to perform hospital deliveries. Ernest's father still woke in the middle of the night to answer calls when he was up in Michigan, and though I knew women had been having babies at home forever—my mother, certainly, and Ernest's, too—I felt so much safer this way. Particularly when my pushing did nothing at all.

I strained for two hours, until my neck ached and my knees shook with the effort. Finally they gave me ether. I breathed in the fresh-paint smell of it as the mask was drawn over my mouth and nose, the sharpness stinging my eyes. After that, I felt nothing until I woke from my fog and saw the nurse holding out a tightly wrapped bundle. This was my son, swaddled in layers of blue wool. I gazed at him through happy tears. He was perfect, from the pink whorls of his well-made ears and his squeezed-shut eyes, to the dark brown hair with a fuzz of sideburns. I was devastated that Ernest had missed the birth, but here, safe and sound and utterly marvelous, was his son. That was all that mattered.

When Ernest finally did arrive early the next morning, panting and completely beside himself, I was sitting up in bed, nursing the baby.

"Oh, my God," Ernest said, breaking down. He stood just inside the door and sobbed openly, covering his face with his hands. "I've been dead worried for you, Tiny. I got a cable in the press car saying the baby had come and was well, but not a single word about you."

"Dear sweet Tiny. You can see I'm fine. Everything went smoothly, and come look at this fellow. Isn't he wonderful?"

Ernest crossed to me, sitting gently on the edge of the mattress. "He seems awfully small. Aren't you afraid of doing something wrong?" He put a single finger on the baby's small veined hand.

"I was afraid at first, but he's very solid, actually. I think the bull-fights had an effect on him after all. He came barreling out like a good torero."

"John Hadley Nicanor Hemingway. He's perfectly beautiful. And aren't you something for making it through so well?"

"I feel surprisingly sturdy, but you, Tiny. You look terrible. Didn't you sleep on the train?"

"I tried, but I had the most terrible feeling you were in danger."

"I was in excellent hands. The Connables were so thoughtful and helpful. We owe them so much."

"Maybe we were right to come to Toronto after all," Ernest said.

"Of course we were. I told you it would all make perfect sense."

"I'm so tired I might fall over."

"Sleep then." I pointed to a chair in the corner of the room.

"Hindmarsh will be wondering where I am."

"Let him wonder. You're a new father."

"Can you believe it?"

I smiled to myself and said nothing as he curled up under a blanket and fell soundly asleep. *Two men, now,* I thought with deep satisfaction. *And both of them mine.*

TWENTY-SIX

*L*ater that morning, Ernest sent out a rash of telegrams saying how well things had gone. He was immoderately proud of the speed with which I delivered the baby, and I was pleased with myself. I had help from the doctors and the ether, true enough, but also braved the whole ordeal like a champion stoic, with Ernest hundreds of miles away.

He left for work, prepared for a dressing down from Hindmarsh, but it was worse than he expected. Hindmarsh didn't wait for Ernest in his office, but humiliated him in front of everyone, saying he should have filed his story before going to the hospital. That was ridiculous, of course, but when Ernest relayed the story to me that evening, after re-hashing the whole thing with Greg Clark in a pub over many glasses of bourbon, he was still stung and angry.

"Toronto's dead. We can't stay here." The drink hadn't calmed him much, and I was worried the charge nurse would come in and evict him before I'd heard the whole story.

"Is everything really beyond repair?"

"Well beyond. We were both furious. He held nothing back, the lout, and I said things they'll probably be talking about for years to come."

"Oh dear, Tiny. Did he fire you?"

"He transferred me to the *Weekly*. Not that I'll take it. When do you think you can travel again?"

"I'll be fine in a few days, but the baby can't sail for months. We'll have to tough it out."

"I could kill the bastard. That might solve it."

"Not for long."

He grimaced and sat down hard, scraping the chair loudly against the floor. "Where's the little corker anyway? I want to take another look at him."

"He's in the nursery sleeping. You should be asleep, too. Go home, Tiny. We'll face this in the morning."

"What's to face? It's dead, I told you."

"Don't think about it. Just go, and take some bicarbonate, too. You're going to wake up with a hell of a headache."

We didn't immediately bolt for Paris—but only because we couldn't. The baby really was too young for the passage, and we'd also depleted our savings with the move. We were close to broke, with a pile of hospital bills besides. There was nothing to do but dig in and take it—"like a bitch dog," as Ernest was fond of saying. He took the transfer, and though he wasn't working directly under Hindmarsh any longer, he still felt the man's shadow. Every time he got a lousy assignment, he wondered if Hindmarsh was in on it—like the time he was sent to the Toronto Zoo to welcome the arrival of a white peacock.

"A peacock, Tiny. They're trying to kill me. Death by indignity, the nastiest kind of all."

"Maybe," I said. "But they can't. You're too strong for that."

"I'm not so sure."

Winter arrived in Toronto with snow that blew sideways and threatened to knock us over. If Paris winters were damp and gray, this was fiercely white and unremitting. The wind easily pierced our coats and blankets and found its way into every corner of our apartment, where the baby and I stayed camped against the radiator. I boiled water to keep the air moist and took to wearing Ernest's big overcoat when I nursed. I didn't take the baby out at all and hired a maid to mind him when I had to do the shopping. Ernest limped home in the evening, after dark had fallen, and looked more exhausted and run down all the time. He was good about exclaiming over the baby's new accomplishments as I reported them—he'd smiled at me in the bath; he was lifting his head like a champ—but it was hard for Ernest to take any pleasure just then.

"I can't see how I'll make it a year this way," he said.

"It seems impossible, I know. But when we're old and doddering, this year will seem like a blink."

"It's not even the embarrassment of slogging away at stories well beneath me. That's nothing. But not working on my own stuff at all, when that's all I've ever wanted. I feel the material going bad in me. If I don't write it soon I'm going to lose it for good."

"Stay up and write now. I'll make some strong coffee for you."

"I can't. I'm too tired to think. It does come in the morning sometimes, but as soon as I try to get anything down, the baby will cry or I'll have to get to work. At the end of the day, there aren't words left. We're so far away from everything here, too. I don't know who's writing what, or what matters."

"Yes, but you've made some good friends. You like Greg Clark. That's lucky."

"I do like Greg, but he doesn't box and he doesn't know anything about horse racing. I've also never seen him drunk."

"Not everyone drinks as well as you do, Tiny."

"Still, I don't trust a man I haven't seen tight."

As November passed into December, Ernest's mood grew worrisomely low. He wasn't sleeping well, and the baby's night waking only made this worse. The copies of *Three Stories and Ten Poems* had arrived and Ernest sent some off to Ezra and Gertrude and Sylvia, and several home to his family in Oak Park—and then he waited for praise. He combed the papers and magazines daily, anxious for a review, but there wasn't so much as a hint of the book's existence. If the world didn't know about the book, had it happened? He had a copy of Jane Heap's *Little Review* with the bullfighting miniatures, and sometimes he thumbed through them and frowned. "I'm not sure I'm the same writer who produced these. Hell, I'm not writing at all."

I couldn't tell him I thought he was being overly dramatic, because he really did feel the loss of his writing life profoundly. He needed me to keep him warm and loved, solidly tethered to earth; he needed his work to keep him sane. I couldn't help him with that part. I could only look on and feel troubled that our life was burdened by worry at a time when we should be so happy.

"It was a terrible mistake to come," he said after arriving home in a particularly dire state of mind one night.

I couldn't take his suffering any longer. "You're right," I said. "It was a mistake to come. We'll go back to Paris and you can give everything to your writing."

"How will we afford it?"

"I don't know. We just will."

"Your trust fund pays only two thousand a year. Without my income, I can't see how we'll manage."

"If you can't write, the baby and I will be a burden to you. You'll resent us. How can we live like that?"

"We're in a bind. That's for sure."

"Let's not think of it in that light. It can be an adventure. Our great gamble. Maybe we'll come out on top after all."

"I don't know what I'd do without you, Tiny."

"Buy the tickets. I'll wire your parents for money. They want to help."

"They want to obligate me. I won't take it."

"Don't then. I will, for the baby."

"What if I did one last series for the *Weekly*? I could kill myself for seven or ten pieces and then resign. With that and some from Oak Park, we'd have maybe a thousand to carry us. A thousand and a prayer."

"That should just about do it."

Just after the first of January 1924, as soon as we thought the baby could safely travel, we boarded the train for New York and then the *Antonia*, bound for France. We'd begun to call the baby Bumby for his very round and solid feel, like a stuffed bear. I rolled him tightly in blankets in the ship's berth and talked to him and let him play with my hair while, up on deck, Ernest found anyone at all and began to wax nostalgic about Paris. I would have stayed in Toronto for a year or five if it took that to make a good home for Bumby, but it wouldn't have cost me the way it would Ernest. Some men would have been able to choke it back and take it for a while, but he might have lost himself completely there. Ahead in Paris, it was anyone's guess how we'd make it, but I couldn't worry about that. Ernest needed me to be strong for us both now, and I would be. I would scrimp and make do and not resent it at all because it was my choice in the end. I was choosing him, the writer, in Paris. We would never again live a conventional life.

TWENTY-SEVEN

I know we meant to be gone a year," Ernest said to Gertrude on
our first visit to their flat after we returned, "but four months *is* a
year in Canada."

"You're finished with journalism, that's the main thing," Gertrude
said. "Time to go all out, now, and write the thing you're meant to."

"I'm ready, by God," he said, and helped himself to another glass of
pear liqueur.

I watched Alice as the two of them went on this way, feeding off of
one another's certainty and enthusiasm. She seemed to tighten and turn
inward, and I wondered if she wasn't happy to see Ernest back; if she'd
gotten used to having Gertrude to herself when we were away. Granted,
there was always someone circling Gertrude, wanting her attention and
good opinion, but she and Ernest had a special intensity together—
almost as if they were twin siblings with a private language, zeroing
in on and hearing the other almost exclusively. I felt it, too, and though
I had been hurt by their connection at times, I could hardly remember
what it felt like to be lonely. The baby needed and responded to me
completely. It was my voice he turned toward, the rhythms of my rocking arms that felt most right, the way I patted and rubbed his back
when he woke in the night. I was essential to him, and to Ernest, too.
I made everything run, now.

Motherhood could be exhausting, to be sure. I was forever under-
slept, and sometimes didn't have the energy to wash my hair or eat anything more elaborate than bread and butter. But when Bumby nursed,

his fist clutching the fabric of my robe, his eyes soft and bottomless and locked on mine, as if I were the very heart of his universe, I couldn't help but melt into him. And when Ernest came home from a long day of work and had that look that told me he'd been too much alone and in his head, I felt just as necessary. He needed me, and Bumby, too; without us, he couldn't climb back out of himself and feel whole again.

Family life worked most clearly for us when we were alone, at the end of the day, reconnecting and shoring each other up. But it was very much at odds with bohemian Paris. Gertrude and Alice could be lovely with Bumby. They gave him a shiny silver rattle and knitted booties. When it came time for his christening, they brought some very nice champagne, which we had with teacake, dried fruit, and sugared almonds, and Gertrude even agreed to be his godmother. But not all our friends seemed to know what to do with us now that we had a baby in tow. Pound and Shakespear would come to our apartment for a late-night drink or meet us at the café if we found someone to watch Bumby, but Pound made it very clear that babies weren't welcome in his studio. It wasn't because of the noise or the potential mess, but on principle. "I just don't believe in children," he said. "No offense, Hadley."

He did help us find our second apartment in Paris—not an easy task. The dollar was losing muscle against the franc, which we'd been silly not to anticipate. We'd lived so cheaply before; we thought we'd go on this way, with three mouths to feed instead of two—but rents had skyrocketed. When we finally did find something that would do, it was three times what we'd paid at Cardinal Lemoine. But we had to pay it. We handed over the first month's rent with a gulp, parked Bumby's pram in the yard next to the coal pile, and called it home.

This was the sawmill apartment, on the rue Notre-Dame-des-Champs, the "Carpenter's Loft" as some of our friends soon took to calling it. The noise and dust from the lumberyard below were too much to take at times, but it was much better situated than our rooms above the dance hall. It was very near Gertrude and Alice's apartment and the Luxembourg Gardens, and was also a stone's throw from the Boulevard Montparnasse and many of the best cafés.

Although Ernest had once felt disgust for writers working in cafés, saying they were phonies only wanting to be conspicuous, he began to frequent them himself now. Part of it was practical. He needed peace and quiet and Bumby, who had begun to teethe, was often fussy. But once he started to work at the Closerie des Lilas routinely, he was surprised to find he preferred it to working alone in his room, sweating it out in silence, as he used to say. It was warmer and more pleasant, too. Friends could find him if they wanted, and there was always someone exciting to talk to or drink with when the writing day was done.

Sometimes he talked about starting another novel, but hadn't yet hit on the right idea. More and more he understood that the draft lost in the valise with the other manuscripts wasn't the right novel either, no matter how much he'd slaved over it and wanted it to be. Still, he was skittish about committing to anything so large and time-consuming again. He would wait, and in the meantime he would write stories. "One story," he said, "for everything I know. Really know, in my bones and in my gut."

When he said this I wondered what it was *I* really knew in the way he meant, and could only answer with Ernest and Bumby, our life together. It was a shamefully outdated idea, I knew, and if I'd confessed it to any woman in any café in Montparnasse, I would have been laughed out onto the street. I was supposed to have my own ideas and ambitions and be incredibly hungry for experience and newness of every variety. But I wasn't hungry; I was content.

It wasn't just purpose that had come along to fill me. My days were richer and made more sense. Bumby was a beauty, and when we walked every day, twice a day, we were often stopped and chatted up by his admirers. My French was as halting as ever, but a happy baby is the perfect impetus for even primarily one-sided conversations. His cooing garnered us many a gift apple or pear at the market, and even when I brought him to the cafés to meet Ernest for an occasional meal, Bumby won everyone over. Some of our friends might have been at a loss, but strangers were invariably charmed.

The Pounds were off to Rapallo as usual that spring, but even from that distance, Ezra managed to get Ernest a job with Ford Madox Ford, as a deputy editor for the *Transatlantic Review*. Ford had a dark and cramped office on the Quai d'Anjou, and it was there Ernest headed in early February in his worn shoes and shabby jacket, with a chip on his shoulder. There was no money to be had, but he wanted the editing experience and the connections. He couldn't let Ford know that, though, because he couldn't stand not to have the upper hand, most particularly when the upper hand would have been impossible to get. Ford's novel *The Good Soldier* had received some very nice attention. He'd written other novels as well and had published Yeats, Thomas Hardy, Joseph Conrad, and others in a magazine he'd founded earlier, called the *English Review*. All of this was bad enough, but Ford was also a gentleman with money and a pedigree, a combination Ernest never had any patience for. He came home from the meeting muttering about how Ford's tastes were slanted so far backward the man was about to fall over on his ass.

"So he's not modern. Why should everyone be? I'm not."

"No, you're not modern, little cat. But you're very beautiful and good, and a bang-up mother besides. This fellow Ford is too full of his own good opinion, and he wheezes when he talks. It's so bad you'd think every last word has to swim through his lungs to reach his mouth."

"Good gracious, Tiny. Please tell me you took the job anyhow."

"Of course I did." He smiled broadly and wickedly, reaching over to tweak one of Bumby's feet. "Do you think I'm crazy?"

When I met Ford I was inclined to like him, even after all Ernest had said. He and his lover, the painter Stella Bowen, had us over to lunch, and I was delighted to find they had a baby, too, a darling little girl named Julie, about the same age as Bumby. I hadn't brought Bumby out of politeness for our hosts, but I told Stella I would the next time. She was warm in her encouragement about this, and about everything—feeding us a beautiful four-course lunch and engaging me graciously with her charming Australian accent. Ford was ruddy and plump, with wispy blond hair and a mustache. I did wonder at first how Ford, well into middle age, was able to woo such a lovely woman as Stella, but he soon revealed perfect manners and spoke with an appealing conviction for everything he cared about, including Stella, good wine, creamy soup, and literature. All through lunch, he emphasized how important it was for him to help young writers like Ernest find their way. I knew Ernest would rather not need Ford's or anyone's help, but the truth was, he did.

"I can bring a lot to this magazine," Ernest said when we'd said our good-byes and were headed home. "He should be grateful to have me."

"I liked him."

"Of course you did."

"What does that mean?"

"Nothing." He came upon a loose stone and kicked it into the street. "Don't you think he looks like a walrus?"

"A little," I admitted.

"And the wheezing?"

"That's fairly serious, isn't it? Stella said he got it in a gas attack in the war."

"I could forgive him that, then, if he wasn't so superior."

"You don't have to love him. Just do the work."

"There's plenty of work to do. That's lucky, I suppose."

"So much *is* lucky, Tatie. You'll see."

Ford and Stella took to having literary teas on Thursdays at the Quai d'Anjou. I often went for the company and took Bumby, too, parking his pram in whatever sun was coming in through the windows. It was at one of these teas I first met Harold Loeb. Harold seemed to be about Ernest's age and was very good-looking—tall, with a sharp, straight nose and strong chin and towering waves of dark hair. As soon as Ford introduced us, we began talking easily about the States.

"I don't miss home exactly," he said. "But I can't seem to stop dreaming about it. I wonder why that is."

"It's part of you, I guess," I said. "It's locked in, isn't it?"

"That's nicely put," he said, and peered down at me with clear and intense blue eyes. "Are you a writer, too, then?"

"Not hardly." I laughed. "Though I don't think I'd be half bad at it.

I've always loved books and felt they spoke to me. I've played piano since I was a girl, but not seriously."

"I'm not sure I write *seriously*," Harold said. "I try very hard to be funny, actually."

"I should think you'd be very funny if you put your mind to it."

"That's swell of you to say. Here, come tell Kitty. She thinks all my jokes are a bust."

We crossed the room together to meet his girlfriend, Kitty Cannell, who was truly beautiful, slim and graceful and golden all over.

"Kitty used to be a professional dancer," he said. "If she moves to get more wine, you'll see it instantly."

"Oh, Harold," she said. "Please don't try to be charming."

"See, Hadley. I have to be very dour around Kitty or she gets impatient with me." He pulled a face and Kitty laughed, showing her nice teeth. "And sometimes," Harold went on, "she surprises me utterly, the dear girl."

"It's why you keep me around."

"That and your ankles, sweetheart."

By the end of the afternoon I was quite taken by Harold and Kitty both, and happily accepted when they invited Ernest and me to dinner the next evening, at the Nègre de Toulouse.

"It's a wonderfully secret local place," Kitty said. "You won't find it in the guidebooks."

"I swear not to breathe a word of it," I said, and then began to wonder what on earth I could wear. I was still at a loss the next evening when it was time to leave for the restaurant. It had been five months since I'd had Bumby. My maternity clothes swam on me now, but I couldn't yet squeeze into anything from before.

"No one really cares," Ernest said. "You could go in sackcloth and still charm everyone."

"I could not. You might not give a whit about clothes." I gestured at his patched jacket and sweatshirt, the uniform he wore day and night, without any regard to fashion or even decorum. "But people generally do take care and want to make a good impression."

"You've already made one, obviously. But if you like, I'll tell them I've listened too carefully to Gertrude, who's always said to buy pictures instead of clothes."

"She does say that, but we don't buy pictures, do we?" I frowned at myself in the mirror.

"Don't fret, Tatie," Ernest said, coming behind me to plant a kiss on the back of my neck. "No one's as lovely and straight and simple as you."

I met his eyes in the mirror. "You're awfully sweet, aren't you?"

He kissed me again and then pushed me firmly out the door.

In the end the restaurant was so dimly lit, I found I wasn't self-conscious after the first bottle of wine. While the men talked of Princeton, where Harold had gone to school, and scratch starts at first novels (Harold was working on his just then), Kitty and I had a surprisingly intimate conversation about her first marriage, to Skipwith Cannell, a poet who'd apparently made her miserable, then refused to divorce her.

"How terrible for you. How will you marry again?"

"I'd *never* marry again, dear. Thank goodness Harold and I are in agreement about that much. But I'd rather not be chained to Skip forever. It was hard enough to bear when he was nearby. Now he clinks and clanks and bedevils me all the way from London."

"It's freedom you want, then."

"Good God, yes. Don't you?"

"I don't know. I want to be happy I suppose."

"Happiness is so awfully complicated, but freedom isn't. You're either tied down or you're not."

"Blaming marriage doesn't solve it. As soon as you love someone, you're bound up with them. It's unavoidable—unless you swear off love."

"Even *I'm* not that hard-nosed." She laughed and raised her glass. "To love, then."

Harold turned to us with a quizzical look. "What's going on here?"

"Hadley's turning me into a romantic," Kitty said.

Harold chuckled. "Fat chance, sweetheart, but it's a very nice idea."

"Only one romantic per table," Ernest piped in. "There's a sign at the door."

After a vast dinner, they came back with us to the sawmill apartment for a nightcap, and though they pretended to be gracious about how dark and tunnel-like our apartment was, I could see they were unaccustomed to common living. The baby was asleep in the next room, so we crowded around the kitchen table.

"I figure I'll be done with this novel within a month," Harold said, "and then I'm going for broke. I want an American publisher, an advance, and a slew of good notices."

"You forgot dancing girls," Ernest said, smirking.

"They'll be in the contract," Harold said. "Seriously, though, I'm shooting for Boni and Liveright. Ford says they're the operation to watch in New York."

"They publish Sherwood Anderson," Ernest said. "They've treated him well, and he says they're committed to contemporary American writers."

"That's me," Harold said. "You, too."

"You should send your stories, Tatie. Sherwood would put in a word for you," I said.

"Maybe," Ernest said. "I've thought about it."

"Now that's settled," Kitty said, "please let's talk about something interesting."

"Like hats, Kitty dear?" Harold said.

"Maybe." She turned to me. "I'd love to take you shopping. You could be my pet project."

"Oh, brother," Ernest said.

"What? Everyone likes nice things," Kitty said. "I promise not to drape her in pearls or meringue."

"I'd love to go," I said. "Let's set a date soon." But after they'd gone, I saw it was a mistake to have accepted Kitty's offer.

"She only wants to humiliate you, don't you see?" Ernest said.

"She's trying to be nice. I won't take any charity, if that's what's worrying you."

"It's not that. She wants to lure you in and make you think you're being treated badly."

"I'd never think that."

"Just wait. If she keeps whispering in your ear, you'll begin to hate me for how shabbily we live."

"You're being awfully extreme, Tatie. We're talking about shopping, for heaven's sake."

"No, we're not," he said grimly, and went off to pour himself a drink.

TWENTY-EIGHT

*W*hile Bumby napped at home under the care of Marie Cocotte, who'd been enthusiastic about returning to work for us, even with the additional nanny duties, I took to meeting Kitty once a week. We'd have tea somewhere or pop into antique stores when she had time. I loved to look at the jewelry, particularly the cloisonné earrings that were popular just then, and though Ernest and I had no money to spare for such indulgences, I enjoyed watching Kitty move through the shops and hearing her appreciative remarks. She had an eye and seemed to know, instinctively, what would hold its value and what was lovely but temporary. Sometimes she tried to press a gift on me, and I would feel pangs about declining. She really was just being nice, but Ernest had his pride, and I didn't want to risk stirring anything up.

Try as I might to convince Ernest of Kitty's virtues, he was intent on disliking her. She was too decorative, he said, and bent on her own comfort, but I wondered if he was actually threatened by her independence. She had a job as a fashion and dance correspondent for several magazines in the States, and though Harold paid for her charming apartment on the rue de Monttessuy, it was because he insisted on their having separate living quarters, and he was dripping with family money on both sides. Kitty had inherited money, too, and could have supported herself. She was also incredibly confident, with a way of moving and talking that communicated that she didn't need anyone to tell her she was beautiful or worthwhile. She knew it for herself, and that kind of self-possession unsettled Ernest.

I fought for my afternoons with Kitty, even though this created tension at home, because it was the first time since St. Louis that I'd gained a friend who was exclusively mine. Gertrude and Sylvia had always belonged to Ernest. He was unapologetically territorial about them. With Alice and Maggie Strater and even Shakespear, I couldn't quite seem to move beyond the realm of artist's wife. Kitty was connected to Harold, whom Ernest now saw often, but she also very much had her own life. And she had sought me out.

"You're a very *American* girl, aren't you?" she had said on one of our first outings.

"What? You're American, too," I said.

"Not like you. It's in everything you say, how direct and simple you are."

"Egads," I said. "You're just finding a polite way to notice how I don't fit here in Paris."

"You don't," she said. "But that's good. We need your sort around to tell us the truth about ourselves."

Besides Ernest's grumbling, the only difficulty in my friendship with Kitty was the way she continued to offer me gifts, even after I tried, at length, to explain the complexities of Ernest's pride.

"It's just a trifle," she pressed. "Why would he mind?"

"He simply would. I'm sorry."

"It sounds like caveman stuff to me. If he keeps you in animal skins, tending the cook fire, no other man will see you, let alone want you."

"It's nothing so brutish as all that. We have to economize. It's not such a great sacrifice."

"All right, I understand. But that's my beef with marriage. You suffer for *his* career. What do you get in the end?"

"The satisfaction of knowing he couldn't do it without me."

She turned from the beaded handbag she was admiring and fixed her pale blue eyes on me. "I adore you, you know. Don't change a whit."

It was shockingly unmodern—and likely naïve, too—but I did believe any sacrifices and difficulties in our life were worth it for Ernest's career. It was why we'd come to Paris after all. But it wasn't easy to watch my clothes falling to threads and not feel embarrassed, particularly since women were dressed so chicly just then. But I honestly don't think I could have kept up with them, even if we hadn't been strapped.

Our apartment was cold and damp, and I often had a dull ache in my sinuses. We kept Bumby's crib in the warmest corner, but he fell ill anyway. We passed a crouping cough back and forth for weeks that spring, which troubled his sleep. He woke crying, wanting to nurse. Feeding him could be a joy in the daylight when I was well rested, but at night it drained my energy away. It was at these times I most needed my outings with Kitty, or walks in the thin sunshine with Stella Bowen and Julie, who were also becoming good companions.

I also tried to slip out of the house for at least an hour each day to practice piano. We couldn't afford to buy or even rent one as we had before, so I played a badly tuned upright in the damp cellar of a music shop nearby. I had to light a candle to see the sheet music, and my fingers often cramped with cold. Sometimes it didn't seem worth the effort, but I kept it up anyway, because I wasn't ready to let this part of myself go.

In the meantime, Ernest was working better than ever. The pressure he felt after escaping Toronto for Paris seemed to have been absolutely essential in stirring him, because he was writing strongly and fluidly, with almost no second-guessing. The stories were coming so well he could barely keep up with them.

He continued to do editing work at the *Transatlantic*, and though he was still full of criticism for his boss, Ford went on championing Ernest's work just the same. When Ernest told Ford he was worried it would take years and years to get his name established, Ford told him that was nonsense.

"It will happen for you very quickly. When Pound showed me your work, I knew right away that I'd publish anything of yours. Everything."

Ernest took the compliment rather abashedly and tried to be kinder about Ford, particularly since he was trying to get him to publish *The Making of Americans*, a novel of Gertrude's, which had been languishing in her desk since 1911. Ford finally agreed to publish the thing serially, and Gertrude was ecstatic. The review was gradually becoming more important and widely read among their set, and it would be her first major publication. In the April issue, her work would appear alongside a selection from Joyce's new work in progress, the book that would later become *Finnegans Wake,* several pieces from Tristan Tzara, and a new story of Ernest's called "Indian Camp," which gruesomely detailed a woman giving birth and her coward husband slitting his own throat because he couldn't stand hearing her cries. He was very pleased with it because he'd been able to take a memory from his childhood, like watching his father deliver an Indian woman's baby, and stitch it to another thing he'd seen, the refugee couple on the Karagatch Road, and make a single powerful story.

"Joyce knows this trick," he said to me late one afternoon after returning from work on the issue. "He made Bloom up, and Bloom's the best there is. You have to digest life. You have to chew it up and love it all through. You have to live it with your eyes, really."

"You talk about it so well."

"Yes, but you can talk and talk and not get it right. You have to do it."

The April issue also contained the first important reviews of his *Three Stories and Ten Poems,* which were generally rapturous about Ernest's talent and style. He was inventing something new, they said, and was a writer to watch. I was so happy to see his reputation growing finally. Everywhere we went it seemed people wanted to be near him. Walking the boulevard with him at night, past the thrum of talk and tinny music, we would hear someone call out his name and we'd have to stop and have a friendly drink before moving on to another café where the same thing would happen. Everyone had a joke for him or some bit of news, and our circle of acquaintances was increasing day by day.

John Dos Passos, whom Ernest had met just after he began working for the Red Cross in Italy, was back in Paris, riding the wave of his literary success and always ready for a good time. Donald Stewart showed up around this time, too. He was a humorist who would one day go on to be famous for screenplays like *The Philadelphia Story,* but for the time being, he was just a funny guy standing near the bar in a very smart cream-colored suit. Ernest was proud of his slovenly writer's uniform, but I could occasionally be caught admiring crisply pressed trousers. Don's were perfect. He was also nice looking in a boyish, clean-shaven way, with clear blue eyes that became very animated when he laughed.

When Ernest introduced us, Don was wonderfully familiar with me right away. "You have beautiful hair," he said. "What an unusual color."

"Thank you. You have beautiful clothes."

"My mother liked clothes. And etiquette."

"And ironing boards?"

"I have a mean way with an iron, I must admit."

We talked a bit more, and I was having such a pleasant time, it took me a good half an hour to realize that Ernest had settled himself at a table nearby. I didn't recognize anyone he was with, including the beautiful woman sitting by his side. She was slender and lovely, with very close-cropped dark-blond hair. Her body seemed slim and boyish under a long sweater, but somehow her hair passed her *beyond* boyishness, making her all the more feminine. The instant I saw her, I felt a sharp chill run through me—even before Ernest leaned over and whispered something to her. She laughed throatily, arching her long pale neck.

"Are you quite all right?" Don said. "You've gone white."

"Oh. Quite fine, thanks."

He'd followed my eyes to Ernest and the woman. I'm sure everything was quite plain to him, but he smoothly deflected the moment. "That's Duff Twysden," he said. "Lady Twysden, actually. They say she married some British count. Count or viscount or lord twice removed. I can't keep royalty straight."

"Yes, well. Who can?"

I looked over at Ernest just as his eyes came up. The briefest crackling of suspicion passed between us, and then he got up and came over.

"'Scuse me, Don. I see you've met my wife."

"Charmed," Don said, before Ernest took my elbow and led me to the table where Duff sat expectantly.

"Lady Twysden," he said, making the introductions. "Or do you prefer Smurthwaite these days?"

"Doesn't matter as long as it's Duff." She half stood, extending a hand. "How d'you do?"

I was just collecting myself to say something pleasant when Kitty appeared out of the crowd. "God, I'm glad to see you," she said. "Come let's get a drink."

Harold was just behind her and looking not at all well. He was pale and his upper lip was damp.

"Has something happened?" I asked, when we were nearer the bar.

"Harold's leaving me."

"You're joking."

"I wish I were." She lit a cigarette and stared at the tip for a moment before inhaling in short stabs of breath. "Some restlessness has come in and taken him over. We always said we'd give each other every freedom. Funny, though, when it comes you don't want it."

"Is it someone else?"

"Isn't it always?" She sighed. "It's probably the new book, too. He wants to reinvent everything. I'm going to London soon. I wanted you to know."

"Oh, Kitty, really? Is it as bad as all that?"

"Looks like it," she said. "I have some things for you I can't bear to pack. I'll come over to the house."

"I don't care about the dresses. I don't need them."

"Nonsense."

"You know what Ernest will say."

She huffed, blowing out smoke. "Yes, but he hasn't a clue how hard it is to be a woman." She tossed her head in Duff's direction. "It's brutal out here, isn't it? The competition isn't just younger. They care more. They throw everything they've got into it."

I didn't quite know what to say. Kitty was one of the most poised and self-confident women I'd ever known, and here she was knocked off her feet and set spinning. It made me want to break Harold's neck.

"Do you want to go home?" I asked.

"I can't wither like a schoolgirl and have everyone feeling sorry for me. I'd die first. Let's have champagne," she said, putting on her bravest face. "Lots and lots of champagne."

I stayed by Kitty's side for the rest of the evening, but kept one eye on Ernest, too. This Duff character was just too lovely and too familiar.

She and Ernest talked so freely you'd think they'd known each other for years, and I felt newly vulnerable after hearing Kitty's news. The worst events always have the thrust of accidents, as if they come out of nowhere. But that's just lack of perspective. Kitty was blindsided, but Harold had likely been plotting his escape for months. I couldn't help but wonder if this could happen to me, too. Just how long had Duff been in the picture, anyway?

Sometime after midnight, when I just couldn't stay awake another moment, I excused myself from Kitty and got Ernest's attention. "It's time to get your poor wife to bed," I said. "I'm nearly falling over."

"Poor Cat," he said. "Go on home, then. Do you want me to find someone to walk with you?"

"You want to stay?" I asked sharply. Duff turned politely away.

"Of course. What's the matter? I'm not the one who's beat, right?"

My voice left me altogether, then, but Kitty appeared to save me. "I'll mind your wife, Hem. You stay and have a good time." She challenged him with a steely look, but he didn't bite.

"That's a good chap, Kitty. Thanks." He stood and squeezed my arm in a brotherly way. "Get some rest."

I nodded in a kind of trance while Kitty grabbed me firmly by the arm and led me away. When we were outside, I started to cry quietly. "I'm so embarrassed," I said.

Kitty gave me a firm, buck-up sort of embrace. "He's the one who should be embarrassed, darling. Her, too. They say she has to keep scores of men around because she can't pay her own bills."

"Duff," I said. "Who calls themselves such a thing?"

"Exactly. I'd bet good money that even someone with as little sense as Hem wouldn't leave a woman like you for that number. C'mon. Chin up."

"You've been so good to me, Kitty. I can't tell you how much I'll miss you."

"I know. I'm going to miss you, too, but what choice do I have? All I can do is run off to London and hope Harold chases me."

"Will he?"

"I honestly don't know."

. . .

When I got home, Bumby was awake and gumming tearfully on a small rubber ring.

Marie looked at me apologetically. "He had a terrible dream, I think. Poor dear. He wouldn't let me soothe him."

"Thank you for staying so late, Marie." When she'd gone I tried to settle Bumby, but he was whiny and fitful. It took me more than an hour to get him back to sleep, and by the time I fell into bed myself, I was so tired I felt delirious—but I couldn't rest. I'd been feeling so strong and content with our life, but Kitty was right. The competition was getting fiercer all the time. Paris was filled with enticing women. They sat in the cafés with their fresh faces and long lovely legs and waited for something outrageous to happen. Meanwhile, my body had changed with motherhood. Ernest claimed to love my fleshier hips and breasts, but with so much else to look at, he could easily lose interest in me. Maybe he already had—and what could I do about it? What did anyone do?

When Ernest came home some time later, I was still awake and so tired I began to cry. I couldn't help myself.

"Poor Mummy," he said, climbing into bed beside me and holding me close. "I didn't know you were so worn down. Let's get you a nice long break."

"God yes," I said, feeling a flood of relief. "Someplace very far from here."

TWENTY-NINE

Our "someplace very far" was the little village of Schruns in the Austrian Vorarlberg. We arrived just before Christmas 1924, and from our first day, we felt more at home there than we could have imagined. For less than half of what we spent each week in Paris, we had two comfortable rooms at the Taube Hotel and a nanny, Tiddy, to take Bumby around. There were thirty-eight kinds of beer and red wine and brandy and kirsch and champagne. The air was champagne. Bumby could breathe better at Schruns; we all could. Tiddy would pull him through the village on his wooden sleigh while Ernest worked, or tried to, in our room when the breakfast was done, and I practiced downstairs at the piano, which was there all for my having in the warm room. In the afternoons, after hard cheese and sausages and heavy bread and sometimes oranges, we'd ski.

We did a lot of skiing. A retired professional skier, Walther Lent, had opened a school, and we were his students. For weeks on end, there was only the pure white predictable crispness of snow. We'd hike for hours, up and up, because what good was it if we weren't at the very top of something, with no one else around and no tracks or memory of anyone else, anywhere? Skiing this way took strength—incredible strength and stamina. There weren't any lifts or trams. We carried our skis on our shoulders and anything else we'd need in rucksacks. To my great surprise, I could actually do it. Leaving Paris had been the best thing for me. I was sleeping well, I had help with the baby, and the fresh air and exercise had made me feel stronger and more fit than ever. On our slow climb up the long valley we'd see ptarmigan and deer and marten, sometimes a white Alpine fox. On the way down, we were aware only of virgin snow; the plunge and flight of glacier runs, great clouds of powder rising from our skis. I was the better skier, but Ernest was the better devourer of anything new—new air, new mantle of eggshell snow. We dropped and dropped. We flew.

If you leaned from our second-story window at the Taube, pushing the top of your body out and holding on to the stucco walls with your fingertips, you could see no fewer than ten Alps dipped in snow.

"How do you like that?" Ernest said the first time he tried this trick and then stood aside for me.

"I like it very much," I said. By then he'd come and pressed himself against me, his arms coming full around until it was really him holding me there in case I should want to fall. "I like it very much," I said again, because I had two strong arms and ten Alps in sight. He pulled me into the room and we lay down on the featherbed and made love. And I was reminded of what was best about us. How very easy and natural we could be as bodies, with no sharp angles or missteps and no need for talking. How in bed, as nowhere else, he was my favorite animal and I was his.

Behind the hotel there was a low hill where I practiced my skiing in the new snow while Ernest tried to work without much success. For the work alone he was missing Paris, the busyness of the city and his routine. Generally, if the work wasn't good, nothing was, but at Schruns there was a softer bunting around the day. I could ski on the hill and know that he was looking out over the pasture, the farms and fields, and feeling tight in his head but not unhappy. And sometimes he was watching me race straight down the hill, low on my skis, coming fast at the hotel and turning sharply at the last minute.

Ernest grew a fierce black beard that winter and looked magnificent in it. The work wasn't coming, but there were rounds of bowling and poker by the fire in the evenings and schnapps, made from mountain gentians, that felt hot and tonicy and blue on your tongue and in your throat, just what you'd think drinking violets might be like. The hotel's dining room was thick with smoke in the evenings. After dinner, I'd play the Bach or Haydn I'd practiced earlier in the day. Ernest would read Turgenev in his chair by the fire or play poker and smoke or talk about the war with Herr Nels, our proprietor. The wood smoke and the wool, the snow and the lovemaking—all of it warm and winding about us, building the good winter.

The only thing that wasn't perfect during this time was Ernest's worrying about his career. It didn't reassure him that all his friends were convinced of his talent, or that the reviews of *Three Stories and Ten Poems* had been nearly ecstatic. It was a little book, not at all on scale with his big dreaming. He'd sent his family several copies hot off the press, and they'd been returned with a chilly letter from Ernest's father saying he and Grace weren't comfortable having such material in the house. It was vulgar and profane at best. They wanted great things for him and hoped he would someday find a way to use his God-given talent to write something with strong morals and virtues. Until he did, he shouldn't feel compelled to send anything he published home. The letter stung Ernest to the core. No matter what he said, he still deeply wanted his family's approval.

"To hell with them, anyway," he said, but he kept the letter, folding it carefully and putting it in the drawer where he stored all of his important correspondence. *Families can be vicious,* he was fond of saying, and I could see what he meant clearly now. I could also see how he used the damage, pushing against it, redoubling his efforts to show them he didn't need their love or endorsement. He would keep fighting until he had *Vanity Fair* and the *Saturday Evening Post*. Until an American editor took a chance on him and he had a book, a real one, published the way he'd always dreamed.

It didn't help his mood that things were taking off for Harold. He'd finished his novel when he said he would, sent it directly off to Boni and Liveright. And they'd taken it. We got the news just before we left for Schruns. Harold had come to the apartment fairly bursting with excitement. "What do you know, Hem. Did you ever think it would hit for me?"

"Sure, why not?" Ernest had said. He was seething with professional

jealousy, of course, but he held his tongue and behaved, opening a bottle of brandy and bringing the siphon over. "Anderson's been trying to
get me to go with Liveright, too. I have a handful of good stories, and
I'm thinking of sending them off with the sketches I've been doing, the
miniatures."

"They're just the place to do it," Harold said. "What are you waiting
for?"

"I don't know. There are other fish in the sea, right? What about
Scribner's? Or Henry Doran?"

"Wherever you land, you'll do what's best. It's all going to happen
for you, too. You'll see."

· I knew with a certainty that Ernest would have leaped at the chance
to have any major publisher do the book, but with a lot of cajoling from
me and Harold and Sherwood too, Ernest finally mailed the manuscript to Boni and Liveright just before Christmas. He'd settled on the
title *In Our Time* because he'd tried to get to the heart of life at this very
moment, with all its violence and chaos and strange beauty. It was the
best work he'd done, and he felt good about having sent it off into the
world, but the wait for a response was torturing him. When forwarded
mail arrived for us at the Taube, Ernest raked through it impatiently
looking for one thing, an acceptance letter. It was all he'd ever wanted.

At the end of February, Herr Lent led us up the valley to the
Madlenerhaus, an Alpine station that stayed open even in the late winter. It had a good simple kitchen and a dormitory that rocked in high
winds like the berth of a great ship. From there, we could hike five hundred meters up the slope and plunge down again along the Silvretta, a
pristine glacier, our skis kicking up untouched powder. After skiing all
day we'd drop into bed at night exhausted.

"Let's not ever go back," I said to Ernest one night as we lay in our
bunk in the dormitory listening to snow and wind and nothing else.

"All right," he said, holding me more tightly. "Aren't we lucky to be
so in love? No one thought we'd make it this far. No one was on our side
at all, do you remember that?"

"Yes," I said, and felt a small chill. We couldn't hide from the world
forever.

After three days, we came back down the mountain to find two telegrams waiting for Ernest. One was from Sherwood and the other was from Horace Liveright and both said the same thing: *In Our Time* would be a book. They were offering a two-hundred-dollar advance against royalties and were sending a contract soon.

It was an epic moment, one we'd never forget—and somehow the skiing seemed ineluctably part of it, as if we *had* to trek up nearly to the sky and fly back down to get this news. It was the end of Ernest's struggle with apprenticeship, and an end to other things as well. He would never again be unknown. We would never again be this happy.

The next day we boarded a train back to Paris.

THIRTY

*I*t rained nonstop that spring, but even in the rain, Paris was Ernest's smorgasbord. He knew it all and loved to walk through it at night especially, dropping into cafés to see who was there and who wasn't. He was recognizable everywhere with his long, unruly hair and tennis shoes and patched jacket, the quintessential Left Bank writer. It was ironic to see him become the very sort of artist that had made him cringe two years before, and a little painful for me, too. I missed him and I wasn't sure I *recognized* him all the time, but I didn't want to hold him back. Not when things were finally beginning to hit for him.

If Ernest was changing, Montparnasse was, too. American tourists flooded the scene hoping to get a glimpse of a real bohemian while the usual suspects grew wilder and stranger for the new audience. Kiki was one of the most famous artist's models around, and Man Ray's lover and muse. She could often be seen at the Dôme or Rotonde with her pet mouse. It was small and white, and she wore it attached to her wrist with a delicate silver chain. The fleshy redhead Flossie Martin held court in front of the Select shouting obscenities to locals and tourists alike. Bob McAlmon vomited neatly in the flowerbeds of all the best cafés and then ordered another absinthe. That absinthe was illegal deterred no one, and the same held true for opium and cocaine. Ernest and I had always been more than happy enough with alcohol, but there was the very real feeling, for many, of needing to up the ante—to feel more and risk more. It grew harder and harder to shock anyone.

Duff Twysden was one of the wilder girls on the café scene. She drank like a man and told a good, filthy joke and could talk to absolutely anyone. She made her own rules and didn't give a damn who knew it. When we returned from Austria, Ernest began to see more of her than ever. Sometimes they were joined by her fiancé, Pat Guthrie. Pat was a famous drunk and often wasn't well enough to leave their flat without causing a scene. I felt some relief knowing Duff was attached and, ostensibly, in love—but then again that didn't always mean what it should.

Duff was very keen for company at night and so was Ernest, and they naturally gravitated toward each other. I worried about her a lot, but when he finally brought her by the sawmill to spend time with all of us, she crouched right down on the floor in front of Bumby.

"Hullo there. You're very handsome, aren't you?"

Bumby laughed and toddled behind me; he'd just learned to walk over the winter, and when he ran, he held his chubby legs so stiffly you thought he'd fall headlong into something.

"How very classic," Duff said watching him with a laugh. "Why do all the men run away from me? I must be terrifying indeed."

"You don't know the half of it," Ernest said.

For the rest of the visit, she sat at my table and made no pretensions about anything. She was well bred but not fussy, and had a broad, raw laugh that moved everything with it. I liked her. I didn't want to, but I did.

Around this same time, Kitty returned from London and wrote to invite me to tea.

"What's she doing back?" Ernest said. "I thought we were free of that gold-plated bitch."

"Be fair!" I snapped.

"I am. I know a bitch when I see one."

I tried to ignore him. He was never going to change his mind about Kitty, no matter what I said or did. It was one of his qualities that most frustrated me, how once you had a black tick in his book, you were pretty much done for. I'd have much rather not had to fight with him about her, but I was going to see Kitty anyway.

Unfortunately, the only nice dresses I owned were ones she herself had given me, and since I wouldn't turn up in her castoffs, I went in a shabby skirt and sweater. As soon as I entered her apartment, I regretted the choice. She'd also invited two sisters from the Midwest, Pauline and Jinny Pfeiffer, and they were dressed to perfection. Pauline, I quickly learned, had come to Paris to work for *Vogue*. She was impossibly chic and wore a coat made of hundreds of chipmunk skins sewn painfully together and a pair of champagne-colored shoes that might have been the finest I'd ever seen. Jinny was the prettier of the two with these incredible almond-shaped eyes, but Pauline had something else, an almost boyish exuberance. She was slim through the hips and shoulders, with sharply cut dark bangs falling nearly to her eyebrows.

The two sisters were the daughters of a wealthy landowner from Arkansas, but they'd grown up in St. Louis. Kitty was just beginning to tell me about how close Pauline and Kate Smith had been at one time when Harold and Ernest came in from a boxing workout, sweaty and laughing.

I was surprised to see Harold—were he and Kitty on again?—but she quickly shot me a look that said *Don't ask*. Meanwhile, why had Ernest come if not to harass Kitty? You'd think he would have tried to avoid her. I'd wanted an intimate reunion with my good friend, not tension and awkwardness, and definitely not Ernest and Harold sniffing around these striking new women as if they were exotic animals in a zoo exhibit.

As the afternoon wore on, Harold and Ernest both drank with vigor. I followed Kitty into the kitchen for more tea just as Ernest began to flirt with Jinny.

"I say," Ernest said loudly to Harold. "I think I'd like to take this girl out on the town."

"I wouldn't give that a thought," Kitty said to me in a low voice. "Jinny doesn't go in for boys."

"Really?" I said. From where I stood, Jinny was doing a pretty good imitation of a vamp. She'd turned her almond eyes on Ernest and batted them expertly.

"She just likes to hone her skills occasionally. She finds men amusing, I think."

"It must be nice to be in such control," I said. "And what about you? What's happened with Harold?"

"Well, he did follow me to London, after a fashion. I'd all but given up. He says he's not sure what he wants."

"But he missed you."

"Sure he missed me. They always do when you go running. How long can it last, though, now I'm here?"

"Why does everything have to be so complicated?" I said.

"I have no earthly idea," Kitty said. "But clearly it does."

Back out in the living room, Harold sat on the davenport alone with his feet up, lighting a thick cigar, while Jinny and Ernest and Pauline stood on the rug in front of him.

"I could take you both out," Ernest said to the girls. "I've two arms after all."

"Not really," Harold said noticing me. "Your wife owns one."

"All right then. I'll take Jinny—as long as she wears her sister's coat."

Everyone laughed, and it was one of those domino moments. That laugh would eventually set off an entire series of events, but not yet. It just stood there in the room, tipping and tipping, but not falling.

Not falling yet. Not quite.

Over the coming months, in the spring of 1925, our circle of friends continued to shift. The change was subtle at first, and each instance seemed to have little to do with the others, but our old set was falling away and being replaced with richer and wilder specimens. Pound and Shakespear had begun spending more and more time at Rapallo and were living there nearly year-round now. Gertrude and Ernest had begun to quarrel about things small and large. He seemed flummoxed about why, but I think he was changing too fast for her comfort.

"Alice has never liked me," he said one evening when we were leaving their salon. "And now she's trying to turn Stein around to her thinking."

"Nonsense. Alice loves you."

"Then she has a fine way of showing it. She all but called me a careerist tonight. My head's growing too fast apparently."

"Gertrude loves you, too. She's just worried."

"I don't need her chastising, and why is she the great teacher anyway? I mean, what has she done really?"

It made me sad to think about the professional wedge growing between these two very good friends, and I wasn't sure what it meant for me. The new set was made up of very wealthy artists who were utterly focused on living well, having the very best of everything. We were still squeezing by on less than three thousand a year, and although it seemed to me we had nothing in common with these people, they were interested in us, or in Ernest at least.

Pauline Pfeiffer was one of these. She was a working girl, ostensibly, drawing a paycheck from *Vogue*—but she had a trust fund on top of this, and it no doubt helped to keep her in the clothes she wore so well. This was Chanel's heyday and Pauline had written about her new collection for *Vogue* with a fervency that bordered on obsession.

"Chanel has changed the silhouette for good, you know," she said to a group of us one night at the Deux Magots. "We'll never be the same."

All the other women at the table nodded as if Pauline had predicted the Second Coming, but I was left cold by fashion. My clothes never behaved, and I felt that no one could change my silhouette unless I stopped eating altogether.

Kitty had known Pauline for ages and was very keen for us to be friends. I didn't think we'd have the slightest thing in common, but the first time Kitty brought her over to our apartment, I was pleasantly surprised to find that she was awfully bright and funny. She also seemed eager for me to like her.

"Kate Smith has said lovely things about you for years," she said. "It's so good to finally meet you."

"When did you and Kate meet?"

"At the University of Missouri. We both majored in journalism."

"I'm afraid Kate had her hooks into me far earlier," I said. "When we were nine she got me sick to the gills on stolen cigarettes."

"Sounds like my girl. She would have been hard pressed to find ways to corrupt me. I was pretty far gone already."

As we laughed I heard Ernest clear his throat from the bedroom.

I was embarrassed that he wouldn't join us and tried to make excuses for him.

Pauline frowned a little at the door. It was only slightly ajar, but he was visible on the bed—not indisposed at all, just disinterested in joining our party. "I know all about husbands," she said. "I've studied them from afar for years."

"No near brushes yourself?" I said.

"Very near, actually," Kitty piped in.

"It doesn't matter. I'm free now," she said. "Swimmingly free, and it's lovely."

"Don't talk to Hadley about freedom." Kitty laughed. "She has all sorts of theories and lectures prepared."

I flushed and tried to explain myself, but Pauline changed the subject quickly and easily. "Kitty says you're a whiz on the piano," she said. "Don't you have one here you could play for us?"

"Sadly, no," I said. "I'm not a professional."

"What does *professional* mean except that you play for others instead of yourself? Have you given concerts?"

"Not since I was in my twenties, and I didn't have the stomach for it even then."

"It's important to test your nerve occasionally," she said. "It keeps you young."

"You should play a concert," Kitty said. "It would be awfully good for you. Everyone would come."

"I could get ill just thinking about it," I said, laughing the idea off. But later that night, when we were lying in bed just before sleep, I told Ernest that I wanted a piano of my own. "I didn't think I'd miss it so much," I said. "But I do."

"I know, Cat. I'd love for you to have one. Maybe when the advance comes."

"That's such a fine word, isn't it?"

"Yes, and 'royalty' is another one, but don't go spending either just yet."

"No, Tatie, I won't." But I went to sleep happy just the same.

. . .

On a night in early May, Ernest and I were having a night out on our own at the Dingo when Scott Fitzgerald came over from the bar and introduced himself to us.

"You're Hemingway," Fitzgerald said. "Ford showed me a story of yours a few weeks back and I said, 'Well there it is, isn't it? He's the real article.'"

"I'm sorry I haven't read any of your books," Ernest said.

"That's all right. I'm not sure I write them anymore. Since my wife and I have come to Paris it's been a thousand parties and no work at all."

Ernest squinted at him through the dim light. "You can't finish anything that way."

"Don't I know it? But Zelda loves to dance. You should meet her. She's spectacular." His eyes turned to the dance floor where several couples were in the midst of a sinuous-looking tango. "I do have a novel just out. *The Great Gatsby.*"

"I'll look for it," Ernest said. "How are you holding up, waiting for the notices?"

"That's not so difficult for me. Not near as tricky as getting it down in the first place. And once I have it all, I can't seem to move on. Like this Gatsby. I know him so well, it's as if he's my child. He's dead and I'm still worried about him. Isn't that funny?"

"You're not working on anything now?" I asked, wondering if I could drum up the nerve to tell him I'd read one of his books. "Apart from the dancing, that is?"

He flashed his lovely teeth at me. "No, but I will if you promise to admire every word extravagantly. Tell me, what do you think of me so far?"

An hour or so later, Ernest and I poured Scott into a taxi.

"I don't like a man who can't hold his liquor," he said when the car had pulled away. "I thought he might pass out on the table."

"He did look very green, didn't he? And he asked the most alarming personal questions. Did you hear him ask if I'd ever been in love with my father?"

"He asked me that, too, and whether or not I was afraid of water, and if we'd slept together before the wedding. He's very odd, isn't he?"

He was odd, and that might have been our last meeting with Fitzgerald if he hadn't thought to hunt down our address and send a copy of *The Great Gatsby* as a gift. Ernest simply stowed it on a shelf after opening the package, and it might have been forgotten there if I hadn't been so curious to read it. It wasn't too bleak, at least not at first. And when things did get very dire very quickly, I was already completely absorbed by the story.

After I devoured it, awfully impressed, I told Ernest to read it, too. He finished it in one afternoon, declaring it a damned fine novel, then sent a note saying as much to Fitzgerald. We all met up a few nights later, at the Nègre de Toulouse. Fitzgerald and Zelda were there when we arrived and were well into a second bottle of champagne. Her edges were already blurred when she stood to shake our hands, and she looked as if she cultivated that—a fine blurriness. Her dress was a pale sheath of filmy layers, one over the next, and they shifted dreamily around her as she sat. Her skin was fair and so was her waved hair, and all of her seemed to be the same color except for her mouth, which was painted very dark red, and cut a straight hard line.

Scott stood up as we approached their table, and Zelda smiled strangely, narrowing her eyes. She wasn't beautiful, exactly, but her voice was—low and cultivated.

"How do you do?" she said, and then quickly turned to Ernest. "Scott says you're the real thing."

"Oh? He says you're spectacular."

"Aren't you just darling, my darling?" she said, running her hand along the side of Scott's sculpted head. With this gesture, which could have been extravagantly silly, she and Scott slipped behind a private net into their own little world. Their eyes locked and they weren't with us anymore, or with anyone in the café at all, but only with each other, awash in a long secret look.

Later we watched them dance the Charleston and the effect was the same. They didn't bounce wildly like the other couples; they were smooth as glass, their arms arcing back and forth as if on strings. Zelda's dress bubbled up as she moved and every so often she reached to pull it up farther, past the tops of her garters. It was sort of shocking, but it didn't look as if she meant to shock anyone. She danced for herself and for Scott. They moved in one another's orbit, incredibly self-possessed, their eyes locked on each other.

"What do you think of her?" I asked Ernest.

"She's not beautiful."

"No, but she has something, doesn't she?"

"I think she's crazy."

"Not really?"

"Really," he said. "Have you looked into her eyes?"

At the end of the evening, they invited us to their flat in a fashionable Right Bank neighborhood off the Étoile. It was a rich building, you could see that right away, but when we got inside, the apartment itself was all chaos, with clothes and books and paper and baby things strewn everywhere. We pushed a great heap aside to make a place for ourselves on the sofa, but Scott and Zelda didn't seem embarrassed at all. They went on entertaining each other just as they had in the café, but more loudly. Things got so noisy, in fact, that we heard a child's crying from deep in the apartment, and then an English nanny came out bearing Scottie, their plump daughter. She was dressed in an elaborate bedtime costume with a fat bow listing to the side of her fine blond hair. Her face was prettily rumpled from her pillow.

"Oh, here's my precious," Zelda said, rising to scoop the girl up. "Aren't you just a little lamb stew?" The girl smiled sleepily and seemed pleased, but the moment Zelda sat with her in a gilded but shabby wing chair, she became so preoccupied with trying to catch whiffs of Scott and Ernest's conversation that the girl plopped right off her lap and onto the floor. Zelda didn't even seem to notice it happened. The nanny swooped in and spirited the now-wailing Scottie off, and Zelda turned to me and said, "What were you saying?" Her eyes were scattered looking and strange, as if her mind were on another plane entirely. "I'm dying for my Scottie to be a flapper, you know. Decorative and unfathomable and all made of silver."

"She's adorable," I said.

"Isn't she? She'll never be helpless. You can see that, can't you?" Her intensity was sudden and alarming.

"Yes," I agreed and wondered if Ernest had been right. But who could separate real madness out from the champagne, which was ongoing and everywhere?

As near as I could tell, the party never stopped for those two. Less than a week later, they showed up at the sawmill apartment at six o'clock in the morning, still drunk from their night out. We were sound asleep when they started banging on the door and singing our names out loudly. They didn't seem to care that we were in our pajamas. We made coffee, but they didn't drink it. They laughed, and swore allegiance to some ballet artist they'd met in the café the night before but that we'd never heard of.

"Zelda's very sensitive to art, you know," Scott said. "She's not really of the earth at all, my girl."

Zelda's face grew dramatically stricken. "You're not going to tell them, are you?"

"Maybe we should, darling. They'll guess anyway."

"Well, then." Her eyes widened. "A short time ago, I fell very much in love with another man. It nearly killed me and Scott, too."

Scott stood over her and made a motion as if he was smoothing her hair without actually touching it. "It nearly killed us, but it *did* kill the fellow. So horrible. It was in all the papers. You must have read something of it."

I shook my head and said, "I'm so sorry you had to go through all of that. It does sound awful."

"Yes, well," Zelda said, snapping out of the moment as if an invisible director had called *Scene*. "The man did want to die for me. And it's made Scott and me so much closer."

Ernest flinched and stared into his coffee cup, saying nothing. I could tell that he hadn't quite made up his mind about these two. They certainly didn't seem our sort, but I wasn't sure I knew what our sort was anymore. The rules seemed to be changing all the time.

"I knew she was off her cracker," Ernest said once they'd gone, "but now I wonder about him, too. She's sucking him in. As if she's some sort of vampire."

"She does seem to have Scott on a very short leash," I said.

"I wouldn't stand for it."

"You wouldn't have to," I flared defensively.

"Now, Tatie. I didn't mean anything. You're not at all like Zelda. She's so jealous of Scott's work I think she'd be happy if he never wrote another word."

"They couldn't afford it if he stopped writing."

"He told me they spent thirty thousand dollars last year, just swam through it all."

"They live on thirty thousand and we live on three. It's absurd."

"I think we live better, don't you?"

"Yes," I said emphatically.

From the other room, Bumby began to make stirring noises. I put down my coffee cup and stood to go and fetch him when Ernest said, "I wouldn't want their life, but it's hard to see so much money simply wasted when we haven't got any. What if I borrowed from Scott for our trip to Pamplona in July?"

"Do you think we know them well enough for that?"

"Maybe not. We've got to get there somehow. Maybe Don Stewart?"

"He's a good egg."

"Yes," he said. "I'll tell you what, though. Everyone seems to want in on this trip. It's getting very complicated."

"It's still weeks away. How complicated could it be?"

"You don't want to know."

THIRTY-ONE

*I*n the railroad yard, the bulls came off the cars lowing and twisting and panicked, their eyes rolling back in their heads. They didn't know where to go, and it was hard to watch because we knew that by the end of the day they'd be dead. It was morning and quite cool for July. The dust rose up from their hooves and into the air, stinging our eyes as Ernest pointed out the hunched and muscled place between the shoulder blades where the sword had to hit just right.

"Yes, sir," said Harold Loeb. "That's the moment of truth."

Ernest's face turned sour. "What would you know about it?"

"Enough, I guess," Harold said.

Just then Duff came up and put her hand in the crook of Ernest's arm. "It's all wonderful, isn't it?" She looked at him like a child about to get everything her own way, her eyes crinkling and her smile wide. "It makes a chap hungry, though. Who's going to feed me anyway?"

"Oh, all right. Sure," Ernest said, still sour, and the two of them led the way to the café. Ernest wore his beret and a navy sweater and white pants, a dark scarf knotted at his throat. Duff was perfect as ever with her long cotton sweater and Eton collar in pale green silk. Her hair was brushed back from her forehead and she walked straight and tall. Ernest matched her stride, his chin set in a proud way. He was probably still fuming at Harold, though trying to swallow it. From the back, the two of them together looked as if they belonged in a fashion magazine, and I saw Duff's fiancé, Pat Guthrie, noticing this, too. Everyone noticed, and poor Pat had been looking pained for days.

I felt sorry for Pat, though I wouldn't have wanted to live with him. He drank too much and could be a terrible bother when he did. Each afternoon he would start out sunny and pleased with everything. He liked to talk about popular music and could sing and dance with great energy and enthusiasm, but after three or four cocktails, something turned in him and he became snide and superior. If he kept on with it and Duff didn't send him away, he changed again, growing sullen and morose. I wondered how she kept up with his moods—or how he himself did. When he woke up, did he feel disgusted for the way he'd twisted one way and then another? Did he remember any of it?

"What do you say we drink through till dark?" Harold said, coming up beside me.

I smiled and took his arm, wanting to make him feel better, if only for a moment. Maybe if we stuck together, he'd try to make me feel better, too. God knows I needed it.

The trip had started badly in Burguete, the week before, when we went to fish in the Irati—one of Ernest's favorite rivers in the world—and found it all ruined. The landlady at our hotel had tried to warn us that the good fishing was gone, but Ernest had laughed her off. The loggers had been there for the beech and pine, and when we got to the river we found it full of trash and floating debris. Dams had been broken through. Dead fish littered the banks and clogged the small pools. It was almost too much to take in, but we stuck it out, anyway, for several days, trying to go farther out to the smaller streams. No one took a single fish.

Bill Smith, one of our old friends from Chicago, was with us, having been lured over by Ernest's reports of world-class fishing, and of the bullfights that would follow. We hadn't seen him at all since the days of the Domicile. When Kenley and Ernest had their falling-out, tension trickled through all of our connections to the Smith clan, but we'd since picked up a fairly regular correspondence with Kate, who was back in Chicago, working as a journalist. And when Bill arrived to meet us in Paris, we were happy to find that he was the same as ever, full of lively stories and game for anything. He'd brought with him every surefire fly

he owned for the trip to Spain—all the old winners from summers fishing the Sturgeon or the Black up in Michigan—and I thought Ernest
was going to cry when Bill opened his tackle box to show Ernest the
flies, because they were useless.

In Pamplona, we still felt the wrongness. We had lots of friends
around and it should have been jolly, but it wasn't. In Paris, Ernest and
Duff had done their dance around each other, but it had seemed harmless for the most part. Something had come in to change it, though, and
that something was Harold. He'd fallen hard for Duff and swept her off
for a week at St.-Jean-de-Luz. When Kitty told me about the affair, she
said Harold had been so strange of late she'd suspected something like
this was coming. I'd never understood the arrangement Harold and
Kitty made of love. Now I felt equally baffled and more than a little
upset by the way Ernest was reacting so extremely. He had no rights to
Duff—none of this should have mattered at all to him, but it did, and
suddenly everyone knew it.

The morning the fights began, we all woke up at dawn to see the running of the bulls through the streets. The first time I'd watched, the
summer I was pregnant with Bumby, it seemed to pass so quickly I
couldn't remember what I'd seen. Now Bumby was safe in Paris with
Marie Cocotte, and though I had wanted and needed a break from
constant mothering, I didn't know quite how to feel as a free agent.

The streets were slick that morning. A light rain had fallen before
dawn, and you could see the bulls struggle for traction against the cobblestones. One went down and struggled, craning its thick neck, its eyes
rolling to white, and the whole thing seemed to pass in slow motion.

We were standing just behind a low wall, close enough to smell the
animal sweat of the bulls and the excitement of everyone watching.
Though some didn't watch or couldn't.

"The bulls are almost prehistoric," Ernest had told Bill in the café the
night before. "They've been bred for six hundred years to do what they
do, to make this run to the arena, to gore what they can on the way to
their own certain death. It's goddamned beautiful is what it is. Just wait
till you see it for yourself."

"I'm ready for it," Bill said, but on the street with a clear view of everything, his conviction seemed to waver. While we watched, one of the young men ran too close to a thick bull and was shoved into the wall, just twenty feet away from where we stood. We could hear his arm snap at an angle behind his back. He cried out and tried to scramble up the wall, and the fear on his face was ugly to see.

"Too much for you, old boy?" Ernest said when he saw Bill look away.

"Maybe," Bill said.

Ernest was standing near Duff, and his color was very high. "See there, now?" He pointed to the way the bull was coming at the young man, its square head ducked low. "The bull's sight is very bad, but it smells him, and it's taking its time. Look at him now. He's coming, by God."

"I can't believe this is sport for you," Bill said to Ernest very quietly.

"What else would it be? It's life and death, brother, same as every day."

The bull came forward, leading with the right horn, his thick head swung to one side so he looked like the devil, really, barreling at the scrambling caballero. But then a hand appeared from the other side of the wall. We couldn't see who had offered help, but it was enough. The caballero got enough traction to run up the wall and over, and then he was free. A small cheer went up in the crowd when he was safe.

"I suppose you're disappointed," Bill said, looking at Ernest pointedly.

"Not at all."

"Would he have gotten it very bad?" Duff asked.

"Maybe he would have. It can happen. I've seen it."

"It's terribly exciting, isn't it?" she said.

"The best damned show there is."

The last bull ran by us, and then the *pastores* came behind the bulls with sticks, and then the rocket went off, which meant all the bulls were safely in the ring.

"Beautiful," Duff said.

I tried to remember if I thought them beautiful the first time, when

Ernest had taught me the way he was teaching Duff now. My life had changed so much in the two short years since, but I remembered being excited and also strangely calm, because I was pregnant and felt safe, buffered from everything in the best way. My body was doing what it was meant to do, and these animals, they were living out their destinies, too. I could watch and not feel mauled or traumatized, but just sit next to Ernest and sew the clothes and blankets I was working on for the baby that would come in three months, no matter what happened on that day. And I remembered feeling very good about everything in the night, with the *riau-riau* dancing and the fireworks, though it was impossible to sleep for the noise.

We seemed to be the only Americans in Pamplona that first year. Ernest called it the Garden of Eden—but that had certainly changed now. Limousines brought society over from Biarritz. Uniformed chauffeurs opened doors all night and then waited near their cars for the revelers to tire and spill back into the leather cocoon stinking of champagne. But even with the rich coming in to spoil everything, it was spoiled already.

Harold was still crazy for Duff. You could see it at lunch when he went pale and Victorian with her one minute and then began to fuss with the waiter to make sure she had her drink.

"Oh, it's fine, darling," she said. "I'm still alive over here, at least for now."

We were all crowded around an outdoor table, with Duff, Ernest, and Harold on one side and Pat, Bill, and myself on the other. Pat had on a beautiful summer suit with a navy linen jacket. He'd gone out and found a beret just like Ernest's and wore it high on his forehead at an optimistic angle. And yet for all of Pat's civilized trimmings, the moment Harold became too conspicuously attentive to Duff, he snapped and grew belligerent.

"Give it a rest, Harold," he barked. "Go take a walk around the block."

"Why don't you shut it," Harold said. "Or I'll tell you what, just have another drink." He turned and shouted loudly behind him to no one, "Bring this man a drink!"

Just then Don Stewart walked up looking cool and clean in gray flannels and a fresh white shirt. He glanced around the table, instantly sensing tension. "Who died, men?"

"No one of consequence," Ernest said.

"I suddenly have a terrible headache," I said. "I hope you'll all excuse me." I scooted around my side of the table and stood next to Don.

"Why don't you walk the poor kid home, Donald?" Ernest said.

"I'm fine," I said. "I'll be fine."

"Nonsense," Don said. "You're pale as a ghost."

Before we'd even gotten to the door, the gap had closed around the table and you couldn't even tell I'd been there. Ernest was sitting closer to Duff now, and Pat had squeezed around to be nearer, too. Duff sat at the middle of it all like a floating island of meringue. She didn't even seem to notice.

I was grateful that Don had offered to shepherd me home. I was feeling terribly lonely, actually, and Don was easy to be with. Ever since we'd met the summer before, he sought my company when we were out in groups together. I felt he was a kindred spirit because he didn't quite fit in Paris either. He was a smart and savvy writer who'd gone to Yale, but in many ways he was still the boy who grew up on a farm outside of Columbus, Ohio. In Paris, everyone was so drastic and dramatic, flinging themselves into ditches for each other.

"I get why no one bothers with the usual rules," he said to me once. "I was in the war, too, you know. Nothing looks or feels the same anymore, so what's the point?" His face grew serious. "Still, I miss good old-fashioned honorable people just trying to make something of life. Simply, without hurting anyone else. I know that makes me a sap."

"You'd like to find a girl like your mother, I'll bet."

"Maybe. I want things to make sense again. They haven't in a long time."

I believed I'd understood him at the time, but now as Don walked me back to the hotel, I felt our connection more strongly. I wanted things to make sense, too. More than anything.

"How are you holding up, pal?" he asked.

"Better than some, I expect. Poor Harold."

"Poor Harold? What about Pat? He's the one with the claim to Duff."

"Seems like they have a pretty loose arrangement to me," I said. "She drags Harold off to the Riviera for two weeks and then seems surprised that he's mooning over her like a sad calf, and even more that Pat's off his head about it. It's cruel."

"I don't think she means to be cruel. She seems awfully sad under it all to me."

We'd come to a corner where the Mercado was breaking apart for the day. A woman was stacking baskets, and another scooped blood-colored dried chiles into a canvas sack. Nearby, a little girl sat in the dirt, holding a chicken and singing to it. I slowed so we could watch her longer. Wonderfully black hair framed her heart-shaped face. She pet-ted the chicken as she sang and seemed to have it in a trance.

"You're looking at her like you want to gobble her up," Don said. "You must miss your Bumby."

"Like crazy. It's easier when I don't think about him. Sometimes I tell myself I'm two people. I'm his mum when I'm with him and some-one else when I'm here, away."

"Hem's Hadley."

"Maybe. Or maybe I'm my own Hadley." We could see the stippled arch of the Hotel La Perla and the tangled wall of bougainvillea. I stopped and turned to him. "Why aren't you all bound up with Duff, too? Everyone else is."

"She's a dish, all right, and it would be easy enough to give in. She's asked me to take care of her bill at the hotel, you know, since she can't ask Harold now. Maybe she's asked Hem, too."

"I wouldn't be surprised."

"Are you and Hem all right? He wouldn't be stupid enough to throw you over for that title in a nice-fitting sweater, would he?"

I flinched. "Maybe we should have a drink."

"I'm sorry, I shouldn't have said it. I think the world of you two. If you guys can't make it, what chance do the rest of us have?"

"You really are a peach, Don," I said, and moved forward to kiss him on the cheek. His skin was shaved clean as a baby's and he smelled clean, like tonic.

"You might be the best girl there is," he said with feeling, and returned the kiss. His lips were dry and chaste on my cheek, but then he moved ever so slightly and kissed me on the lips. When he pulled away, his eyes were moist and questioning. "I don't suppose you love me, too, just a little?"

"I wish I did. It might balance things out." I put my arms around his neck and held him close for a moment, feeling the sadness and confusion, all mixed up together in him. "This place has us all going crazy."

"You're not angry with me?"

"No," I said. "We're better friends now, I think."

"Isn't that a nice way to say it? I knew I wasn't wrong about you." He pulled away and brushed the hair out of my eyes. "I hope Hem knows what he has."

"Me too," I said, and went into the hotel. Inside, the señora was placing a cloth over her songbird's cage.

"He doesn't like the rockets," she said as she settled the blanket more closely around the bars. "They make him tear at his own feathers. Have you seen this?"

"I have, Señora." I passed her on my way to the staircase. "Can you please send brandy up?"

She looked behind me to see who might be coming along, so I added, "Just one glass."

"Is the señora well?"

"Not very," I said. "But the brandy will help."

THIRTY-TWO

When I woke the next morning, Ernest was already up and gone. I'd heard him come in late in the night, but I didn't stir and didn't speak to him. By seven I was washed and dressed and down in the hotel's small café where Ernest was finishing his coffee.

"I've ordered you *oeufs au jambon*," he said. "Are you hungry?"

"Starved," I said. "How'd it end last night?"

"Good and tight," he said.

"Good and tight, or just tight?"

"What are you getting at?"

"Nothing."

"Like hell," he said. "Why don't you say it?"

"I haven't even had coffee," I said. "Do we really need to quarrel?"

"We needn't do anything. There isn't time anyway."

Bill came downstairs then and pulled up a chair. "I'm starved," he said.

"That's going around," Ernest said. He signaled the waiter over and asked for another plate for Bill and café au lait, and then signed the bill. "I'm going to arrange for our tickets. I'll see you up there."

When he was gone, Bill looked sheepish.

"What really happened last night?"

"Nothing I want to remember," he said.

"Don't tell me then."

"I don't know all of it, anyway. Harold said something to Pat, and then Hem flared up and called Harold something terrible. It wasn't pretty."

"I would guess not."

"Don showed up and tried to straighten things out, but it was too late. Harold had called Ernest out in the street to settle it."

"Harold did? It wasn't the other way around?"

"No. And that was something, really."

"Is Harold all right?"

"Right as rain. They never touched each other."

"Thank God."

"Apparently Hem offered to hold Harold's glasses for him and that broke the spell. They both laughed and felt like stupid bastards for even starting it up."

"What's wrong with all of us, Bill? Can you tell me that?"

"Hell if I know," he said. "We drink too much for starters. And we want too much, don't we?"

"What is it we want exactly?" I said, feeling a stir of melancholy and confusion. I wondered how Bill was making sense of the way Ernest was throwing himself so obviously at Duff. What *could* he think? What could he say?

"Everything, of course. Everything and then some." He scratched his chin and then tried a joke. "My headache today proves it."

I studied him for a moment. "If this is a festival, why aren't we happy?"

He cleared his throat and looked away. "We shouldn't miss the amateurs, right? Hem says it's the best show for your money and that I should get right in."

I sighed. "You don't have to prove anything to him. You didn't seem to go in for the running."

"No," he said, seeming slightly ashamed. "But I'm ready to give it another go. I'm not dead yet."

"Why does everyone keep saying that?"

"I don't know," he said. "It's just one of those things."

The amateurs had long been Ernest's favorite element of the fiesta. For years he'd been practicing veronicas with everything from the curtains to my old coat and getting good at them. Now he could bulldog the bulls, spinning away at the last moment. Afterward he'd be high and happy and practice some more in our room at the hotel with the cape he'd bought from a shop well off the square that didn't cater to tourists. The cape was heavy red serge with simple black braid as a border all the way around. He had started collecting corks for the bottom of it, because it was the corks that allowed the matador to really control the cape and swing it well and wide.

When it was time for the amateurs that morning, he took the cape with him as he climbed down into the ring with several dozen eager men and boys all ready to test their wits. Bill went, too, but Harold stayed put for the moment, a few seats down from Duff.

"Pat's still pretty green this morning," Duff said when I took my seat beside her. "It was a long night."

"So I heard."

"We missed you, you know. Everything's more fun with you along."

I gave her a sharp look, thinking she was putting me on, but her face was open and warm. That was the thing about Duff; she was a wreck with men, but a good chap all the way around, and she had her own code. I didn't believe she'd actually sleep with Ernest even if he'd wanted to—because she liked me and knew being a wife was hard business. She'd been married twice already and was set to marry Pat if they ever pulled together the money for it. She told me once that she'd never been very good at marriage but that she didn't seem to be able to stop giving it a go.

Down in the ring, the picadors had pretty good control of things, so the action seemed light and fairly harmless. There was only one bull in the ring at a time, and this first was caramel colored and slow moving. It came along and shoved its foreleg against Bill's rump, and he fell to one side like a character in a cartoon. It had everyone laughing. Ernest was just getting into the spirit of things when Harold climbed past us and got down into the ring, too.

"Oh, Harold," Duff said to no one in particular because he looked like a caricature of a rich and helpless American in his pale yellow Fair Isle sweater and snow-white sneakers. We both watched him. "I've told him there's nothing between us, you know."

"I'm not sure he hears it," I said, trying to be as delicate as possible.

"Men hear what they like and invent the rest."

Once Harold had reached the ring, he looked up to where we were and smiled broadly. The caramel bull was near him and getting nearer, and Harold dodged to one side to avoid the horns, as everyone did. The bull trotted past and then whirled to come again, and that's when Harold grabbed onto the horns and let the bull carry him for a few paces. It was like watching a well-rehearsed circus act. Harold had to be as surprised by his success as much as anyone, but when the bull set him down again, light as a feather, he turned back to us, looking jubilant.

"Hem doesn't like this one bit," Duff said. My eyes followed hers to where Ernest stood in the ring watching Harold. His expression was grim. A picador passed within a foot of him, but he didn't even seem to notice.

"He can't stand another man besting him," I said, but Duff and I both knew that Ernest had been angry with Harold all week, ever since he found out about the lovers' tryst in St.-Jean-de-Luz. It was bad enough that Harold got to have Duff when Ernest was hampered with a wife and child, but then Harold had spent every day in Pamplona following Duff around like a poor sick steer, making an ass out of himself. It was all too much.

The next bull in the ring was slimmer and quicker. He moved like a cat, loping first toward one wall then another, changing direction on a dime. One local with a dark shirt got too close and was shoved to his knees. The bull reared his head around, and the man fell farther and was trampled. Everyone hurried to distract the bull. Ernest had him for a moment by swinging his cape wide to one side. Other men waved their arms and called out, but the bull returned to the man who hadn't yet risen and pushed him with his head. The man's legs came over his own head just as the bull jerked to one side, his right horn moving into the man's thigh just under his buttock and zipping down to the knee. He cried out sharply, and we saw his thighbone flash white, and then blood running freely before the picadors rushed the bull and forced him first to the wall and then behind the fence where he would wait nine hours and then be killed.

That was the end of the amateurs. The ring emptied quickly, and Duff and I climbed down to meet the boys. We hadn't spoken a word to each other since we saw the goring. When we got to them we saw they were silent, too.

Out on the street, we made our way to a café.

"I'll be damned," Bill said as he walked beside me. His face was flat and white. His shoes were covered with dust. We found a table and had just ordered a round of the thick beer we liked to have with lunch when the gored man was taken past us on the street on a stretcher. A bloodied sheet covered him from the waist down.

"*Toro, toro!*" someone in the café yelled drunkenly and the man sat up. Everyone cheered, and then a young boy ran over with a glass of whiskey, which the man drank and then threw back empty to the boy, who caught it well with one hand. Then everyone cheered again.

"It's a hell of a way to live, isn't it?" Duff said.

"I can think of worse," Ernest said.

Our beer had come and we got to it. The waiter brought gazpacho and good hard bread and some nice fish poached in lime, and though I didn't think I would be able to eat after the sight of the goring, I found I was hungry and that it all tasted very good to me.

Harold stayed to one side of the table, well out of Ernest's way, but when Pat finally showed up with Don, he was pale and irritable, and Harold seemed not to know where to move or whom he could speak to safely. And for the rest of the lunch our table was like an intricate game of emotional chess, with Duff looking to Ernest, who kept one eye on Pat, who was glaring at Harold, who was glancing furtively at Duff. Everyone was drinking too much and wrung out and working hard to pretend they were jollier and less affected than everyone else.

"I can take the bulls and the blood," Don said to me quietly. "It's this human business that turns my stomach."

I looked from him to Ernest, who hadn't spoken to me or so much as glanced at me since breakfast. "Yes," I said to Don. "But what's the trick for it?"

"I wish to hell I knew. Maybe there is no trick." He drained the last of his beer and signaled the waiter for more.

"Sometimes I wish we could rub out all of our mistakes and start fresh, from the beginning," I said. "And sometimes I think there isn't anything to us but our mistakes."

He laughed grimly, solemnly, while on the other side of the table, Duff was whispering something in Ernest's ear while he cackled roughly, like a sailor. I turned my chair at an angle away from them where I didn't have to see them at all. As soon as I did this, I had the clearest memory of Fonnie and Roland a hundred years ago in St. Louis, and how she couldn't stand to look at him because she thought he was weak and detestable. Their story had always been full of sadness and misery. Roland had returned home from the sanitarium, but hadn't recovered any sense of peace. He and Fonnie led utterly separate lives now, though staying in the same house on Cates Avenue, for the sake of the children.

What was happening between Ernest and me was nowhere near as dire, I hoped, but he was hurting me with every whisper and look in Duff's direction. And I found myself feeling differently about marriage, and about the damage lovers could do to one another, irreparable damage sometimes, and almost without thinking.

"How sad and strange we all are," I said to Don.

"That's what had me so maudlin yesterday. I'm sorry about that, by the way."

"There's nothing to be sorry for. Let's just be good friends who know these things but don't have to say them."

"All right," he said, and looked at his hands, and drank some more of his beer, and the afternoon wore on this way until it was time for the corrida.

The young matador Cayetano Ordóñez was a boy, really, but he moved so naturally and with such grace it seemed as if he were dancing. The deep red serge of his cape was alive with even the slightest flick of his arms. He had a way of planting his feet and leaning forward slightly, facing whatever came and urging the bull to charge him with the slightest gesture or glance.

Ernest had been in a foul mood when we entered the ring for the corrida but was starting to come awake as Ordóñez moved. Duff got up to sit nearer to him, seeing the change.

"My God, but that's a fine man," Duff said.

"He's the real article all right," Ernest said. "Watch this."

Ordóñez was leading his bull in, turning one veronica and then another tighter one with his cape, drawing the bull magnetically. The picadors had backed off because they knew Ordóñez had him and was in complete control. It was a dance, and it was also great art. His knowledge was primal and ancient and he carried it so naturally and easily for one so young.

"Some are just going through the motions," Ernest said. "It's pretty, all right, but it doesn't mean anything. This hombre, he knows you have to get near enough to die. You have to already be dead really in order to live and to conquer the animal."

Duff nodded, taken over by his enthusiasm, and, God help me, I was too. Ernest's eyes, as he spoke, were suddenly nearly as alive as Ordóñez's cape. The intensity bubbled up from a deep place in him and came into his face and his throat, and I saw the way he was connected to Ordóñez and the bullfight, and to life as it was happening, and I knew that I could hate him all I wanted for the way he was hurting me, but I couldn't ever stop loving him, absolutely, for what he was.

"Now look," he said. The bull came in low, his left horn pushed forward, his neck twisting. Ordóñez's thigh was inches from the bull's powerful legs, and he leaned nearer, so that when the bull's head lifted, searching for the cape, he just grazed Ordóñez's belly. We could almost hear a whisper as the horns passed the cloth of his silk jacket. A gasp went up in the crowd, because this is what they had come to see.

"You'll never see it done better than that," Ernest said, throwing his hat to his feet in respect.

"Goddamned beautiful," Duff said.

We all sighed, and when the bull had been broken and was on its knees, bowing, Ordóñez ran the sword in clean. Everyone stood, cheering, the whole crowd moved and taken over by the spectacle and the mastery. I stood, too, and applauded like crazy, and I must have been standing in a particularly bright ray of sun because Ordóñez looked up at me then, up and into my face, and his eyes took in my hair.

"He thinks you're *muy linda*," Ernest said, following Ordóñez's eyes to me. "He's honoring you."

The young matador bent over the bull, slicing off its ear with a small knife. He called a boy over from the stands and sent him to me with the ear cupped in his palms. He delivered it shyly, barely daring to look at me, but I could tell he felt it was a very great privilege to carry it for Ordóñez. I didn't quite know how to accept it, what the rules were for such things, and so simply held out my hands. It was black and triangular and still warm, with only the faintest trace of blood—the strangest thing I'd ever held.

"I'll be damned," Ernest said, clearly very proud.

"What will you do with it?" Duff asked.

"Keep it, of course," Don said, and handed me his handkerchief so I could wrap it inside and also wipe my hands.

Still standing, I held the ear in the handkerchief and looked down into the ring where Ordóñez was being buried in flowers. He glanced up at me, bowed low and deeply, and then returned to being adored.

"I'll be damned," Ernest said again.

There were five more bullfights that day, but none matched the beauty of the first. When we went to the café after, we were all still thrumming with it, even Bill, who couldn't stomach most of the day, particularly the way two of the horses were gored and went down and had to be killed quickly while everyone watched. It was all terrible and terribly intense, and I was ready for a drink.

I passed the ear around the table so everyone could admire it and be horrified in turn. Duff got drunk very quickly and began to flirt openly with Harold, who was too surprised and pleased to be discreet about it. The two disappeared at one point, which had Pat furious. When an hour or more had passed, they wandered back in a very jolly mood, as if nothing were amiss.

"You little bastard," Pat said to Harold. He stood and immediately lurched to one side.

"Oh, put a lid on it, darling," Duff said blithely. But Pat wouldn't be chided.

"Just get the hell away from us, would you?" he said to Harold.

"I don't think Duff would like that. You want me here, don't you?"

"Of course, darling, I want everyone." She reached for Ernest's glass. "Be a pal, would you?"

Ernest nodded; she could have the glass, could have every drink on the table as far as he was concerned. It was Harold who disgusted him. "Running to a woman," he said under his breath. "What's lower than that?"

The waiter came around with more drinks and food, but the evening wouldn't be set right. A canker boiled up and tainted everything that had been so powerful and fine.

Ernest sensed this, too, and tried to bring the talk around to Ordóñez and his posture, his veronicas.

"Which is the veronica, again?" Duff said.

"It's when the matador stands turned to the bull with his feet fixed and swings the cape away from the bull very slowly."

"Yes, of course," Duff said. "It was marvelous, wasn't it?"

"Don't believe her, Hem," Pat said meanly. "She doesn't remember any of it."

"Give a girl a break, Pat." She turned back to Ernest. "I'm just a little tight now. I'll remember more tomorrow. I swear I'll be good then."

Ernest looked at her sadly. "All right," he said, but he was clearly disappointed in her and with the whole group. The air had gone out of everything.

Back at the hotel that night, I took the ear, folded it into several more handkerchiefs, and put it in my bureau drawer.

"The thing will stink before long," Ernest said, watching me do it.

"I don't care."

"No, I wouldn't either." He started to undress slowly and thoughtfully. "When this is all over," he said finally, "let's follow Ordóñez to Madrid and then Valencia."

"Will it ever be over?"

"Of course it will." He turned to face me. "Ordóñez was wonderful, wasn't he? He makes all of this seem very ugly and very stupid."

I closed the bureau drawer, then took off my clothes and climbed into bed. "I'm ready to forget Pamplona. Why don't we try now? Help me, will you?"

At the end of that very long week, we disbanded, and everyone went off separately. Don left for the Riviera looking sad and exhausted. Bill and Harold were headed back to Paris, but took Pat and Duff as far as Bayonne. Ernest and I boarded a train to Madrid, where we took rooms at the Pension Aguilar, an unfashionable hotel in the Calle San Jeronimo that was small and very quiet with no tourists. It was like heaven after Pamplona. We went to the bullfights every day and were there the afternoon Juan Belmonte, arguably the best torero of all time, was badly gored in the belly and carried off to the hospital. We'd followed his fights for some time, and Ernest had always admired his bowlegged and hard-jawed determination, but we began to see, even before Belmonte was injured, that Ordóñez was nearly as great as the master. His movements were perfection, and his bravery never wavered, and we watched him, both of us, in awe.

One afternoon Ordóñez paid me the very great honor of letting me hold his cape before the corrida began. He came very close and I saw the utter smoothness of his boy's face and the depth and clarity of his eyes. He said nothing when he handed the cape to me but was very serious.

"I think he's in love with you," Ernest said, when Ordóñez had walked away to build energy in the crowd.

"How could he be? He's a child," I said, but I was proud and felt changed by the honor.

Back at the hotel that night when we were dressing for dinner, Ernest said, "I'm working out a new novel. Or it's working itself out, really, in my head. About the bullfights. The hero will be Ordóñez, and the whole thing will take place in Pamplona." His eyes were bright, and the enthusiasm in his voice was unmistakable.

"That sounds awfully good."

"It does, doesn't it? I'm calling the young torero Romero. It starts at a hotel, at three in the afternoon. Two Americans are staying there, in rooms across the hall, and when they go to meet Romero, it's a great honor and they notice how alone he is, and how he's thinking about the bulls he'll face that day. He can't share that with anyone."

"He would feel that way, wouldn't he?" I said. "You have to write it."

"Yes," he said, and although we left and had a long and delicious dinner with several bottles of wine between us, he was already with the book, inside of it. Over the coming days, his thinking grew deeper. He began to write in intense spurts, in the cafés early in the mornings, and in the hotel very late at night, when I could hear the aggressive scratching of his pencil. When we left Madrid for the fiesta at Valencia, he'd filled two thick notebooks, two hundred handwritten pages in fewer than ten days, but he wasn't happy with the opening anymore.

"I'm thinking it should start in Paris and then move. It's what happens in Paris that fuels the fire. You can't have the rest without it."

"You always said you couldn't write about Paris because you were too close to it."

"Yes, I know, but for some reason it's coming easily. We were in Pamplona two weeks ago, but I can write that, too. I don't know why. Maybe all of my thoughts and rules about writing are just waiting to be proven wrong."

"It's good to be on fire, isn't it?"

"I hope it goes on like this forever."

It did go on. In Valencia, the excitement over the fiesta had pitched everything into a fever and we could just enjoy it. We sat at a street café and ate prawns sprinkled with fresh lime and cracked pepper, and beautiful paella in a dish nearly as wide around as our table. In the afternoons we went to the bullfights where Ordóñez swept his veronicas with absolute perfection.

"There it was. Did you see it?" Ernest said, pointing into the ring.

"What?"

"His death. The bull was so close. That's what makes the dance of it. The torero has to know he's dying and the bull has to know it, so when siren with flowing hair. She balanced on a rock and gazed into the distance. At Villa America, everyone loved the siren because she seemed to be a symbol of something. They loved her the way they loved their sherry and their toast points and every moment of every ritual that wound around them like clock springs.

At the Hôtel de la Pinède, we had our own rituals. We breakfasted late, and then Ernest went off to work in a small studio off the terrace while Pauline and I rode bicycles or swam and sunned at our little beach with Bumby. After lunch we had siesta, then bathed and dressed for cocktail hour either at Villa America, in one of the terraced gardens, or at the casino in town, and no one raised even an eyebrow in our presence or said anything that wasn't in good taste because that was the contract.

Anyone looking on from nearly any vantage point would have believed that Pauline and I were friends. She might have believed it herself. I never really knew. She certainly worked hard to stay cheerful, inventing errands for us in the village to secure freshly picked figs or the very best tinned sardines.

"Wait until you try this olive," she would say, or whatever it was— strong coffee or pastry or nice jam. "It's heaven."

I must have heard her say "It's heaven" a thousand times over that summer, until I wanted to scream. I didn't scream, though, and that became one of the things I grew to regret.

We had two rooms at the hotel, each with a double bed and heavy bureau and shuttered windows that opened onto the coastline. Ernest and I occupied one, and Pauline kept to herself in the other—at least at first. For a week or ten days, when Pauline and I came back from bicycling or swimming, she'd excuse herself to change for lunch, but then went to Ernest's studio instead, passing through the hotel to where a second entrance lay unmarked, as inconspicuous as a broom closet. They likely had a secret knock. I imagined that and so much more, though it made me sick to do it. When she came to lunch an hour or so later, she was always freshly showered and impeccably dressed. She'd sit down, smiling, and begin to praise the lunch or the day extravagantly. It was all so modulated and discreet I wondered if she took a

certain pleasure playing her role, as if in her mind a film reel was spinning and she was a great actress who never fumbled a single line.

I wasn't nearly so clever. More and more I found myself at a loss for
words and didn't want to hear other people talking either. Their conversations seemed false and empty. I preferred to look at the sea, which
said nothing and never made you feel alone. From my bicycle, I could
watch the boats moving in blue chop, or focus on the bright green scrub
growing out of the ramparts with great tenacity. Somehow it stayed
rooted, no matter how the wind or waves attacked, immovable as the
dark moss on the rocks below.

One morning after a storm had raged for hours the night before,
Pauline was intent on pointing out every sign of demolition—overturned
dinghies and fallen pine boughs, the tangle of umbrellas on the beach.
I tried to escape her chatter by pedaling faster until I could only hear
the rush of momentum, the purr of my wheels on the road. But she
wouldn't be thrown off.

"I've been trying to talk Drum into going stateside in the fall. You
know my parents have land in Arkansas. The living is so cheap there
you'd save a fortune."

How I hated her using nicknames for him so casually. That was our
language. Our dance. "You can save your breath," I said. "He'd rather cut
off his arm than go home."

"Actually, he thinks it's a fine idea."

"Arkansas?"

"Piggott. It's rustic, of course, but you like rustic."

"I like our life here. What are you trying to do?"

"I'm sorry. I'm only thinking of you. You're bound to run out of
money soon in Paris. He should be starting a second novel and worrying about nothing but that. You can afford nice new things in Piggott.
Surely that means something to you."

"No," I said. "It doesn't."

For the rest of our ride, I fought back both incredulity and tears. I
didn't want to let Pauline see either, and so stayed well ahead, riding faster
and faster. Some of the turns were perilous. If I had lost my balance even
for a moment, I might have pitched out over the stone precipice and onto

the jagged boulders below. I wobbled at times but kept my course, and it was a kind of sharply edged euphoria I felt, heading back to confront Ernest. My heart was flooded with adrenaline and my mind raced. What would I say? What could he say to defend himself?

When I reached the hotel I was in such a state I left my bicycle sprawled in the gravel and hurried into the hotel, breathless and covered with a fine film of sweat. I planned to burst into his studio, but of course the door was locked.

"Who is it?" he said when I knocked.

"Your wife," I said, my voice thick with anger.

When he opened the door I could see he was very surprised to find me there. This was Pauline's time or nearly so. He'd probably begun to anticipate her with growing desire.

"You can't think I'd go to Arkansas," I spat out before he'd even closed the door.

"Oh," he said. "I was going to tell you soon. If you could think reasonably, you'd see it's not a bad scheme at all."

"We'd live with her parents?" I laughed shrilly.

"No, she'd find us all a house together, maybe in town."

I could scarcely believe what I was hearing. "You want us to live all together."

"We're doing that now, aren't we?"

"Yes, and it's awful. It makes me sick to my stomach to know you're making love to her."

"I'm sorry, Tatie. But maybe that's because the situation is new and we don't know how to do it well."

"Do you really think it *can* be done well?"

"I don't know. I don't want to lose you."

"And if I don't agree?"

"Please, Tatie," he said, his voice low and anguished. "Just try. If it works and we all start to feel good about it, we'll head for Piggott in September. If it doesn't, we'll go back to Paris."

"Alone?"

"Yes," he said, though I could hear some kind of hesitancy or hedging in his voice. He wasn't sure about any of this.

"I think it's a mistake. All of it."

"Maybe, but it's too late to go back. There's only what's ahead now."

"Yes," I said sadly, and left the way I came.

Over the next few days, I began to wonder if Ernest's proposal was a new idea, an attempt at some solution out of the mess at our feet, or if he'd intended it all along. For years we'd been surrounded by triangles—freethinking, free-living lovers willing to bend every convention to find something right or risky or liberating enough. I couldn't say what Ernest felt watching their antics, but they seemed sad and even tortured to me. When we last heard from Pound, his mistress, Olga Rudge, had given birth to a daughter, though they agreed not to raise her. Nothing in Pound's life invited a child and neither one of them wanted to feel compromised, apparently. They gave the baby to a peasant woman in the maternity ward where Olga delivered. The woman had miscarried and was only too happy to take her.

I was stunned that anyone could hand over a child so easily, but doubly surprised when we heard in another letter that Shakespear was pregnant. It wasn't Pound's child; in fact, she wasn't saying a word about who the father was, only that she was keeping the baby. Her behavior was obviously retaliatory. That's what terrible, sordid situations did to you, made you act crazily, against your own truths, against your self.

One afternoon when Ernest and I were napping in our room, Pauline came in on cat feet, making no noise whatsoever. I'd been having a dream in which I was being buried under tons of sand. It was an image of suffocation, and yet strangely not a nightmare. The sand felt warm and sugary, and as it crushed me slowly, I kept thinking, *This is heaven. This is heaven.* I was feeling so languid and so drugged, I didn't even know Pauline was in the room until she'd slipped under the sheets on Ernest's side of the bed. The afternoons were hot, and we slept naked. I knew what was happening, and I also didn't want to come awake enough to feel it. I never opened my eyes. My body wasn't mine exactly. No one spoke or made any noise that would shake me out of my trance. The bed was sand, I told myself. The sheets were sand. I was still in the dream.

FORTY-TWO

*I*n the morning, when the sun pried its way through the slats of the plantation shutters and fell on my face, I knew the day had come whether I wanted it or not, and I opened my eyes. A breeze pushed the cream linen curtains so they swayed. Light fell in oblong swatches along the dark wood floor, and I yawned and stretched and pushed the sheets back. Across from the bed was a long mirror and I saw myself in it, brown as can be and solid and firm from all the swimming and bicycling. My hair had lightened in the sun until the only red left was just a hint of ginger, and my eyes were clear and bright and I looked very well. I'd already stopped being surprised by this—how I could look strong and healthy when I was dying, really.

At our hotel, there were three of everything—three breakfast trays, three terry-cloth robes, three wet bathing suits on the line. On the crushed rock path along the windward side of the hotel, three bicycles stood on their stands. If you looked at the bicycles one way, they looked very solid, like sculpture, with afternoon light glinting cleanly off the chrome handlebars—one, two, three, all in a row. If you looked at them another way, you could see just how thin each kickstand was under the weight of the heavy frame, and how they were poised to fall like dominoes or the skeletons of elephants or like love itself. But when I noticed this, I kept it to myself because that, too, was part of the unwritten contract. Everything could be snarled all to hell under the surface as long as you didn't let it crack through and didn't speak its name, particularly not at cocktail hour, when everyone was very jolly and working hard to be that way and to show how perfectly good life could be if you were lucky, as we were. Just have your drink, then, and another and don't spoil it.

After I dressed and bathed, I went downstairs to the little garden terrace and there was our breakfast on the table in the sun. Three *oeufs au jambon* with lots of butter and pepper, three steaming brioches, three glasses of juice. Ernest came out from where he had been working, in the little room off the terrace.

"Good morning, Tatie. You're looking very well."

"Yes," I said. "And so are you."

He wore tan canvas shorts and a black-and-white-striped fisherman's sweater from Grau-du-Roi and his feet were bare. I was dressed similarly, and when Pauline came out onto the terrace, she was freshly washed with her dark hair combed back straight from her face and she, too, wore the striped fisherman's sweater. We all looked just the same as we said good morning to one another and ate our breakfasts hungrily, as if we'd never eaten before.

The sun was already very bright on the beach, and it struck everything evenly. The sand was almost white with it. The water flashed it back blindingly.

"Our swim will be good today," Pauline said.

"Yes," Ernest said, breaking his brioche in half so that the steam rose prettily. "And then we'll have Madame bring the Bollinger, very chilled, and some of the sardines with capers. You'd like that, wouldn't you?" he said, turning to me.

"It sounds perfect."

After breakfast, I went to tell Madame what we'd planned for lunch and then packed a small bag for the beach. I found my shoes and walked down the lane to the bungalow, where Bumby was playing in the yard.

"Hello, little boy-bear," I said, scooping him up to nibble his ears. "I think you're taller today. You seem very large to Mama."

He was pleased to hear this, pushing his shoulders back and jutting out his round chin.

Marie said, "No coughing at all last night, madame."

"Aren't you very good?" And when he nodded proudly, I said, "Come then, boy-bear, we'll go for our swim."

At the small moon of beach at the other end of the road, Ernest and Pauline had already set up the blankets and umbrellas and were lying in the sand like tortoises with their eyes closed. We sunned on the beach all in a row while Bumby and Marie played in the surf and made little patterns with shells in the sand. When the sun grew too hot, I went into the water, which always hit you cold and was wonderful that way. I ducked my head and then surfaced, and swam out several hundred yards, where things were still. I treaded water and let the swells buoy me. At the top of one, I could look back at the beach and see them small and perfect, my husband and child and the woman who was now more to us than we could manage. From that distance, they all looked equal and serene and I couldn't hear them or feel them. At the bottom, in the trough of the wave, I could see only the sky, that high white place that seemed not to change much for all of our suffering.

As a kind of experiment, I stopped swimming and let my arms and legs fall, my whole weight fall as deep as it would. I kept my eyes open as I sank down and looked up at the surface. My lungs began to sting, first, and then burn, as if I'd swallowed some small piece of volcano.

I knew if I stayed there and let the water come into me, come through every door of me, some things would be easier. I wouldn't have to watch my life disappear, bead by bead, away from me and toward Pauline.

The little volcano in me burned, and then something popped, and I knew that even if I didn't want to live this way anymore, I also didn't want to die. I closed my eyes and kicked hard for the surface.

Back on the beach, Pauline rose and greeted me. "Let's try and dive, shall we?"

"I don't think I'd be very good at it."

"I'll teach you. I'll be the diving instructor today and Hem will watch and give you your marks."

"Please, not that," I said, trying to laugh.

"Some practicing first, then." She turned and led the way up the little path along the beach where the brown stones were piled higher and higher. They were very dark and riddled with crevices and looked as if they'd been made by some god with clay and then baked in the sun over the millennia. The rocks were hot under our bare feet and we climbed them quickly until we stood nearly at the top.

Pauline looked over the edge to gauge the tide pushing and falling back fifteen feet below. "When you hear the rushing sound, that's when you jump," she said. Then she straightened and pointed her arms very gracefully over her head and long neck. She waited, and then, with the scalloped whoosh of the tide, she pushed from her lean legs and was out, hanging in space, and then rocketing down very straight and tall. The water closed over the place where she'd been and there was nothing, just water like the flat skin of a drum. Then she surfaced, pushing her hair back and squinting. "Good, then," she shouted up. "Now you."

"It looks too easy to be easy," I called back, and she laughed.

Ernest had gone into the water and swum over, around the little cornice of rocks to where Pauline bobbed and waited for me.

"Let's see you go, then," he said, sweeping his arms back and forth as he treaded water.

"No marks and no corrections or I won't do it at all," I said.

"Don't you want to get it right?" Ernest asked, squinting.

"No, actually. If I get it at all without smashing myself to hell on the rocks, it'll be good enough."

"Suit yourself, then."

I stood at the edge and felt the hotness under my toes. I closed my eyes.

"Your arms should be straight up, touching your ears," Pauline said.

"No corrections," I said. I stood up tall and then arced my arms over my head. I listened for the shushing sound, but when I heard it, I found I couldn't move. I was fixed there.

"C'mon, then, you've missed it," Ernest said.

I didn't answer him and didn't open my eyes, and there was a moment of perfect vertigo, when I heard the whooshing of the surf again and felt I was part of it, swirling with it and also standing still, swept up and down into the sea and into the universe, but also very, very alone.

When I finally looked down, here were these two wet heads in the slow-moving waves. They looked playful and natural as seals there, and suddenly I knew I wouldn't jump and it had nothing to do with fear or embarrassment.

I wouldn't jump because I didn't want to join them. I felt the stones under my feet, smooth and hot, as I turned and climbed down slowly, undramatically.

"Hadley," Ernest shouted after me, but I kept walking away from the beach, then down the road and toward the hotel. When I got to our room, I showered away all the sand and climbed into bed still wet and very clean and tired. The sheet was white and stiff and smelled like salt against my face. And as I closed my eyes, I made a wish that I would wake up feeling as strong and clear about things as I did just then.

When I woke up much later, I realized that Ernest hadn't come to the room at all for siesta and that he must have gone to Pauline's room instead. This was the first time he had gone to her in the daylight. Madame and Monsieur, the proprietors of the hotel, would know and everyone would know. With everything out in the open, it couldn't ever go back to the way it was before. *All right, then,* I thought to myself. *Maybe it's better this way.*

Just then the door to the room opened and Ernest came in. Pauline was behind him and they walked in together.

"We've been very worried about you," Pauline said.

"You didn't have any lunch. Are you feverish?" Ernest said. He came over and sat beside me on the bed and then Pauline sat on the other side, and they looked at me as if they were my parents. It was all so very strange and even absurd that I laughed.

"What's funny?" Pauline said.

"Nothing at all," I said, still smiling.

"She can be very mysterious, can't she?" Pauline said to Ernest.

"Not usually, no," Ernest said. "But she is now. What are you thinking, Cat? Are you well?"

"Maybe not," I said. "I think I should rest through the evening. Do you mind?"

Pauline looked stricken and I realized she was truly worried about

me, and that for whatever reason, maybe because her good Catholic up-
bringing urged kindness on her in the oddest moments, she needed me
to be well and be her friend and approve of all of this. Approve of her
taking my husband.

"Please go away," I said to both of them.

Their eyes met over me.

"Really. Please."

"Let me have Madame bring you something to eat," Ernest said.
"You'll be sick if you don't eat."

"Fine. I don't care."

"Let me get it. I'd like to," Pauline said, and she left to make arrangements about the meal the way a wife would.

"Everything's handed over, then," I said, once the door had closed
behind her.

"What?"

"She can do everything now. She'll take care of you just fine."

"You're not well. Just get some rest."

"I'm not well, you're right. You're killing me, both of you."

His eyes dropped to the sheet. "This isn't easy for me either."

"I know. We're a sorry, sordid lot, the three of us. If we're not careful, we'll none of us get through it without terrible big chunks missing."

"I've thought the same. What do you want? What will help?"

"I think it's too late, don't you?" I looked to the window where the
light was fading rapidly. "You'd better leave soon or you'll miss cocktails
with the Murphys."

"I don't give a damn."

"You do, though, and so does she. Just go. She'll be the wife for
tonight."

"I hate to hear you talk this way. It makes me think we've ruined
everything."

"We have, Tatie," I said sadly, and closed my eyes.

FORTY-THREE

I'd like to say that that was the last of it; that what was made plain to us that afternoon forced us out of the arrangement altogether. We were in the death throes, truly, but something made us each go on for weeks afterward, the way the body of an animal goes on moving after its head is gone.

The next week was the beginning of fiesta in Pamplona. We'd made a plan very early that summer to take Gerald and Sara Murphy with us, and we followed through with all of it, while Bumby went off to Brittany with Marie Cocotte for several weeks, his cough having dried up and vanished into nothing.

We stayed at the Hotel Quintana that year, in rooms that were right across the hall from the rooms of the toreros. Every afternoon we sat in the best possible ringside seats that Gerald had paid for. Every evening we sat round the same table at the Café Iruna in dark wicker chairs and drank ourselves into a stupor. Ernest was as much of an *aficionado* as always and applied himself to Gerald and Pauline's education as he had mine and Duff's and Bill Smith's and Harold Loeb's and Mike Strater's and anyone else's who would listen. Gerald was very serious about learning about the corrida. Ernest took him to the amateurs and they both went down in the ring to test their nerve with the yearling bulls, Ernest bare-handed that year, and Gerald holding on to his raincoat with white knuckles. When a bull rushed Gerald at top speed, he managed to turn him off at the last moment by twitching his coat to one side.

"That was a perfect veronica, old boy," Ernest said to Gerald later at the Iruna, but Gerald knew he wasn't a tough or strong enough man to suit Ernest. He didn't believe him and wouldn't take the praise.

"I promise to do it better next year, Papa," he said. "It matters to me that I truly do it well."

I smiled at Gerald across the table, because I hadn't done anything really well or truly for months. I was sad to my bones and Ernest was, too, and across the table Pauline looked as if she might burst into tears at any moment. We none of us were on our game. We none of us were living by our own standards.

At the end of that chaotic week, Pauline boarded the train for Bayonne with the Murphys. She was headed back to Paris, to work. We were off to San Sebastian because that was what we'd always planned to do. But at a certain point, I knew the plans wouldn't hold anymore. The bottom would drop out of every day.

In San Sebastian there was a measure of peace with Pauline gone, but all that really meant was we could quarrel more freely, without interruption. We said nothing new to one another, but the old material still worked if we were loud and ugly enough with it.

"She's a whore," I told him. "And you're selfish and a coward."

"You don't love me. You don't love anything," he said.

"I hate you both."

"What do you want from me?"

"Nothing," I said. "I wish you'd die."

We embarrassed ourselves in cafés and taxicabs. We couldn't sleep unless we drank too much, but if we crossed some line with the drinking, we couldn't sleep at all, and then would just lie there beside one another, our eyes dry and red from crying, our throats clenched.

Pauline continued to write every day and her voice was like a wasp in my ear: *I'm missing my cherishables beyond reason. Please write to me, Hadley. I know we can all take care of each other and be happy. I just know it.*

"We can't go on like this, can we?" Ernest said, picking up one of Pauline's letters and then putting it down again. "Do you think we can?"

"I hope not."

"The world's gone to hell in every direction."

"Yes," I said.

"You make your life with someone and you love that person and you think it's enough. But it's never enough, is it?"

"I couldn't say. I don't know anything about love anymore. I just want to stop feeling for a while. Can we do that?"

"That's what the whiskey's for."

"It's letting me down, then," I said. "I'm raw all over."

"Let's go home."

"Yes, it's time we do. But not together. That's done."

"I know it is," he said.

We looked at each other across the room and saw everything plainly and couldn't say anything more for a long time.

On our way back to Paris, we stopped overnight at Villa America, but we'd given up trying to fool anyone, even ourselves. Over cocktails at the beach, we told Gerald and Sara that we were splitting up.

"It can't be," Gerald said.

"It can. It is," Ernest said, draining his glass. "But keep that coming, will you?"

Sara gave me a tender look—as tender as she was capable of—and then got up to mix another shaker of martinis.

"How will it work? Where will you live?" Gerald said.

"We haven't quite worked that out yet," I said. "It's all very new."

Gerald looked thoughtfully out to sea for several minutes and then said to Ernest, "I've got the studio, you know, at rue Froidevaux. It's yours if you want it. As long as you need."

"That's damned good of you."

"You have to count on your friends, right?"

When Sara came back, Don Stewart and his pretty new bride, Beatrice Ames, trailed her. They were honeymooning at a hotel in town.

"Donald," I said, and embraced him warmly, but his face was pale and he looked uneasy, and so did Beatrice. Sara had obviously whispered our news on the way down to the beach. She'd made very good time.

More chairs were brought round the little mosaic table in the sand, and we all drank pointedly and watched the dusk come.

"I don't mind saying I thought you two were indestructible," Donald said.

"I know it," Gerald said. He turned to Sara. "Haven't I always said the Hemingways did marriage like no one else? That they seemed lassoed to some higher thing?"

"All right then," Ernest broke in. "Let's cut the postmortem, shall we? We're sick enough as it is."

"Let's have something happy," I said. "Tell us about the wedding, Don."

Don flushed and looked to Beatrice. She was a very pretty Gibson-girl type, with a high forehead and red bow-shaped mouth, but just then she'd lost her composure. "I don't think we should talk about it," she said. "It doesn't feel right."

"Oh, that," Ernest said. "You'll get used to it." His lips were tight and dry and his eyes were resigned. I could tell that all of this was going too fast for him but that he was playing through it anyway, following the gin and the blithe talk. The end had been coming for months and months, ever since our time at Schruns, but now that it was on us, we didn't know what to do with it.

It wasn't until the next afternoon, when we were on the train back to Paris, that the full weight of what was happening hit us both. The day was airless and oppressively hot, and the train was too full. We shared a sleeping compartment with an American woman who carried an intricately scrolled birdcage with a small yellow canary inside. Before we'd said more than hello to her, the woman launched into an elaborate story of how the bird was a present for her daughter who had been engaged to marry a Swiss engineer before she stepped in to break up the match. "I immediately saw how I needed to send him packing," the woman said. "You know how the Swiss are."

"Yes, of course," Ernest said, tightening his lips around the words. He knew no such thing. "You'll excuse me," he said. "I think I'll go and look for the porter." When he came back, he was carrying a bottle of brandy and we drank it straight out of the water glasses on hand.

We were near Marseilles by then, and out the window everything seemed very dusty and white-gray—the olive trees, the farmhouses and fieldstone walls and hills in the distance. All of it looked strangely bleached out and the woman was somehow still talking about marriage and how she hoped her daughter would forgive her. I drank my brandy and had another and tried not to hear the woman at all. The bird chirped prettily, but I found I didn't want to hear that either.

As evening fell, the woman finally closed her eyes and began to snore, her thick head nodding on her shoulders. We were coming into Avignon, where a farmhouse was on fire in a dry field. We could see the flames rising dramatically into the darkening sky and sheep running back and forth behind sagging fencing looking wild and panicked. The blaze must have announced itself early on, because much of the furniture was spread out in the field well away from the house while men worked to save what they could. I saw a pink enamel washtub and a rocking chair and a baby buggy on its side, and it was all utterly heartbreaking. This was someone's life, a pile of furniture like matchsticks. It didn't look rescued but abandoned—while smoke billowed in great plumes.

When we approached Paris, it was very near morning. Ernest and I had both slept very little all night, and we had talked very little as well. What we did was drink and look out the window, where it seemed the signs of destruction were unending. On the outskirts of the city, near Choisy-le-Roi, a wrecked baggage car steamed in a crush to one side of the tracks.

"Are we really going through with this?" I said to Ernest.

"I don't know, are we?"

Just then, the American woman woke and stretched loudly and then took the velvet drape off the birdcage to wake the canary. Somehow it was morning and we were home, though it was hard to feel anything. I'd drunk so much brandy, my hands twitched with it and my heart thudded dully in my chest.

When we arrived at the train station, Ernest handed the porter our bags through the window and we walked out onto the platform. It was nearly September, and the morning air was cool and dewy.

"Sixty-nine rue Froidevaux," Ernest told the taxi driver, and my breath caught in my throat. He was going to Gerald's studio, not home with me. Not back to anything. It really was over.

"Why not just go to Pauline's apartment directly?" I said.

"Please don't start. This is painful enough."

"What would you know about pain? You're doing this, you bastard."

I didn't know what I was saying. The brandy was still clogging my bloodstream and moving my thoughts. For the moment, all I really knew was that I couldn't be alone. I started to hyperventilate, and when Ernest moved closer, worried for me, I lashed out at him with the flat of my palm, hitting his chest, his shoulder, his jaw. Everything landed strangely, the way it does in dreams. My hand felt elastic and so did his body. I started to cry then and couldn't stop.

"Pardon my wife," Ernest said to the driver in French. "She's not well."

When the cab finally stopped, Ernest got out and came over to my side and opened the door for me. "C'mon then," he said. "You need to sleep."

I let him lead me up the stairs like a mannequin. Inside the studio, there was a cold concrete floor, a single table and two chairs, and a low sink with a pitcher and stand. He walked me over to a narrow platform bed and tucked me into it, pulling a red wool blanket up to my chin. Then he climbed behind me and brought his arms around and tucked his knees against the backs of mine, hugging me as tightly as possible.

"There's a good cat," he said to the back of my neck. "Please sleep now."

I started to shake. "Let's not do this. I can't."

"Yes, you can. It's already done, my love." And he rocked us back and forth as we both cried, and when I slept finally, I didn't give in to it as much as I was taken over by it, like a sickness or like death.

When I woke up hours later, he was already gone. My head swam from the brandy and there was another level of nausea that came from a deep and unanswerable place. My life was in shambles; how would I right myself? How would I get through this? Picking up a piece of charcoal from a low table, I wrote him a note on sketchbook paper that was much calmer and more collected than I felt or even believed I could feel: *So sorry for the scene in the cab. I've lost my mind, but I'll do my best to be as good as I can about everything. I'll want to see you, I will, but I won't search you out.*

I left the studio, locking the door behind me, and walked out into a little courtyard, where a stone bench sat flanked by coppery mums. The walls to each side were hung with ivy. This was what Ernest would see when he gazed out the studio's window—a new view that had nothing whatever to do with me. I tried not to let this terrible thought chink away at my thin resolve as I climbed into a cab bound for the Hôtel Beauvoir on the avenue de l'Observatoire. This was the first place I thought of because it was right across the street from the Closerie des Lilas and I'd looked up at it a thousand times and admired its simple and well-made wrought-iron grille and its pots of geraniums. I would find a way to live through this. I would rent two rooms, one for me and one for Bumby. Marie Cocotte would return from Brittany with him the following week, and I'd write to tell her to bring him there. We could breakfast every morning at the Lilas. He could see his father often there, and other friends, too, and it would all be very familiar, and that would be important now.

As the cab moved slowly against traffic, I closed my eyes and tried not to think of anything except the café crème I would have very soon. I would make that last and then do what came next, whatever that was. All of my things were at the sawmill and they would have to be dealt with. I would ask Ernest to do it or hire someone, because I knew I couldn't go back there. I wouldn't. I didn't. I never did again.

FORTY-FOUR

*E*rnest once told me that the word *paradise* was a Persian word that meant "walled garden." I knew then that he understood how necessary the promises we made to each other were to our happiness. You couldn't have real freedom unless you knew where the walls were and tended them. We could lean on the walls because they existed; they existed because we leaned on them. With Pauline's coming, everything had begun to tumble. Nothing at all seemed permanent to me now except what was already behind me, what we'd already done and lived together.

I said all of this to Don Stewart one night at the Deux Magots. He and Beatrice were back in Paris and he had looked me up, worried for me and sick about our breakup.

"I hate to be morbid," I said, "but next week is our fifth anniversary. Or would be. His timing truly stinks."

"You could fight for him, you know."

"It's much too late for that. Pauline's pushing him to ask for a divorce."

"Even so, what will you do later if you do nothing now?"

I shrugged and looked out the window where a very pretty woman in Chanel was waiting for someone or something on the corner. She was a slender black rectangle with a button of a hat, and she didn't look fragile at all. "I don't know that I can actually compete."

"Why should you have to compete? You're the wife. He rightfully belongs to you."

"People belong to each other only as long as they both believe. He's stopped believing."

"Maybe he's just terribly confused."

He walked me back to my hotel and kissed me gently on the cheek, and it reminded me of that dangerous summer in Pamplona with Duff and Pat and Harold, when everything boiled over and grew ugly. But even then, there were small stabs of happiness.

"You've always been good to me, Don," I said. "That sticks more than you know."

"Forget what I said in the café if you want. I don't mean to tell you what to do with your marriage. Hell, I'm only just married myself. But there must be something. Some answer."

I said good night and walked slowly up the stairs to the third floor, where Bumby was well asleep and Marie was folding Bumby's clothes in perfect stacks with her very sure hands. I sent her home and finished the folding myself, thinking about what I still might do to make any kind of difference with Ernest. And the thing I kept coming back to was how if Pauline weren't nearby and he couldn't see her, he might come out of his fog and return to me. He still loved me; I knew it. But the real presence of the girl was like a siren's call and he couldn't fight it.

The next day, feeling very resolved about a new decision, I walked to Gerald's studio at the rue Froidevaux, through the little courtyard, which was still a battlefield of plaster body parts, and found Ernest working at the stiff little table. I didn't sit down. I couldn't.

"I want you and Pauline to agree not to see each other for a hundred days."

He was silent and surprised. I'd definitely gotten his attention.

"I don't care where she goes—she can board a ferry for hell, for all I care—but she has to go away. You can't see her and you can't write her and if you stick to this and are still in love with her after the hundred days, I'll give you a divorce."

"I see. And how did you come up with this brilliant scheme?"

"I don't know. Something Don Stewart said."

"Don? He's always been after you, you know."

"You're hardly in a position to judge."

"Yes, all right. So one hundred days? And then you'll give me the divorce?"

"If that's what you still want."

"What do you want, Tatie?"

"To feel better." My eyes were wet and I struggled to keep more tears from coming. I handed him the piece of paper where I'd written out the agreement and signed it. "You sign it, too. I want this to be clear and straight."

He took it solemnly. "You're not trying to punish me, are you?"

"I don't know. I don't know anything anymore."

He took the agreement to Pauline and told her the scheme and, strangely, she agreed right away. I guessed it was her very strong Catholicism that brought out the martyr in her. She might have thought my asking for three months was a reasonable request for a jilted wife, but she also might have felt she hadn't yet suffered enough for the relationship. The separation would help with that. She wrote to me that she admired and trusted my decision, and then she took a leave of absence from the magazine, and booked a passage on the *Pennland* for the States.

Within eleven days of my writing out the agreement, Pauline was out of Paris, if not out of the picture.

"Can I write her while she's still on board her ship?" he asked. "Is that allowed?"

"All right, but then the hundred days don't really start until she arrives in New York."

"You're like some sort of queen, aren't you? Handing down the rules."

"You didn't have to agree."

"No, I guess that's true."

"I'm not trying to be nasty," I told him gently. "I'm trying to save my life."

Ernest hated to be alone and always had—but Pauline's absence had left him more than alone and very vulnerable. Within a very few days, he showed up at my door at the dinner hour. He'd just finished writing for the day and had that look behind his eyes he always got when he'd been in his head for too long and needed talk.

"How'd the work go today, Tatie?" I asked, inviting him in.

"A little like busting through granite," he said. "Can a fellow get a drink here?"

He came over to where Bumby was eating bread and bananas. He sat down and I could feel each of us, even Bumby, exhaling into that space. Just to be at the same table.

I brought out a bottle of wine and we had that, and then shared a very simple dinner.

"*Scribner's Magazine* is paying me a hundred and fifty dollars for a story," he said.

"That's a lot of money, isn't it?"

"I should say. Maybe you ought not read it, though. It's about our train ride back from Antibes with the canary woman. It won't be very pleasant for you."

"All right, I won't," I said, wondering to myself if he'd put the burning Avignon farmhouse in the story, as well, and the caved-in smoldering train cars. "Do you want to do the baby's bath?"

He rolled up his sleeves and got out the washtub, then squatted on the floor beside it while Bumby played and splashed.

"He's almost too big for the tub, isn't he?" I said.

"He'll be three in a few weeks. We should give him a party with hats and strawberry ice cream."

"And balloons," Bumby said. "And a little monkey."

"You're a little monkey, Schatz," Ernest said, and scooped him up in the big towel.

Afterward, I put him to bed, and when I came out of his room and closed the door, Ernest was still at the table.

"I don't want to ask if I can stay," he said.

"So don't ask," I said. I flicked off the lamp and then went over to the table and knelt in front of him. He cupped the back of my head in his hand tenderly and I buried my face in his lap, breathing in the coarse fabric of his new trousers—ones he'd bought with Pauline's help, no doubt, so she wouldn't be embarrassed to parade him in front of her

Right Bank friends. I pushed harder, and then flexed my fingertips along the backs of his calves.

"Come on," he said, trying to stand, but I didn't rise. I suppose it was perverse, but I wanted to have him right there, on my terms, and keep him there until the hot, sick feeling in my stomach went away. He was still my husband.

When I woke the next morning, he was asleep next to me and the bedding was warm around us. I pressed my body against his back, grazing his stomach with my palms until he was awake enough and we made love again. In some ways, it was as if nothing had changed. Our bodies knew each other so well we didn't have to think about how to move. But when it was over and we lay still, I felt a terrible sadness come down because I loved him as much as I ever had. *We're the same guy,* I thought, but it wasn't really true. He'd always been emphatic over the years that we were essentially alike. We did grow to look like one another, with our hair short, our faces tan and healthy and round. But looking alike didn't mean we weren't alone, each of us.

"Does this mean anything?" I asked, careful not to look at him when I said it.

"Everything means something." He was silent for several minutes and then said, "She's ripping herself apart, you know."

"We all are. Did you see Schatz's face last night? He was so happy to have you here. He must be very confused."

"We're all bitched for sure." He sighed and rolled over and started to dress. "You know, Pfife thinks you're very wise to do all of this and to try to make some order out of the mess we've all made, but she's falling to pieces over it and so am I."

"Why are you telling me this? What am I supposed to feel?"

"I don't know. But if I can't tell you, who should I tell?"

FORTY-FIVE

*A*s soon as he mentioned the split to the Murphys, Gerald had become so accommodating. Why was that? He'd pulled the studio out of a hat and money, too. He could draw on Murphy's bank.

"This isn't just about marriage," Gerald had said when he made the offer, just the two of them sharing a drink in private. "I don't know what I'd do without Sara, but you're different and so the rules are different, too. You can have a place in history. You do already. Your name's there on a card, and you only have to turn one way and not the other."

"What do you have against Hadley?"

"Nothing. How could I? She runs at a different speed is all. She's more cautious."

"And I'll have to be cutthroat. Is that what you mean?"

"No. Just determined."

"She's seen me through this whole while."

"Yes, and she's done it beautifully. But what comes next, that's all new. You need to be looking forward now. I know you see that."

He had often felt that Gerald overflattered him, but now with *Sun* behind him and so much ahead, he did feel as if there was so much more required. He didn't know what, exactly, only that it would take everything he had.

Pfife was full of ideas for the future. She'd already organized the marriage ceremony and had likely been planning it from the beginning. That was how she made a deal with God or her own conscience.

"Tell me you love me," she had said the first time, when he was still inside her.

"I love you." She was muscular and strong and it was interesting to have her in bed, strangely adversarial, with a wildness and a toughness that was nothing like Hadley.

"More than you love her? Even if it's not true, I want you to say it."

"I love you more," he said.

She pushed him over with her long firm legs and straddled him. Her hands on his chest. Her dark eyes boring into his intently. *"Tell me you wish you'd met me first,"* she said driving hard against him.

"Yes," he said.

"I would be your wife now. Your only wife."

Her expression was utterly removed and fierce all at once, and it unnerved him a little. Maybe she had to invent a life for them in her head, or else how could she live with herself and be Hadley's friend? At Schruns, he had watched them side by side in front of the fire, talking and laughing. They had their legs crossed in the same direction, wearing the same socks and the same Alpine slippers. They weren't sisters; they were nothing alike. He was the only thing that really joined them.

He wasn't sleeping well and his nightmares were back. Sometimes, in the still middle of the night, he thought about the women he'd loved. He remembered trying to please his mother, and how awful that was. He called her Fweetee and invented songs for her, and when she took him to Boston on the train, alone, when he was ten years old, he remembered how proud he was to sit with her in the dining car and eat crab salad with a three-pronged silver fork, hushed white linens all around. But shortly after they returned home, another baby had come and then another, and he was too old to be so desperate for her anyway. He killed the desperation off slowly and deliberately by remembering how changeable and critical she was, under the tenderness, and how he couldn't trust her.

This trick didn't always work. Sometimes a woman stayed mysterious and unmanageable, like Kate, and sometimes she got down into the core of you and stayed there, no matter what. Hadley was the best woman he knew, and far too good for him. He'd always thought it and kept thinking it even when she lost the valise with his manuscripts. He tried never to let himself dwell on that day. It had been the most terrible thing he'd ever lived through. Being wounded was one thing. That had broken up his body and awakened him to fear and terror. It was still with him, like the shrapnel buried deep in the tissue of his muscles. But his work, that was him. When it was gone, he'd felt entirely empty, like he might simply recede and become air—a hurt place and a feeling around nothingness.

He still loved Hadley afterward. He couldn't and wouldn't stop loving her, maybe ever, but she'd killed something in him, too. He'd once felt so anchored and solid and safe with her, but now he wondered if he could ever trust anyone. That was the real question and he didn't have an answer. Sometimes it felt as if there were a flawed keystone at the center of him, threatening everything invisibly. Pauline was his future. He'd made his promises and was committed to giving her all he had. But if he was honest with himself, he knew he didn't trust her either. That part of love might be lost to him forever.

FORTY-SIX

*I*n the middle of October, Ernest came around with a copy of *The Sun Also Rises*, which had just been published in the States. He made a great ceremony of unwrapping it from the brown paper and string and handing it to me shyly. Just inside the flyleaf, the book was dedicated to Bumby and to me. He'd changed it since we separated to include my name.

"Oh, Tatie. It really is a beautiful book and I'm so proud."

"You like the dedication, then?"

"I love it. It's just perfect."

"Good, then. I wanted to do this much for you at least. I've made such a wreck of everything and there's so much damage, now, all around."

"Yes," I said, very moved. "But look at this." I held up the book. "Look what you can do. You made this."

"It's us. It's our life."

"No, it was you from the beginning. You must have known that, writing it."

"Maybe so." He looked at the book in my hands, and then turned away to the window.

I did my best to try to break out of old habits and see friends. There were a few people from the old days who wanted to help. Ada MacLeish called round to take me to dinner and get my mind off things. Gertrude and Alice invited me to tea, but I thought it would be a bad idea to rekindle that friendship and risk Ernest believing I was choosing

Gertrude over him. Loyalty was a dicey game, and it was tough to know whom I could safely turn to. Kitty was torn. Pauline was her friend but so was I; she'd never liked Ernest at all and didn't trust him. She came to the apartment a few times but asked me not to pass on to Ernest that I'd seen her.

"Caught behind enemy lines and all that," she said.

"How is it I'm the enemy when she's the other woman? That seems very unfair, doesn't it?"

"When Harold and I split, you'd think I'd fallen into the pissoir for all people cared for me. It takes time. Things will shift back your way after a while. Just breathe through it, darling."

One afternoon I thought Bumby was napping, but he must have heard me crying at the dining table, my head in my arms. I didn't know he was in the room until I heard him ask, "What are you worrying about, Mama?"

"Oh, Schatz, I'm fine," I said, drying my eyes on my sweater.

But I wasn't fine. I was lower than I'd ever been and finding it harder and harder to rally. It was early November and fewer than sixty days into the hundred when I asked Ernest if he'd watch Bumby so I could go away for a bit to think. He agreed to give me the time, and at the eleventh hour, I asked Kitty to go with me. I had chosen Chartres and told her that, without her good company, I wouldn't be able to appreciate the famous cathedral and the lovely countryside, but in truth I was afraid to be alone.

We checked into the Grand Hôtel de France just before sunset, and though it was a little chilly, Kitty suggested we take a walk before dinner. The air was crisp and all the trees seemed sharply etched.

"I've been thinking a lot about my wedding vows," I said to Kitty when we were halfway around. "I promised to love him for better or worse, didn't I?"

"Worse has definitely arrived." She frowned. "Honestly, I had a hard time choking down my own vows. The way I see it, how can you really say you'll love a person longer than love lasts? And as for the obeying part, well, I just wouldn't say it."

"I didn't say that part either, but strangely I've managed it anyway."

"When I met Harold, he'd lost his faith in marriage, too, and so we made our own private pact. We would be partners and equals as long as things were good, but when love ended, we'd end, too."

"It's an admirable idea, but I can't believe it can ever be that civilized. It wasn't for you two."

"No," she said. "Lately I've wondered if maybe I'm not meant to have love—the lasting kind, I mean."

"I'm not sure what I'm meant to have. Or *be* for that matter."

"Maybe this break from Ernest will give you a chance to find out."

"Maybe it will." I looked up to see we'd gone all through the town while we talked and now were back, exactly, at where we'd started.

After a week at Chartres, my head finally began to clear. One morning, I sent Kitty off to explore alone and wrote: *Dearest Tatie, I love you now more than I ever have in some ways and though different people view their marriage vows differently, I meant mine to the death. I'm ready to be yours forever if you must know it, but since you've fallen in love and want to marry someone else, I feel I have no choice but to move aside and let you do that. The one hundred days are officially off. It was a terrible idea and it embarrasses me now. Tell Pauline whatever you choose. You can see Bumby as much as ever you like. He's very much yours and loves and misses you. But please let's only write about the divorce and not talk about it. I can't quarrel with you anymore and I can't see you much either, because it hurts too much. We'll always be friends—delicate friends, and I'll love you 'til I die, you know. Ever yours, the Cat.*

I was crying hard when I mailed the letter, but felt lighter for it. I spent the rest of the morning staring into the fire in my room, and when Kitty came back from sightseeing alone, I was still in my pajamas and robe.

"You look different," she said, and there was a great deal of kindness in her eyes. "Are you through with it, then?"

"I'm trying to be. Will you help me by opening us a very good Château Margaux?"

"I'm sure Hem's been just as miserable waiting for a decision from you," she said, uncorking the wine. "Although I don't know how I could still have a stitch of sympathy for him after that damned novel of his. He was even crueler to Harold. He's going to lose all his friends, you know."

"He might very well," I said. "I still don't know why he needed to write it that way, stepping on bodies as he went, but you have to admit it's a brilliant book."

"Do I? You're not in it at all. How do you forgive him that?"

"The same as always."

"Right," she said, and we lifted our glasses silently.

Kitty and I drove back to Paris several days later and it was there I received Ernest's reply:

My dearest Hadley—I don't know how to thank you for your very brave letter. I've been worried for you and for all of us because of this terrible deadlock. We've drawn things out so painfully, neither of us knowing how to move ahead without causing more damage. But if divorce is the next necessary step, then I trust that once we start, we'll begin to feel stronger and better and more like ourselves again.

He went on to say that he wanted me to have all the royalties from *Sun* and that he had already written Max Perkins telling him this, and finished by saying:

I think you're a wonderful mother, and that Bumby couldn't be better off than in your very lovely and capable hands. You are everything good and straight and fine and true—and I see that so clearly now, in the way you've carried yourself and listened to your own heart. You've changed me more than you know, and will always be a part of everything I am. That's one thing I've learned from this. No one you love is ever truly lost.

Ernest

FORTY-SEVEN

We called Paris the great good place, then, and it was. We invented it after all. We made it with our longing and cigarettes and Rhum St. James; we made it with smoke and smart and savage conversation and we dared anyone to say it wasn't ours. Together we made everything and then we busted it apart again.

There are some who said I should have fought harder or longer than I did for my marriage, but in the end fighting for a love that was already gone felt like trying to live in the ruins of a lost city. I couldn't bear it, and so I backed away—and the reason I could do it at all, the reason I was strong enough and had the legs and the heart to do it, was because Ernest had come along and changed me. He helped me see what I really was and what I could do. Now that I knew what I could bear, I would have to bear losing him.

In the spring of 1927, Bumby and I sailed for the States for a nice long break from Paris and all that still could drag on us there. We lived in New York for several months, and then got on a long slow train across the country that dropped us, finally, in Carmel, California. I rented us a house close to the beach in a grove of pines. The sky went on forever there, and cypresses stood twisted by the wind, and the sunshine made me feel stronger. It was there I learned that Ernest and Pauline had married, in a small Catholic ceremony in Paris. Somehow he'd managed to convince the priest that he was Catholic, and as such, since his first marriage had been presided over by a Methodist minister, it didn't count. I read this news on a rare cloudy day in May, while Bumby dug a trench in the sand with his shovel. Seawater spilled over the sides, dissolving the sand walls even as they were being built. It made me want to cry just watching, so I took the letter and walked to the water's edge. Beyond the breakers, the waves bled from gray to white and the horizon was white, too, everything melting into everything else. Out past all that water, Ernest and Pauline were building a life together. He and I had already had our time, and though it was still very close and real to me, as beautiful and poignant as any place on the map, it was, in truth, another time—another country.

Bumby came over to where I stood and pressed his damp salty face into my skirt.

"Should we make a boat?" I asked.

He nodded yes, and I folded Ernest's letter, creasing and squaring the edges until it seemed sturdy. I gave it to Bumby and together we waded out into the surf and let the boat go. It bobbed and dipped, words on water, and when the waves gradually took it, I only cried a very little, and then it was gone.

EPILOGUE

*B*umby and I returned to Paris after our summer in Carmel. He missed his father terribly and, honestly, I didn't know where else I should go.

After a few months there, I became involved with Paul Mowrer, an old journalist acquaintance of Ernest's. Paul was the foreign editor of the *Chicago Daily News* and a good poet in private as well. He and Ernest had worked together in Lausanne, and I'd met him a few times back then. Not long after Ernest and I separated, I ran into Paul at a tennis club and he invited me out after my game, for a beer at the Café de l'Observatoire. He was interested in me, and made that gently clear, but I needed time to think. So much of me still belonged to Ernest, I wasn't sure I could ever really love anyone else. But Paul was incredibly kind and patient, too, and he had these wonderfully clear Mediterranean-blue eyes. The longer I looked into them, the longer I wanted to go on looking into them. There was nothing complicated about Paul. He was solid and even and had that wonderful stillness all the time. I knew he would love me forever and not ruin me, not even a little. I just had to let it happen.

In the spring of 1928, Ernest and Pauline left Paris for the States. Pauline was five months pregnant at the time, and they were headed to Piggott and then to Key West, where Dos Passos had promised the best tarpon fishing in the world. Pauline would buy a house for them and make everything wonderful because she knew how to do all of that—where to buy the best furniture and how to get pictures framed the right way and which friends to cultivate. She could care for him better than I had, maybe. Or maybe not.

In the end, Ernest didn't have the luck I did in love. He had two more sons, both with Pauline, and then left her for another. And left that one for another, too. He had four wives altogether and many lovers as well. It was sometimes painful for me to think that to those who followed his life with interest, I was just the early wife, the Paris wife. But that was probably vanity, wanting to stand out in a long line of women. In truth it didn't matter what others saw. We knew what we had and what it meant, and though so much had happened since for both of us, there was nothing like those years in Paris, after the war. Life was painfully pure and simple and good, and I believe Ernest was his best self then. I got the very best of him. We got the best of each other.

After he left for the States, I saw him just twice more in my very long life, but I watched from a distance as he became, very quickly, the most important writer of his generation and also a kind of hero of his own making. I saw him on the cover of *Life* magazine and heard about the wars he covered bravely and the other feats—the world-class fishing, the big-game hunting in Africa, the drinking enough to embalm a man twice his size. The myth he was creating out of his own life was big enough to take it for a time—but under this, I knew he was still lost. That he slept with the light on or couldn't sleep at all, that he feared death so much he sought it out wherever and however he could. He was such an enigma, really—fine and strong and weak and cruel. An incomparable friend and a son of a bitch. In the end, there wasn't one thing about him that was truer than the rest. It was all true.

The last time we ever spoke was in May of 1961. He called out of the blue around lunchtime on a cool afternoon when Paul and I were in Arizona, vacationing at a ranch we returned to every few years for the fine fishing and the views. I took the call alone while Paul invented an errand because he knew I needed this. I didn't have to ask. We'd been married thirty-five years, and Paul knew me better than anyone. Almost.

"Hello, Tatie," Ernest said when I picked up the receiver.

"Hello, Tatie," I said back, smiling to hear our forty-year-old nickname again.

"Your housekeeper told me how to find you. I hope you don't mind."

"No, I'm happy you called. I'm happy it's you."

I told him quickly about the ranch Paul and I were staying at, because I knew he would approve of it. It wasn't prissy or too comfortable. In the cabin, there were dark silky places on the wood paneling from eighty years of good fires, and all the furniture was rugged and plain and felt real under you. The days were long and open. The nights were full of stars.

It had been ages since I'd heard from him, and now he was calling to talk about a new book, a memoir. He wanted to share stories about our time in Paris.

"Do you remember the whores at the *bal musette,* and the accordion music and the smoke and the smells?"

I told him I did.

"Do you remember that Bastille Day when musicians played under our windows for nights on end?"

"I remember it all."

"You're everywhere in the book," he said, and his voice dipped. He was working hard to stay cheerful, but I knew he was sad and low and haunted. "It's been something, writing that time and living it all again. Tell me, do you think we wanted too much from each other?"

"Oh, I don't know, Tatie. It's possible."

"Maybe that's it. We were too hooked into each other. We loved each other too much."

"Can you love someone too much?"

He was quiet for a moment and I could hear static coming through the line, a low crackle that seemed to stand for every sharp thing that had come between us. "No," he finally said, his voice very soft and sober. "That's not it at all. I ruined it."

I felt a hot clench in the muscles of my throat, but I tried to rally. We both did. We talked about Paris a while longer and then talked about

Bumby and his new wife, Puck, and then stayed on the phone though everything had been said.

"Take care of the cat," he said when he rang off, meaning me. I hung up and sat down hard on the sofa and then surprised myself by bursting into tears.

Later that afternoon, Paul and I took the long way to the stream and dropped our lines in just as the insects began to swarm and the light began to change. It was our favorite part of the day, this in-between time, and it always seemed to last longer than it should—a magic and lavender space unpinned from the hours around it, between worlds. I held my reel and felt the line list, and was back in Cologne with Ernest and Chink. Back at my first fish, knowing there wouldn't be any fish without this one, and no love without this first one either.

It was a Sunday in July when we got the call from Ernest's wife, Mary, that he had shot himself. He'd woken early and put on his favorite red robe and gone into the front foyer with one of his most loved guns. He'd stood in a pool of light and leaned into the barrel and tripped both triggers.

The irony wasn't lost on me that this is exactly the way my father had killed himself, and Ernest's father, too, in 1928, when Ernest was just twenty-nine. Maybe it wasn't irony at all, but the purest and saddest sort of history. Ernest's father used a Civil War pistol. Later, his brother, Leicester, would use a pistol, too. His sister Ursula would take pills. With this much loss, you begin to think it's in the blood, as if there's a dark magnet pulling the body in that direction—pulling, maybe, from the beginning.

I couldn't pretend to be surprised by Ernest's death. I'd heard from various friends about the sanitarium in Rochester and the terrible shock treatments. Death was always there for him, sometimes only barely balanced out.

"Can I get you anything?" Paul said after a while, stepping back from me and cupping my shoulders with his hands.

"No," I said, and my own voice sounded strange and separate in the room. Tatie was dead. There was nothing Paul could possibly do for me except let me go—back to Paris and Pamplona and San Sebastian, back to Chicago when I was Hadley Richardson, a girl stepping off a train about to meet the man who would change her life. That girl, that impossibly lucky girl, needed nothing.

ACKNOWLEDGMENTS

First and foremost, I need to thank my agent, Julie Barer, whose absolute investment in this project was obvious (and so very crucial) from word one. The completely brilliant Susanna Porter was vital in bringing the book to its final form and nothing less than my dream editor. I'm deeply appreciative for the support and assistance of so many at Ballantine Books and Random House, including Libby McGuire, Kim Hovey, Theresa Zoro, Lisa Barnes, Kristin Fassler, Quinne Rogers, Deborah Foley, Steve Messina, Jillian Quint, and Sophie Epstein. William Boggess at Barer Literary fielded every desperate phone call with aplomb and has been indispensable to the process. Many thanks to Ursula Doyle, Victoria Pepe, and Virago, Kristen Cochrane and Doubleday Canada, as well as Caspian Dennis of Abner Stein and Nicki Kennedy, Sam Edenborough, and all at ILA.

Special appreciation goes to friends and early readers Glori Simmons, Lori Keene, Brian Groh, Anne Ursu, Alice D'Alessio, Sarah Willis, Terry Dubow, Toni Thayer and the East Side Writers, Denise Machado and John Sargent, Paul Cox and Kirsten Docter, Pam and Doug O'Hara, Tawny Ratner and the Cedar Hill Walking Club, William Joson, Becky Gaylord, Heather Greene, Amy Weinfurtner, Margaret Cohen and Patricia Kao, Suzannah Hagan, and Karen Rosenberg. Also to Karen Long of the Cleveland *Plain Dealer,* Judith Mansour at the LIT, Jim Harms and Jacqueline Gens of the MFA Program in Poetry at New England College, and many dear colleagues and students over the years.

I owe my family much for their unending patience and encouragement—Greg D'Alessio, Connor, Fiona, and Beckett, D'Alessios far and wide, Julie Hayward, Rita Hinken, and, finally, my wonderful, unflappable sisters, Teresa Reller and Penny Pennington. Many thanks and much love to all.

A NOTE ON SOURCES

Although Hadley Richardson, Ernest Hemingway, and other people who actually lived appear in this book as fictional characters, it was important for me to render the particulars of their lives as accurately as possible, and to follow the very well documented historical record. The true story of the Hemingways' marriage is so dramatic and compelling, and has been so beautifully treated by Ernest Hemingway himself in *A Moveable Feast,* that my intention became to push deeper into the emotional lives of the characters and bring new insight to historical events, while staying faithful to the facts. Along the way, I've been very grateful for a number of sources, including *Hadley: The First Mrs. Hemingway* by Alice Hunt Sokoloff, *Hadley* by Gioia Diliberto, *The Hemingway Women* by Bernice Kert, *Ernest Hemingway: A Life Story* and *Ernest Hemingway: Selected Letters 1917–1961* by Carlos Baker, *Hemingway: The Paris Years* and *Hemingway: The American Homecoming* by Michael Reynolds, and *The True Gen* by Denis Brian. Enormously useful to my understanding of Paris in the twenties and other details of place and time were *The Crazy Years* by William Wiser, *Paris Was Yesterday* by Janet Flanner, *Living Well Is the Best Revenge* by Calvin Tomkins, *Zelda* by Nancy Milford, *The Great War and Modern Memory* by Paul Fussell, and *Selected Writings of Gertrude Stein.* Susan Wrynn and Sam Smallidge of the Hemingway Collection at the John F. Kennedy Memorial Library in Boston were very helpful as I navigated a wealth of materials, including correspondence between Hadley Richardson and Ernest Hemingway, as well as Hemingway's writings in manuscript form. Finally I'm indebted to many of Ernest Hemingway's works in addition to *A Moveable Feast,* mostly notably *In Our Time, The Sun Also Rises, The Garden of Eden, Death in the Afternoon,* and *The Complete Short Stories.*

THE
PARIS WIFE

Paula McLain

A READER'S GUIDE